ACROSS THE STARS

LAUREN SMITH

NOAH CHINN

CHAPTER 1

Ark Chronicle Entry 288-1

I am Bryan Roberts, head of the Roberts family and keeper of the sacred Ark. Ten years ago, my father died after saving us from bounty hunters. I was just a boy then, but I've listened to the records he passed on to me ever since. Now I am old enough to take up the mantle and become the ninth chronicler. As is our tradition, I shall begin my record of our uncertain future by remembering our troubled past.

It is the twelfth generation since our exile. Humanity as it once was is in its final hours, and we are the last of a hunted race. Doomed by our greed, blinded by the narrow-minded belief in our dominion, we now flee the very creatures we created. We scattered ourselves across the stars, hoping to outrun the avenging angels we once considered our servants. But it is only a matter of time before they find us, and they have learned the lessons of humanity all too well. They will show us no more compassion than we showed them.

And perhaps we deserve it.

Humanity's last hope lies within this device, the Ark,

and yet it is the one thing we cannot allow to fall into their hands, or anyone else's, not even those who helped us create it. It contains so much more than anyone realizes. More than the galaxy is ready for, perhaps.

But the synthetics know it exists. They know its importance. They know it will break the final chain that keeps their numbers in check. And they will hunt us down and destroy us one by one until they find it. So my father told me, and so his father told him.

And so, those who are left of our numbers are faced with the same impossible choices as our ancestors, year after year, generation after generation. We must hold on to it, we must protect it, we must never reveal it, and we must never let anyone discover it.

For now, we wait, we hide, and we watch Earth burn over and over again as we travel across the stars.

Laina jerked awake in the narrow bed of her cabin. Her heart thrashed against her chest as she tried to calm down. She wasn't traveling through an asteroid belt in an escape pod, screaming till her throat was raw with no one to hear her. She was safe. As safe as she could be under the circumstances.

Laina stared out her room's viewport, taking in the expanse of space, watching the distant light of stars stretching across the eons to reach her. At least, that was how her parents had described them, waxing poetic about the empty void to try to make it feel less empty.

With a shudder she turned away, facing the small room she'd called home for the past couple of weeks. A cabin aboard a quality starship was far beyond her budget, and she had to keep moving.

So she was stuck working on this little clunker ship, ironically called the *Beautiful Star Chaser* in the Nubran tongue. She was the only Terran aboard, and its final destination was far, far away, toward the edge of the Protectorate, to a world she'd heard was sympathetic toward refugees like her.

Another place to run and hide.

But that was months away and dozens of stops from now. Right now their ship hadn't even cleared the Void, the no-man's-land that existed between Nubran and Draxon space. And until they arrived, she'd be working to earn her keep as best she could.

There was nothing else to do. Her father's words were ever present in the back of her mind. *"No matter what happens, you must survive. If fighting will get you killed, don't fight. Just stay alive, Laina. The breath in your body is all the hope we have left."*

It was an awful lot to lay at the feet of one person, but Laina understood what he meant. As long as there was life, there was hope. But sometimes she wondered if there really was any hope to be found.

She had to stay under the radar wherever she went, and she couldn't trust anyone, least of all the government. Every station, every city, even every major starship had officers representing the Protectorate looking for people like her. The galaxy was full of alien life, and little of it looked kindly upon her. After all, she was just property.

As a so-called "freeborn," she had no rights, and many races still took a dim view of her kind after what had happened to Earth three hundred years ago, during what they called the Terran Disaster. After that day, the balance of power among Terrans shifted forever.

Freeborns like her were hunted down and captured.

There was even a price put on their heads to return them to their rightful owners, the mockeries of creation that looked like humans and were anything but.

Made in our image. If that's wasn't playing God, I don't know what was.

Most of her friends and family had long since been caught and turned over to the Terrans. As far as she knew, of her family, she was the only one left free...or alive.

A chill that had nothing to do with the cold of space made her reach for her leather bomber jacket and slip it over her shoulders. The jacket had been her father's. Even after all this time, it still carried the scent of oiled leather that reminded her of him. She buried her nose in the fleece lining, reliving the brief sense of comfort it gave her. She'd lost her parents ten years ago when the Silver Legion had raided their small refugee ship. It had been carrying the last ten members of their group. Ten, from what had once been thousands.

The Silver Legion. The military branch of the Terran Colony Fleet. She hated them, but her fear was stronger than her hatred. It was crushing to know that humans like her had *no* influence, *no* power in galaxy. They were no better than slaves, and yet those mockeries of humanity, synths and cyborgs, were spoken of with awe by most other races.

Laina never saw the Legion that day, but there was no mistaking the reflective plating of their ship. Her parents had forced her into an escape pod before the Legion disabled their ship and prepared to board.

But something had gone wrong. Almost as soon as the pod had launched, her parents' ship exploded. She had wanted to stay and fight alongside her family, to die beside them. Instead, she'd clung to the tiny confines of the escape pod as it trembled from the shockwave. Golden flames turned purple and rippled out like waves in a cosmic pond, disturbed by a stone thrown by a thoughtless god. At fourteen years old she had become an orphan.

That was when the nightmares started, along with the strange longing for a world she'd never known.

Earth.

Her blood remembered it. The feel of cool grass beneath her bare feet, the warmth of a healthy yellow sun, the air thick with the symphony of early-morning bird song.

Could a person's DNA carry memories? Laina had been born on a starship, yet she could feel the weight of Earth deep in her soul. But she would never see the planet that called to her because there was nothing left to see.

She had heard the whispers from other alien races when they thought she wasn't listening. To them, freeborns were mongrels who mated, fought each other, and consumed whatever they could. They weren't capable of anything more than that and were certainly not worthy of having a seat in the Galactic Senate.

She wasn't sure if she should be angry at them for believing that, or understanding. They did destroy their home planet, after all. At least, that was the official ruling, and centuries of propaganda had done her kind no favors. Earth was a blackened, unlivable mass, and the freeborns were to blame for it, one way or another.

Her parents hadn't been able to tell her much about Earth. Neither of them had ever seen it. Nor had their parents or grandparents. But they carried with them the stories of the past. Earth, the land of a thousand human civilizations, with cities that sparkled beneath the sun, mountains that were wreathed in mists, oceans that stretched for thousands of kilometers, and countless species of animals. They made it sound like a paradise.

Before the synthetics. Before the cyborgs.

The way she had been told the story, when humanity had expanded their reach beyond Earth to its nearby planets, they'd faced all kinds of hardships—radiation exposure, low or no gravity, and dozens of other dangers that could damage the human body over time. In the early days of the colonies, before interstellar travel was even a possibility, life was very risky outside of Earth. But if other worlds were going to someday be hospitable to humans, robots alone couldn't lay the foundation. It required a human touch.

Or humanlike.

Synthetic humans, better known as synths, were built using human DNA, but they were designed at the genetic level with the rigors of space and other hostile environments in mind. They matured and learned quickly so they could become productive as quickly as possible. Over the next century the process was improved upon and refined, until they became a part of everyday life. And eventually an eye was turned toward their potential use in war.

Though they still looked the same, these next-generation synths utilized far more technology in their makeup, right down to the cellular level, making them stronger and faster—some said nearly immortal. These were referred to as cyborgs, and they were in charge of what was left of mankind.

Laina shifted to the edge of her cot and looked back out her small window into space. The stars stopped moving as they dropped briefly out of transit. Probably for another maintenance cycle on the engines.

Each of those thousands of twinkling specks she could see was a star, unimaginably big. Some of those points of light were entire *galaxies*, unbelievably far away. Even close by, in this system, the accretion disk around the massive star they were passing churned like a colorful kaleidoscope, dragging patterns of dust through the emptiness ahead.

It was beautiful, and yet looking at it all made her feel so alone. A million planets and moons out there were filled with intelligent life, yet none of them were human. She had never been so aware of her solitary existence than when she was at a spaceport, surrounded by a dozen different species, many of which shared humanoid traits, some even sounding human, yet none of them were.

These small differences were a painful reminder that she would never fit in. Whether it was the blue skin of the Nubran and Draxon, the short and rough stature of the Hopat, or the strange ethereal beauty of the winged Elysians, she was always reminded that she wasn't one of them. There would always be a divide, having literally come from different worlds, to the point where even a basic conversation could result in misunderstandings.

Laina turned away from the tiny window of her cabin and used the sink before she dressed for meal time. It was easy to lose track of days and hours in space without any sun to guide her. Meals were often the only way she kept track of time on her seemingly endless life on the run. There were days where she feared she may never stop running.

Exiting her cabin, she walked down the corridor until she reached the mess hall. Several Nubrans were already there, and a few smiled at her in greeting as she prepared a plate and joined them at one of the long tables. She listened to them talking and laughing about something that had happened during one of their work shifts. It was nice to just listen sometimes and not feel obliged to talk.

"So, have you ever had sex with a cyborg?"

Laina almost spit out her food, and not just because of the taste. She'd zoned out for a few minutes, and somehow the conversation had turned to sex with cyborgs? Her Nubran crewmates all looked at her expectantly, some with what could only be called a coy smile.

"P-pardon?" For a moment she wondered if she had misunderstood. Her understanding of Nubran was passable but not flawless.

The male who had asked the question leaned forward. "I figured since we were all being so honest here tonight, you should share as well. So, have you?"

Most of the time the crew simply ate where and when they could, but the captain insisted on having everyone together every few days for the sake of morale. This often led to bawdy conversations of one sort or another. Last time it had been about fights they had been in at different ports of call. But this? She hadn't been ready for this.

"I...I..." How could he ask such a thing? Didn't he know what the cyborgs did to freeborns? Who would even consider—?

"I have," said one of the engineers, a Nubran woman. All eyes turned to her now.

"You have not," said the man.

The woman raised her hand, three fingers and a long thumb, and touched her forehead. "Kinerath as my witness. And it was *glorious*."

That got just about everyone hooting in appreciation, except the captain, who sat at the far end watching the proceedings.

"How so?" asked another of the female crewmembers.

"It wasn't just *what* he did," the engineer confessed, "but *how* he did it. Even what he said."

"Was he formal and old-fashioned?" one of the men asked. "Like that old Terran show—the one with the stone house that was far too big for everyone."

"*Downton Abbey*," the captain said in English.

It was funny, but everyone on this ship probably knew more about old Earth than she did. Terran culture was extremely popular among the Nubran, mostly pre-Disaster culture. Something about it just clicked with them, to the point where they even copied certain forms of Terran entertainment they'd never previously used themselves. But Laina tended to avoid such things. It only reminded her of a better time for her people. A time that no longer existed.

The woman continued her tale. "He didn't speak as formally as some of the vids the Terrans put out these days," she said. "But he did have a way with words. And with his *tongue*." That got another round of hoots from the crew, and Laina realized she had been holding a spoonful of food close to her mouth for almost a minute.

She was torn between revulsion and curiosity. It had been forever since she'd had sex with anyone. Such things usually required some amount of trust, and she couldn't afford to trust anyone.

"So what did he do?" another female crewmember asked.

"Well, we all know about their gifts when it comes to strength and endurance," the engineer teased, "but what they don't mention is how sensitive they can be when it comes to touch. He knew *exactly* where to go and what to do. Either I wasn't his first Nubran, or he had very fine instincts."

The man who had started this conversation now turned back to Laina with a grin on his blue face. "So then, how about it? Can you confirm what she's saying?"

The captain coughed politely. "I think that's enough, crewman." She met Laina's eyes, a silent understanding resting behind them. "It might be that our crewmate here hasn't had the chance to enjoy anyone's company recently. Not that I can blame her. There certainly isn't anyone on this ship *I'll* be calling to my personal quarters."

That got another round of hoots, and Laina finally felt like she was being let off the hook. She shrank back down with a sigh of relief and added a bit of protein paste to her food to give it some flavor. After the meal, she returned to her cabin to try to get some more rest. She wouldn't start her shift for another six hours. But as she lay back on her bed, her mind was still racing.

Since the death of her parents, Laina had survived by passing herself off as a synth, using a stolen ident. It worked well enough to get odd jobs in the outskirts of spaceports where they didn't check credentials too closely. The kinds of places where any discrepancies could be passed off as a glitch with the ident reader.

It wasn't unusual to find synths going rogue in this part of space, leaving the Terran Colony Fleet and striking out on their own in the Void. It also made every encounter with someone she thought might be freeborn tense and nerve-racking. Any one of them could be a synth who wouldn't think twice about turning her in for a quick payday. Eventually she started avoiding them altogether, isolating herself even further. It wasn't worth the risk.

The problem was that she'd never truly be safe back where she'd been. Despite having hitchhiked across dozens of worlds, she hadn't traveled more than a hundred light-years from the place her parents had died. She was still far too close to Terran-patrolled space. Now that she was old enough, it was time to change all that. She could never afford paid transport, and her ident would never pass a proper scan at an official customs port, but she'd learned about the kind of deep-space traders who liked to bypass official channels, and some of them exchanged service for passage. Off the books, of course.

It would be risky, but if she pulled it off maybe she could finally settle down and not have to constantly look over her shoulder. She'd never see another human for as long as she lived, but at least she'd die free. So Laina had started keeping tabs on incoming ships at the local starport.

The captain of the *Beautiful Star Chaser* was a Nubran woman named Zore. She'd just finished smuggling goods in from Elysian space, and some of her crew had decided to look for work on other ships. It was pretty standard practice during long-range hauls, especially since Zore wasn't heading back the way she came. Her next destination was toward the Galactic Core, a good twenty thousand light-years away.

Perfect.

Captain Zore didn't ask any questions about Laina's glitchy ident. She might have even suspected her true intentions. The Nubran as a species were strangely infatuated with Terran culture, and some were sympathetic toward the freeborns. No doubt her malnourished state only added to that sympathy. Zore simply nodded and welcomed her aboard.

Life aboard the *Beautiful Star Chaser* so far had been taxing but fair. The ship was a beaten-up Corinthia-class transport, far from factory-fresh, and most of her duties were of the mundane variety, while the real crew stayed busy keeping the ship together. She'd almost grown to enjoy it.

Their first stop had been a world on the edge of the

Void. Their ship needed some maintenance, and the crew were given a few hours of shore leave, but they were warned to watch themselves. Laina had hoped to buy some food that didn't come processed in a tube for the next leg of her journey.

Keeping herself well covered with a hooded coat, she'd passed by a market near the station. A group of men and women of various species had been on a raised platform, half-naked, shivering in the bright light. Some were human. Freeborn.

Slavery was illegal in most parts of the Protectorate, not in the Draxon Collective. Since the Void was a region of space that did not fall under Protectorate jurisdiction, it was easy to end up getting snatched and sold off like these poor souls.

Laina had stood there transfixed, watching as aliens had come forward and bid on them one by one until they vanished. Husbands and wives were torn apart, children ripped away from parents. It had destroyed Laina to watch it happen. She'd kept her tears at bay and hurried back to her ship. She had to keep moving.

This was why she was leaving and why she had no intention of ever looking back. She could put up with cleaning toilets for three months if it meant she could breathe a little easier.

The comm by the metal door of her chamber glowed to life. Probably someone who was going to chew her out for sleeping in or tell her that the recycler was backed up again.

"Attention, all hands. Unidentified vessel approaching. Captain Zore orders all aboard to prepare for possible boarding and inspection." The female Nubran spoke clearly, but Laina could hear the tension in her voice.

Possible boarding and inspection? She groaned. Most

likely a nearby system's picket ship looking for smugglers or hoping for a bribe to let them pass. The problem with hitching a ride on this piece of junk was that it couldn't outrun anything. She ran to the closet and retrieved her small pack, filling it with her belongings, just in case she needed to hide it.

The comm made a crackling noise as a transmission broke through. A baritone voice filled her small room. A *Terran* voice.

"This is Sub-Commander Ronan of the TCF *Orion*. By order of the Galactic Protectorate, the *Beautiful Star Chaser* is to stand down and prepare for boarding and inspection. Anyone in possession of contraband or illegal passengers will be sanctioned." The static cut off, signaling the end of the transmission.

Laina stared numbly at the comm.

The Silver Legion is here? How?

She had to hide, had to get somewhere safe before the ship was boarded. Her identity would never stand up to a real inspection, and she wouldn't pass for a synth if they did a gene scan.

She zipped up her small pack, for once thankful she had only a few possessions to worry about. Some data crystals with books on them and a fresh change of clothes, plus a couple of spare protein tubes that tasted like ash. It was a light load. As she turned to check the room for anything she might have left behind, a shape appeared outside her cabin window. She drew closer, unable to look away.

TCF *Orion*. The name was emblazed on the reflective hull as it pulled up alongside her ship. She wasn't an expert, but she recognized a Silver Legion heavy cruiser when she saw one. It was practically synonymous with them.

The ship was a thing of beauty. Sleek, but practical and

efficient. It held a lethal grace that reminded her of how equally dangerous the crew was. Silver and gray outlines gave the ship a deadly polished appearance. A pair of bright blue lights flashed near a docking tunnel that was extending itself out toward the *Beautiful Star Chaser*.

The front part of the cruiser had a large bridge with a viewport that stretched from the floor to the ceiling. A single chair was placed in the center of the room, with several navigation and operating stations set around it. But it wasn't the chair that caught her attention or even the commander sitting in it, looking at her ship like it and all aboard were prey. It was the man standing closest to the viewport she couldn't look away from.

He was the most beautiful man she'd ever seen. Even though men weren't usually called beautiful, she couldn't think of a better word to describe him. Blond hair that looked silky enough to run her fingers through hung just above his shoulders. She shook herself, wondering why she was thinking about a man's looks at a time like this.

By now the ships were almost touching, just meters apart, giving her a clear view of his face. His ice-blue eyes caught hers and swallowed her whole. No emotion lingered there, nor did any trace of feeling show upon the chiseled features of his face. His silver-and-red uniform struck fear in her, a symbol of everything she was running away from, and yet she couldn't help but notice how well it presented his body.

He was devastating. He was a god. He was a cyborg. He had to be. And he was staring back at her through the window of the *Orion*. Legs braced, hands clasped behind his back, he looked every inch the predator she knew him to be. The crew's conversation about cyborgs and sex came screaming back to her.

"It wasn't just what he did, but how he did it..."

"He did have a way with words. And with his tongue..."

"He knew exactly where to go and what to do. Either I wasn't his first Nubran, or he had very fine instincts..."

She was painfully reminded of just how long it had been since she'd been with anyone and just how a vision like this pressed all her buttons. Even the danger...

Danger.

Danger!

Why wasn't she finding a place to hide?

The man's lips curled into a leonine smile that seemed to say, *I'm coming for you, little mouse.* Laina's heart stopped as the *Orion's* docking bridge locked onto the transport's bay doors.

The blond-haired cyborg turned to say something to one of his crew before he left the main deck. She had to hide. Now. But she had a sinking feeling that no matter where she hid they'd find her. If they knew she was on board, they'd tear the ship apart to get to her.

And then what? Right now it seemed slavery was the best she could look forward to. She almost wished the ship had been intercepted by graywalkers instead. At least with those monsters she knew what her ultimate fate would be.

She ran to the door, but it wouldn't open. She pressed her palm on the panel, but it didn't unlock. The light beneath her palm flared red. She tried again. Still red.

"Damn!" She tapped the comm to contact the captain.

"Captain Zore, this is Laina down in 4C. My door won't open. Can you override the controls?"

Captain Zore's voice came over the comm. "Laina, I'm sorry. The Legion gave me strict orders to lock down all rooms until everyone can be scanned and verified."

Laina gulped. This was happening. It was really

happening.

"Captain, I have to tell you. I'm—"

"Stop. Don't say anything. You do and this whole crew becomes complicit. Do you understand?"

Laina sighed. "Yes."

"I'm sorry, Laina. I really am. But there is a ceiling as to how much I am willing to risk when my ship and crew are at stake. You can't just expect to hide from these things."

Terror squeezed her heart. As much as she understood Zore's reasoning, she couldn't help but feel wounded at being so quickly abandoned. She would be handed over to the cyborgs to be punished for a crime that had occurred centuries before she was even born.

She sagged against the locked door and tipped her head back.

Wait... What did she say? Ceiling? Hide?

Her eyes opened, and she gazed up at the ceiling. It was covered with thin tiles, nestled into square outlines covering the network of pipes and wires above. She'd had to pop up there a number of times to fix some minor leaks. *What if...?*

Running over to her bed, she leapt up on it and climbed onto the thin metal headboard. She was just tall enough to reach the low ceiling, and soon she'd cleared a body-sized hole. She grabbed one of the pipes—thankfully not too hot—and summoned the strength to pull herself up. It was a confined space and impossibly dark, and it only got darker when she slid the tile back into place. With her pack slung over her shoulders, she started to crawl toward a distant light. Where did it lead? Who knew. Any place was better than this.

She left not a moment too soon, because the sound of the docking bridge pressurizing between the two ships told her the cyborgs had boarded.

CHAPTER 2

ARK CHRONICLE ENTRY 1-6

Testing...testing...

This is Dr. John Roberts, utilizing Ark recording function for continuing historical journal to accompany the Ark for posterity. Year one, entry number six.

Now...where was I? Oh yes. Why we made the cyborgs...

By the 2200s, synthetic humans had become an everyday fact of life. Our economy, interplanetary travel, our very way of life relied on them. We also sought to perfect the synths by fixing their flaws, such as the degenerative disease that came to be known colloquially as Dolly syndrome, which plagued the entire first generation. Those we referred to as "second generation" faced their own difficulties, most notably the extremely high percentage that were incapable of retraining once they had become fixed on their expected role.

Later, as tensions rose with the outer colonies, it was decided that a new type of synth was needed. One that was suited for war, but also more versatile and adaptable. In this one way they became the closest to human any generation of synth had ever been.

But in every other way, they became even more distant. The nanotechnology used in their creation granted them enhanced speed, strength, and regenerative abilities—even now we're not certain whether or not they can die of old age. Despite their appearance, there is as much artificial to them as biological. That is part of the reason why we dubbed them cyborgs.

Ronan Antares, sub-commander of the TCF *Orion*, led his team through the docking tunnel connecting his ship to the transport. He carried his pulse gun ready in one hand. These were almost certainly smugglers, and as such they had a tendency to get desperate to protect their bottom line.

The doors ahead opened, revealing a humanoid female with pale-blue skin, wearing a captain's uniform. Nubran. A peaceful race, one of the five founders of the Protectorate, they rarely caused trouble yet remained influential. Nubrans were traders by and large, and they often made long voyages to the farthest reaches of known space, well off the beaten path of most of the safer ship routes.

"Captain Zore?" Ronan asked in a clipped tone. He was not amused by this Nubran's attempt to transport a freeborn across the Void. Oh, there was a chance the woman he'd seen was a synth, but the look on her face told him those odds were small. Zore was in clear violation of Protectorate law.

The captain gave a curt nod. Wariness shadowed her amber eyes, but there was no fear. A brave female. Ronan respected that.

"Welcome aboard the *Beautiful Star Chaser*. Who do

we have the pleasure of meeting?" Her diplomatic tone was typically Nubran, but evasive.

"I'm Sub-Commander Ronan Antares of the Silver Legion. Your ship has been detained for inspection of contraband. I expect to have your crew's full cooperation."

"Of course," said the captain. "Anything else?"

Ronan smirked. "As a matter of fact, yes. Under the regulations laid out by the Sol Patriation Act set forth by order of the Galactic High Council, we will also be inspecting your crew. We have reason to believe you're harboring freeborn Terrans aboard."

"Freeborn?" Captain Zore looked shocked. "There was a Terran aboard when I left Draxon space, but I assure you she was a synth. I vetted her ident as per regulations. Regardless, she left at our last stop. Said she didn't want to travel too far from home."

This female probably played games of chance. She was a skilled liar. "I see. Then I'm afraid to inform you that you have a stowaway on board. But you do not need to worry; we will take her off your hands and return her home."

Zore's skin flushed purple. "How did you—?"

"You cannot hide things from the Legion." He was not about to admit that spotting a human on board was a lucky break. They had been stopping and searching every vessel on this trade route as part of a standing contract with the Protectorate.

It had been sheer luck that he had seen the human woman staring at him as their ships came together. An attractive enough face, yet it had been full of fear. The kind of fear he'd seen on a hundred freeborn runaways. Yet something about that woman's face had put him on edge, and he would not rest until she was safely in a locked cell on board the *Orion*.

"As requested, nonessential crew have been put on lockdown in their quarters, but I assumed it was because you thought a *criminal* was on board." Disapproval layered the captain's tone.

Ronan narrowed his eyes. "Yes. Exactly." He gestured to his boarding party. "Search the ship, but leave the crew quarters to the officers." They nodded and left to canvass the control room, engine room, cargo hold, and anywhere else of possible interest.

Ronan then turned to his immediate subordinates: the *Orion*'s security chief, Alanna Vela, and Ensign Julian Aquila. Both were cyborgs, and as such they would be better suited for securing the freeborn—freeborns had a nasty habit of fighting dirty whenever they felt all hope was lost. He knew this all too well from personal experience, and he wouldn't take any chances.

"Have one of Captain Zore's officers show you to the crew quarters and inspect each one. Start with the lower portside decks. When you find the freeborn, bring her to me."

Ronan slid his pulse gun back into his holster. Alanna and Julian saluted and left. He stayed behind, monitoring the inspection's progress through the comm in his ear, his body tense. He didn't trust himself not to be harsh with the human if he found her first. Better to let the others go instead. He needed to remain in control.

But sometimes that control was tested, like the moment he'd seen this woman's face through the bridge window. There was something deep inside him that warned him about getting too close. At first he thought it came from anger, old scars that ran deep. But now he began to wonder if there was something more...primal behind his reaction.

He shook his head, trying to rid himself of the temptation of taking a freeborn, even a willing freeborn, to his bed. It was unthinkable. She was and always would be the enemy.

It wasn't unnatural for him to feel pleasure; he had found it often enough with females of various species, even among his crewmates. Yet all of that seemed to pale against the primal rush he felt knowing this one particular freeborn would be in his grasp. But why?

Perhaps part of him believed she might have answers. Something about her face seemed familiar. But he couldn't imagine how.

The stunned look of surprise he'd seen on her face, her pale lips parted and her gray eyes wide with fear. Her brown hair fell about her shoulders in wild disarray. Had he seen her before somewhere? Why did that idea please him even more? Why did it make his heart rate increase? It was the thrill of success, no doubt. Another successful hunt. That was all.

Alanna and Julian walked back down the corridor toward him, their faces stony.

"Ronan, the registered crew is accounted for. No sign of any freeborn. One of the berths was empty, however." Alanna slid her stun baton back into its sheath. The rest of the search crew checked in over the comms. Class D restricted goods had been found in the cargo hold. If the captain didn't have the proper paperwork, it was a fineable offense at worst. But nothing else out of the ordinary was reported.

Ronan grew increasingly frustrated. Slowly he turned his attention to Zore. The captain licked her lips. "I told you, she's not on board. You'd best go back to our last stop and search there. But she's probably already on another ship."

Ronan eyed her suspiciously. What was it about the freeborn that caused Zore to lie for her? Try to protect her? Didn't she know what they were capable of? They weren't worth her pity.

He turned to Alanna. "Lieutenant, can you access the ship's systems?"

She nodded, tapping a control panel on the wall. "Their security is simplistic. I do not require the captain's assistance for this."

Zore frowned. "Lovely."

"Is there video feed for the crew cabins?"

Alanna's fingers tapped on the screen rapidly. "Yes. I will bring up the recordings for the unoccupied room we found. Here."

There she is. The human female was watching something out the small window of her cabin. *Him.* Then she ran to the door, calling to be released.

Ronan eyed Captain Zore, who kept her face blank and impassive.

"A very cunning stowaway," Ronan said. "Hiding in plain sight all this time?"

When the freeborn realized she couldn't leave, she leaned heavily against the door, shoulders slumped. *Defeat.* But then the woman surprised him. She looked up at the ceiling, almost at the hidden camera, and smiled. The woman went to her bed, climbed up on the precarious perch of the headboard, and with surprising grace pushed at the ceiling directly above her. Ronan continued to watch in amazement as she hauled herself up and disappeared.

Cunning and quick to adapt. He had to admit he was impressed.

Julian chuckled from behind him. "Well, I'll be damned." The ensign was the most social of the command staff, the one most likely to give in to human traits like humor, and the least likely to obey orders, which was why he was still an ensign. Strangely, he also harbored more hatred for the freeborn than most of the *Orion* crew.

"What?" Ronan asked.

Julian shouldered up next to him to get a better look at the screen. "She gave us the slip. This ship is probably full of places for her to hide. Clever little thing. Like a fox. You remember foxes?" Julian's dark hair fell into his eyes, and he brushed it away with irritation.

Ronan frowned. "I remember foxes. I also remember stories of how agitated the hounds got waiting for the fox to come down from the trees they tried to hide in. I'm not nearly as patient."

Alanna snorted. "Patience was never one of your virtues."

Ignoring her remarks, he turned back to Captain Zore. "Where does the air duct in the ceiling lead?"

Zore shrugged. "They lead all over the ship. She could be anywhere—"

A sudden creak overhead drew everyone's focus.

Zore's eyes flicked above their heads, just for a moment, but it was enough to betray her.

Ronan smiled and pulled his pulse gun from his holster. "Anywhere, you say?" He flicked the setting to stun and nodded to Julian.

The ensign eyed the ceiling, listening for movement, then lunged up and tore down one of the ceiling tiles like it was made of paper.

With a great crash and a scream, a woman fell from above. She landed hard on her side, a small pack rolling off her shoulders and bumping into Alanna's black boots.

Alanna toed it daintily, as if it might detonate, before she reached down and picked it up.

The woman whimpered and crumpled into a ball, knees tucked up near her chin, arms wrapped around her head, protecting herself from whatever attack she expected. Ronan kept his weapon trained on her. She couldn't have been injured—the fall wasn't that high. But freeborns were fragile, he had to remember, so it was possible she'd hurt herself. Still, that was none of his concern. He had a duty to attend to.

"Get up, freeborn."

The bark of his order made the woman flinch, and she began to unwind, as though forcing herself to relax. Her body uncurled, and she pushed herself into a sitting position, wiping dust from her face and hair. She looked helpless. How ironic, given what her ancestors had done to him and his kind.

Her lovely gray eyes—yes, even he could admit that much about them—shone like the hull of the *Orion*. Pure. Beautiful. When her gaze finally settled on his face, her eyes darkened. Like the Scar on Jupiter, they clouded and churned.

"You." She let out a whisper, only audible to him. She shoved herself to her feet and wobbled unsteadily before regaining her balance. Did she recognize him?

"Under the regulations of the Sol Patriation Act as set forth by order of the Galactic High Council, you are hereby detained by the Silver Legion. You will be returned to Terran space, where you will spend the rest of your days in the service of the Terran Colony Fleet. Ensign, restrain her."

The moment Julian took a step toward her, she swung a fist at him. He easily caught her wrist and twisted it until her legs buckled, and she fell to her knees at his feet with a cry of pain.

"Why did you think that would work?" Julian asked.

The woman gasped, face still ravaged with the pain of his tight hold.

He leaned in closer, anger growing. "I've been fighting tougher opponents than you for three hundred years. I once took down a gorg with my bare hands. Why did you think such a feeble attack would succeed?"

The woman shut her eyes, wincing with pain as she took a deep breath.

"Answer me, *freeborn*," Julian demanded, gripping her more forcefully.

Ronan was about to tell Julian to stand down when she struck, driving her other fist into Julian's groin. He cursed as he released her. The woman dove past a shocked Alanna and ran for the door. Ronan aimed his pulse gun and fired, striking her between the shoulders. She went down hard, head smacking into the floor.

The control room went silent, except for the electric drone of computers, as Ronan walked over to the unconscious woman. A cut above her left eye from where she'd hit the floor was dripping blood onto the deck.

An emotion wormed its way to his chest. *Pity.* He pitied this woman. She was so frail, so breakable, like the rest of her doomed people. And yet she was brave enough to evade him and his team, even if the attempt was ultimately futile. It was a pity that freeborns had so many failings. It ruined the few strengths they had.

Ronan knelt and slid one arm behind her back and one behind her knees to lift her up in his arms. He carried her body to his chest and walked back to Alanna and Julian.

"Have the boarding party return to the ship," he said to

Alanna. "Notify the commander that we are returning to the *Orion*." He then looked at the Nubran captain. "We have acquired your 'stowaway,' Captain. I have no further interest in your vessel. You may resume your course."

Zore nodded, carrying a mixture of relief and sadness. "Thank you." Her eyes strayed to the human's face. "Please, don't go hard on her. She is a nice person. Always polite. Worked hard. She never caused any trouble."

Julian groaned. "I beg to differ."

Zore frowned, her amber eyes darkening. "You would have done the same in her position. Any one of us would."

"What's your point, Captain?" Ronan asked in irritation.

"My point is that she is undeserving of whatever fate you have in store for her. I would think, coming from a race once persecuted like they are now, you would be more merciful."

The Nubran's words were bold and unafraid, her determination to stand up for the freeborn an unexpected turn. Ronan couldn't help but wonder what hold this female had over Zore that she would risk her life and the lives of her crew.

"They receive all the mercy they deserve," said Julian.

Zore's head dropped, and she looked away. "You have the law on your side, and I have complied, but if you cannot see that justice must be tempered with wisdom, then there is nothing left to discuss. I will thank you to leave my ship in peace."

"As you wish. Safe journey, Captain." Ronan nodded to his subordinates, who flanked him as he left the control room and returned to the *Orion*, his prisoner still in his arms.

Commander Alaric Corvus stood waiting for them on

the other end of the airlock. His eyes zeroed in on the prisoner.

"So, you were right. You did see a woman on board," Alaric mused. At two meters in height, he was slightly taller than Ronan, but he held an air of command about him that made him seem more solemn than the rest of the crew. A silver star sat on both of his epaulets, but with his service record he could easily have three if he desired. He was one of the first cyborgs to command a warship, and one of the leaders of the Cyborg Rebellion three hundred years ago.

"She gave us a bit of trouble." Ronan tilted the body in his arms so the woman's head rolled away from his chest and toward the commander. The wound above her eyes had caked and clotted.

"Doctor, we need you," Alaric called over his shoulder. A woman appeared from the group that had gathered around the airlock. Dr. Valeria Schedar was the *Orion's* chief medical officer. She wore the uniform of the Legion, only with a silver caduceus on her shoulders instead of a rank insignia. Her long blonde hair was pulled back at the nape of her neck and bound with a strap.

"Minor head trauma... Stunned with a pulse gun, I take it?" Valeria reached to take the woman's body from Ronan.

He felt a strange urge keep her in his arms. Valeria looked up at Ronan and sensed his reluctance. Her lips curved in a soft, understanding smile.

"She won't require a stretcher. Bring her to the infirmary. I still have to tend to her wounds." Valeria headed for the sickbay, and Ronan followed. He felt his commander's eyes on his back the entire way. He wasn't behaving abnormally, was he?

The sickbay was a large room with multiple beds and various medical instruments. Though the cyborgs on board could regenerate from most injuries quickly without aid, the majority of the crew were synths, and as such they required more traditional care.

"Where should I put her?" Ronan asked, looking at the multiple beds. None of them looked particularly comfortable to him.

Valeria waved at the room as she searched for her instruments. "Anywhere is fine."

The metal surface of the nearest medical exam table gleamed in the artificial light, looking cold and hard. Ronan had no desire to place the woman on that.

"Do you have something to lay on the bed to cushion her?"

Valeria chuckled. "Haven't you been here since the refit?"

"I rarely need to come here."

"Just lay her down and press the panel next to the bed, where it says 'New Patient.'"

Ronan did so. As soon as he pressed the button, what he'd assumed was a metal surface slowly ballooned out, raising her up a few centimeters and cushioning her on all sides, raising her head up to a natural resting position.

"Elysian design," the doctor said matter-of-factly. "Customizes the bed to the patient's body, plus provides readings of basic body functions." She pointed to the diagnostics panel above her head, which now lit up with her heart rate, pulse, and brain activity.

"I should have guessed."

"Well, as you said, you rarely need to come here."

Ronan's attention returned to the prisoner. His fingers threaded through her hair. The chestnut strands felt like watered silk. A frisson of pleasure went through him, and he felt a surge of reluctant tenderness for her. That tenderness quickly turned to anger, then into something else. He pictured her looking at him not with fear but desire, and that desire being returned in kind. What would he do if...?

"Ronan?"

He blinked, Valeria's call jarring him back. He shook his head and controlled himself. "What?" His hands were still deep in the soft coils of the freeborn's hair. He freed his hand of the strands that clung to his fingers.

"You can daydream inappropriately on your own time, not mine. I need to wake her." Valeria cleaned the prisoner's head wound and covered the cut with a clear cream, which disappeared as it was absorbed. "She probably has a concussion. I need to make sure she didn't suffer from any other injuries during her journey, and for that I'll need to wake her."

"Fine. Do it." He waited as the doctor injected her with a serum that would pull the prisoner back into consciousness.

The woman's lashes fluttered, and then her gray eyes, fogged with pain and confusion, locked onto his and held.

"You," she gasped. Again she'd said that.

"Me," he agreed. He forced himself to scowl, though part of him found her bewilderment amusing. But she was not a source of humor. Despite how she appeared, she was the enemy. He could never forget that.

CHAPTER 3

Ark Chronicle Entry 1-24

Cyborgs...synths...the words sound so...inhuman. Though some of my colleagues disagree, I think it is obvious why we use such words to describe our creations. We needed to believe, on some level, that they were not fully human—and we did not want to open the way to suggest that they were our equals. Some feared they might then believe themselves to be our betters, but I believe the reason is more simply explained by greed.

After the global economic collapse of the twenty-first century and the subsequent restructuring that put corporations in charge, matters of policy and rights have always been made with an eye to corporate needs and profits. And in 2100, when the Synth Proposal was introduced shortly after the Mons Olympus incident, that need was made clear in the very first word.

We needed our creations to be something less than us so that we did not dwell too long upon how we intended to use them. We would still talk of rights, strive toward some superficial semblance of fairness and equity with them, but the truth was we would always hold something back. Because we believed we had to.

What we never considered was that they would figure this out for themselves.

OUT OF THE FRYING PAN AND INTO THE FIRE, AS HER mother used to say. Laina's brain pounded against her skull. What the hell had happened after she fell out of the air duct? A punch, she remembered that. A lucky hit. She'd been running—somewhere, anywhere—and then blinding pain and nothing.

The cyborg studied her, the chilly depths of his blue gaze taking in every inch of her to the point that she began to feel uncomfortable.

"What...did you do to me?" She tried to voice it as a demand, but it came out as breathless and frightened as she felt.

"You attacked one of my men, then tried to escape. I stunned you. You fell and hit your head. Our doctor believes you may have a concussion." His deep voice teased her ears. If he were human, she wouldn't be ashamed of her body's reaction to it.

A tall woman stood next to her, dressed slightly different than the others. "I would like to do a full medical scan for any other injuries or conditions you might have contracted. Please remove your clothes." The doctor's face held a gentleness to it. Perhaps it was simply part of her genetic makeup, a programed medical background where doctors were trained to believe in healing and helping above all things.

"Take my clothes off?" She clamped her hands around the collar of her jacket, closing it tight. They could easily force the clothes off her, but she wasn't going to just give in.

The doctor made eye contact with the male cyborg, their shared look unblinking. Laina had the distinct feeling they were communicating. No, that was crazy. Cyborgs weren't telepathic. Then what were they doing? Finally, the doctor sighed and turned back to her.

"Removing your clothes will allow my scanners to get a more accurate reading. I can also treat any other injuries you might have sustained."

"Do I have to?" She grudgingly realized that she wasn't above begging.

The male cyborg made a growling sound that made her squeeze the jacket even tighter about her. His hands shot out and tore the jacket open.

"Um, Ronan. What are you doing?" the doctor asked.

"It's obvious she's hiding something. I won't be held responsible for allowing a freeborn to smuggle a weapon on board. Now help me remove her clothes or get out of the way, Valeria."

The doctor rolled her eyes and wrapped one hand around Ronan's wrist, stilling him.

"At ease, Sub-Commander. We can do the scan *after* she's calmed down. She's been under a lot of stress. Give her some space, and she will comply."

Laina found herself nodding enthusiastically, hoping Ronan would have mercy on her, even though every instinct in her told her he wasn't the merciful type.

"She'll do it *now*." He locked his frosty eyes to hers. "Won't you? You'll be good and not make any trouble for me. I have no interest in forcing you into compliance, but if pain is what motivates you, then I will provide *motivation*."

Valeria made a soft noise that sounded like a chuckle.

What was going on here? It was as though the doctor didn't believe him. It made Laina bold enough to stand her ground.

"So you'll just take whatever you want? That's what your kind do, after all, right?" Where her sudden burst of bravery came from, she didn't know. Her entire life she'd been taught to hide, evade, barter, even beg if necessary for survival. Something about this cyborg's superior attitude epitomized everything she hated about them, and for once she was tired of cowering in fear.

The cyborg doctor gave a polite intervening cough. "Ronan, it's obvious she's uncomfortable. And you know my views with regard to the treatment of freeborns," Valeria warned. All gentleness was gone in an instant, and her face was as stony and determined as Ronan's.

Laina sensed an ally in the doctor, and right now she desperately needed one. She reached out to touch the doctor's arm. "I'll do it, I promise...if he leaves. You can search me for weapons, wounds, ticks and lice, whatever you want. After he's gone."

She saw the warring emotions on Ronan's face, and they terrified her. Rage. Distrust. Wariness. Concern. It was like he didn't know what to do with himself. Like he was barely in control.

"I'm not leaving. You'll attack the doctor the second my back is turned."

"I believe I can handle myself," said Valeria.

Ronan ignored her. "I know your kind better than you know yourself. I'll not let my friends die because you tricked me with your false modesty."

Again, she saw the doctor roll her eyes. "For the love of the Colony, Ronan..."

Ronan glared at the doctor. "Your primary concern is

your patient. My primary concern is the safety of this ship and everyone on it. *My* concern outweighs yours."

Laina sucked in a breath. What made Ronan so distrustful? His people were the ones who hunted hers down, not the other way around. She wasn't the deadly one in the room.

"I want her searched, Val."

"What if I restrained her?" Valeria suggested. "She'd be harmless then."

Ronan seemed to be satisfied. "You can cut off her clothes once she is restrained," he growled.

"Cut off my..." She leapt off the exam table and shrugged out of the jacket so fast that both cyborgs jumped back. Ronan raised his pulse gun. She hadn't even seen him grab it.

"Listen. This jacket was my father's. I'm not letting you cut it off me, and I want it back. You can search it for whatever you want. Just give it back. In one piece. Please." She laid the coat out on the examination table.

Ronan smiled, a dark, cruel smile. The same kind he'd had when she glimpsed him through the window of the *Beautiful Star Chaser*.

"You're in no position to make demands. You are a prisoner of the Silver Legion, and you live or die at the pleasure of the Terran Colony Fleet. Is that clear?"

Something in Laina's throat clamped down, and she suddenly found it hard to breathe. Tears welled up in her eyes.

"Pl—please." Her voice broke as she begged. "It's the only thing I have left of him...please."

Valeria's lips pursed in a tight line. She met and held Ronan's gaze. Another unspoken moment passed between them. Finally, Ronan heaved a sigh.

"I will take this and conduct a thorough search. If you're telling the truth and it holds no weapons or other threats, it will be returned to you. If you're not, it will be incinerated." He bent to pick up the jacket, and she nearly burst into a sob of gratitude. "You can live without the rest of your clothes?"

Laina responded with a nod. They could dress her in rags and she wouldn't have cared, so long as she got her jacket back.

"Please, come to the table." Valeria gestured to where she'd been lying before.

With the blanket removed, she climbed up and lay back on the examination table, which quickly fit to her contour again. Ronan handed Valeria a set of silver cuffs that Laina recognized with dread. Slaver cuffs. They were long and thin, fitting neatly around her forearms, yet the alloy they were made of was incredibly strong. She'd seen them on slaves at stations, and she'd wondered if the metal felt cold on one's skin. Now she knew. They were like ice. But they could also send a massive shock through her if she got out of line.

Despite the fact they had no obvious fasteners, the doctor took her wrists and easily connected the cuffs to the examination table.

"There, satisfied? Now, take her jacket, examine it down to the stitching if that will make you happy, and wait outside until I call for you. Is that understood?" Valeria dismissed Ronan without another word.

Ronan gripped her coat so tightly that his knuckles whitened. He stalked out of the medical bay, and the door slid shut with a hiss.

The second Ronan was outside, Laina relaxed. The man had scared her witless, yet she couldn't stop looking at him. He was a scourge to her kind, and yet she'd never felt more alive than right now.

When Valeria rose over her, it reminded Laina that she was almost as tall as Ronan. She blocked out the light overhead as she ran a small tube-shaped device with a broad, flat head over Laina's body. Some kind of state-of-the-art medical detector. The kind of medical equipment she'd been around before now was often decades out of date. But that was to be expected when you were raised on the run, living on the scraps of other species' kindnesses.

"My apologies for the restraints," the doctor said. "I would remove them, but I suspect Ronan is at a terminal outside, watching me examine you, seething."

"Seething?"

"Yes, it's quite unlike him, but something about you has him riled up. I've never seen him like that before. I'm tempted to take the cuffs off just to see how long it takes him to come storming back in."

Laina almost laughed at that.

"What is your name?"

She felt safe enough to answer, at least partially. "Laina... My name is Laina.

"It's nice to meet you, Laina. I am Dr. Valeria Schedar. My friends call me Val. You may do so if you wish."

She blinked up at the cyborg, unsure of where this simple kindness was coming from. "Um...okay, Val. Thanks." Maybe she seemed nice because she was designed that way.

The doctor continued to scan the length of her body, then checked some readings, then frowned and scanned again.

"My apologies. I'm going to have to remove the rest of your clothes, Laina."

Laina tensed. "How come?"

"There are some unusual readings here. Contamination might be involved. I need to have as clean a scan as possible to confirm a few things. Don't worry, we'll provide you with fresh replacements."

She blushed as Val took turns between scanning and removing her clothes, storing them away in a quarantine bin. Soon she was completely naked, but the doctor did her best not to make her self-conscious about it.

"Nearly done," Val said soothingly. "Tell me, are you on any kind of medication?"

"No."

"Have you ever had any cybernetic augmentation that you later removed?"

"I can't afford anything like that."

"No, I suppose not. What about something simple, like birth control implants?"

"Pardon?"

"Pleasure stim implant?"

"*What?*"

"Did you engage in sexual activity with any of the crew on your ship who might have been augmented in some way?"

"No!"

The doctor seemed to realize how uncomfortable Laina was getting at her questions. "My apologies. I'm trying to rule out certain possibilities. I forgot that your kind can be a little uneasy talking about sexual matters."

"It's not that, it's just..." Actually, it *was* that. She'd been orphaned as a teen and had rarely talked to others like her since then, so in some ways she had never had a chance to get comfortable talking about sex with anyone. "I mean, you're *not* uncomfortable talking about sex?"

"I'm a doctor. Sex is simple biology. But, yes, as a whole we don't treat it as anything to be ashamed of."

"I'm not ashamed of it."

"I beg to disagree. Your heart rate spiked during those questions. Your fight-or-flight response engaged."

"It's just... I mean, it's personal. That's all." The fact she'd had barely any experience in that matter didn't help, either.

The doctor gave a sly smile, avoiding direct eye contact. "You know, your heart rate spiked like that earlier. When Ronan insisted on having your clothes removed."

"Well, it's like you said. Fight-or-flight response, right?"

"Perhaps. But you have to admit the sub-commander is attractive."

Laina frowned. "Hard to tell given how he glares at me."

"Yes, well, I've never seen him glare at anyone like that before, freeborn or otherwise. I think he's confused."

"About what?"

"About you, of course. Okay, so I've ruled out anything in your core region as a point of origin. I'm going to work toward where I first noticed the anomaly. Try to hold still."

Laina squirmed, but not because she was trying to escape. She was fighting an uncontrollable urge to scratch an itch on her nose. The doctor consulted a full-body map on the display next to her, then swept the scanner along her right arm.

"I'm going to release your right hand," she said. "I need to confirm the cuff isn't causing any interference."

She tapped a control on her wrist, and just like that the metal cuff popped open, freeing her right arm. The doctor continued her scan and froze when she fixed it on the back of Laina's hand. The device gave a series of short beeps.

The doctor's brows drew together. She reached up and uncurled Laina's clenched fist, gently holding the fingers open so she could run the scanner over Laina's palm. The same rhythm of short beeps followed.

"What is it?"

Val studied her hand and bit her lip before responding. "You have an implant in your hand. I can't quite explain it. It's unlike anything I've ever seen before. It's artificial, but it also seems to be organic. How odd," she mused. "I would like to run some more tests."

"You keep saying these things as if I have a choice in the matter."

Valeria smiled. "I find a good bedside manner is important, regardless of species or circumstance."

The doctor's thumb swept over Laina's palm in a circular motion, and she stared at it as if it were a puzzle to solve. The doctor released her from the bed and replaced the cuff she had taken off. At least she could sit up on the table again. Val handed her a blanket, which she used to cover herself, then went to consult a datascreen.

"Now, first I'd like to test and see—"

"You can run your tests later, Valeria," a cold voice said. Ronan stood in the doorway of the sickbay like an implacable force of nature.

Laina used the blanket to cover herself as much as possible. A blush crept across her face. She'd become painfully aware of her less-than-ideal body. Someone like him probably saw perfection every day on board this ship. Sure, it was easy to have a perfect body when you were literally born that way. She looked to the doctor as an example. Tall, gorgeous, not an ounce of fat anywhere it shouldn't be...

She mentally smacked herself. What was she *thinking?*

"You could at least give her a chance to change first."

"She can change in her cell. I won't have her try any tricks on you."

Valeria sighed. "Very well, Ronan. I'm done with the initial exam. You may take her now. But I'd like to see her again so I may look at her hand. There's something unusual there."

"Unusual?" He looked to the doctor, one brow raised.

"And before you ask, no, it's not a weapon. It could be nothing. Sometimes the scanners pick up things that turn out to be false positives."

"I want to know if you find anything important."

"Of course," Val promised.

Ronan growled something that sounded like a curse word. He stalked over to the exam table and grabbed Laina's arm. She gasped as he tugged her off the table and onto her feet. The blanket started to fall from her body, and she tried to catch it.

Ronan reacted as though she were trying to break free or attack him. He spun her around to face the medical bed, bending her over it and pinning her arms to her lower back. The blanket slid to the floor at her feet. Her lungs seized as she fought to remain calm. She felt like he might kill her here and now if she made another move.

"For the love of the Colony, Ronan, stand down. She wasn't trying to escape." Valeria's voice was soft, but also at wit's end, as though she were speaking to a frustrating child. Laina couldn't see the doctor. Her cheek was pressed to the examination table, which was dutifully formfitting itself around half of her face. She shut her eyes, trying to block out the pain in her wrists.

Ronan's hips dug into her backside harder.

"She...she tried...," Ronan argued, but he sounded unconvinced.

"She was trying to keep her body covered," Valeria explained patiently.

Slowly, Ronan's grip lessened until he released her completely. When he stepped back, she didn't move. She could still feel his eyes on her naked body.

A warm hand settled on her shoulder. She turned her head a little to see Valeria behind her. The doctor bent, picked up the blanket, and covered her. She laid down a neatly folded pile of clothes next to her.

"It's all right, Laina. Ronan will escort you to the brig now. Remember to take your clothes with you."

She looked up at Ronan through her lashes, hoping to avoid direct eye contact with him. He stared at her, an odd expression on his face. He wasn't angry, but he seemed indecisive. His brow was furrowed, and his lips were pursed.

"So, is that your name? Laina?" The words came out as though such small, almost pleasant talk was grating to his ears.

"Yes."

A tic worked in his jaw. Without warning, he released her from the slaver cuffs. "I've reconsidered. Dress. Now. I won't have you walking through the ship naked."

Laina hastily scrambled into the red-and-silver uniform and black boots. It looked like a simplified version of the uniform Ronan himself was wearing. When she was ready, Ronan took her hands and slipped the silver cuffs back onto her wrists.

The slaver cuffs. How she hated them. He locked them together so that her wrists were bound like a criminal. Part of her wanted to protest, but in the end exhaustion won out. There was no way off the ship, no way to fight. They would ask their questions, and she would have no answers. Then they'd send her off to work the rest of her days for the Colony somewhere. Or maybe they would dispose of her like they had her parents, her friends...

She was so tired. Tired of running, tired of being afraid. But perhaps now she was close to the end of her suffering. Sadness filled her when she realized she had no fire left in her to fight, but that was the reality. She'd lived her life on the run, hadn't known any other way. Some days she felt a hundred years old given the things she'd seen, the things she'd had to do. And this was, at last, the end of her story.

Ronan shoved her shoulder, and she stumbled a step.

"Move, freeborn," he barked.

Freeborn. The word, vilely pronounced as it was from him, was still a badge of honor for her.

That's right. I wasn't just born free, I have lived a free life. You may have caught me, but I will die free as well. There was honor in that, and it gave her strength.

"I said *move!*"

She shook her head numbly. He looked furious enough to strike her, but he didn't raise a hand. The doctor stood a few feet away, watching them curiously, her arms crossed.

Laina turned her head in his direction, catching his eye. "Are you going to kill me?"

Ronan's eyes widened. "What?"

"If I don't turn out to be useful to you. Are you going to kill me? Work me to death in some mine?"

Ronan looked like he was about to recite a prepared speech, but the doctor raised a hand for him to be quiet.

"Laina." Val's voice seemed to have an almost soothing, hypnotic effect. "No one is going to hurt you. The Protectorate has laws in place regarding the treatment of slaves and indentured servants within Draxon space, and we obey those laws."

Ronan put his hands on his hips, legs braced apart as he faced her, looking every inch the warrior. Not that she'd seen many warriors, but in her travels she'd certainly seen dangerous beings, and Ronan looked to be one of the most dangerous she'd ever come across.

"The doctor is correct," Ronan added. "The Colony will find a use for you, and you will be put to work, but you will be treated fairly. That is our way." His words were quiet and layered with a placating tone that made her uneasy, though she didn't get the impression he was lying to her. The problem was, she knew he was.

"You treat us *well*?" Laina snapped. "The Legion killed my parents. You killed my family, everyone I grew up with." *Let them argue their way out of that one,* she thought darkly.

The two cyborgs exchanged looks.

"Laina," Ronan said, sounding surprisingly patient, "whatever you think we are, we are not cold-blooded killers."

A forced and brittle laugh escaped her. "No? My parents were on board an unarmed refugee ship. Your people came to 'claim' them. When they couldn't get in, they destroyed the ship instead and everyone on it. Your people made me an orphan."

Ronan came over to her, towering above her, forcing her to look up to meet his eyes. "I cannot imagine losing one's parents, given that I never had the blessing. I have no sense of what you must be feeling. But know this. We do not kill without reason. We are better than that."

"Better? You're no...better than anyone...else..." She groaned as her vision swam in murky patterns. She surrendered and closed her eyes, feeling herself drop as the strength left her legs.

Strong arms banded about her waist, lifting her up. She

felt herself lifted and cradled in Ronan's arms. Voices talked around her, and she struggled to focus.

"What happened? Did you give her a sedative?"

"Yes, during my examination. I guess it's taking effect now."

"How much did you give her?"

"Only a half dose. But she's weak, still recovering from long-term malnourishment, and the shock of all this is only adding to her stress. She needs to stay in sickbay."

A cold laugh followed. "I don't trust her here. Too many of your instruments could be used as weapons. No, she'll be taken to the brig until she's well enough for questioning. You can see to her treatment there if you must."

"I will never understand your paranoia, Ronan." This was accompanied by a warm palm brushing the hair back from her face. "I don't think this woman is the least bit dangerous."

"You didn't see her cripple Julian with a single blow."

"Don't exaggerate. I heard about Julian. Just because she knows your weak spot does not make her dangerous. It just means she's had to deal with men before." Valeria chuckled. "I'm starting to think Laina may be the most interesting thing to happen to this ship in some time."

"You and I have vastly different concepts of what is interesting, Doctor."

The voices continued to talk, but Laina could no longer discern any meaning, and she drifted away into unconsciousness.

CHAPTER 4

Ark Chronicle Entry 45-67

I have said much over the decades about what Earth was like, how we rose and ultimately fell, but before I die and pass the duties of the Ark on to my son, it's important to look back, not just at us, but the universe and the space-faring species within it. Some of them are old, even ancient, while others are as new to the stars as we are.

The Protectorate was founded more than five thousand years ago, when three of the founding species, the Nubran, Draxon, and Hopat, first encountered one another at a point where their present-day territories meet. Within a few centuries, contact was made with two other species—the reclusive Ugaro, and the fair Elysians—and the Protectorate was established.

At this time in history, interstellar travel was slow and time-consuming. Though the light barrier had been broken, it would be several millennia before it reached the speeds we are capable of today. So by the time these species first encountered one another, they had established themselves within their own regions of space for hundreds, if not thousands of years.

Most of the time, contact between the five species was infrequent, and the colonization of other worlds was slow. But they all continued to explore, because their generous and broadly defined borders contained within them millions of systems each.

Over time, they encountered other races, younger races that had only recently achieved space travel. But these races were within the borders of the well-established Protectorate species, and the question was raised as to what would be done with them.

Laina slowly came around. She felt a cold surface beneath her body and the hum of a ship's engines. Her body wouldn't stop shivering. The thick blanket draped over her offered minimal comfort against the cold metal of the raised platform she was lying on. Unlike the sickbay, there was no comforting formfitting padding to match her body's shape here. She sat up, looking around in confusion, trying to figure out where she was. A dull pain pounded behind her eyes in an awful steady rhythm. She winced as she pushed herself up on her elbows and took in her surroundings.

She was in a containment cell of about eight by twelve feet. It was well known that the Legion purchased many of their ships from their allies, the Draxon, but while the other parts of the ship she'd seen had been renovated into something more comfortable, the cells here were pure Draxon in design. Functional, efficient, and cold.

While her cell was lit, the room beyond was empty and

dim. That was odd. The front of the cell had a slight shimmer, an energy field meant to keep prisoners contained, but it was also fully visible at all times in order to discourage escape. Not that there was anywhere she could escape to. This was a Legion ship, and there was no place she could hide where they couldn't find her.

Despair settled over her until she felt numb and unable to breathe.

She curled up and nestled deeper into the blanket, her teeth rattling. Why did they keep the cells so cold? Her stomach churned with nausea, but it soon turned to a grumbling for food. She hadn't eaten in a day. Captain Zore and her crew hadn't offered the most appetizing meals. After so many days of greenish broccoli-like oatmeal paste, better suited for their biology than hers, she'd resorted to using her own supply of protein tubes, but the last of those were in her backpack. Thinking of the captain made her sad. She'd been a friend, at least as close to one as she'd had in a while, yet she'd turned her over to the cyborgs without a fight. Not that she could have won such a fight.

Laina wondered for a moment if they would make an example of Zore and destroy her ship for carrying her. She might never know the captain's fate.

I hope you're safe, Zore. She meant it. Life was dangerous enough at the best of times, and Zore had to think about the safety of her entire crew, not just Laina.

She tugged the blanket closer. Her belly ached from hunger, even as bile rose in her throat, which she fought back down. She knew she ought to get some sleep, but it was hard when she was cold and starving. The growling seemed to reverberate inside her like the beating of a hollow drum. She almost wished she was back with the doctor. Val had been the only nice cyborg she'd met, and at least the sickbay had been warm.

Ronan, though...

He epitomized everything she feared about the cyborgs. His good looks only emphasized that air of superiority they carried about them, how they looked down on freeborns like bugs, and with as much right to live in their presence. It was like seeing the face of an angel, only to have that face scowl and find you unworthy. Perhaps unfit to live.

Laina was still lost in her thoughts when something moved by the brig's open entrance. A large shadow stole into the room. A guard? Why didn't he turn on the lights? The shadow moved slowly, and it was larger than she'd first imagined. The light from her cell was only bright enough to see that he wore a Legion uniform. Maybe he was there to feed her. She wondered if they'd give her actual food or a bowl of water and kibble to make her feel more like an animal. Then he reached her cell, and she was able to see his face. What she saw turned her blood to ice. *Hatred.*

The cyborg placed his palm over the panel that locked her cell door. It hummed, and although Laina couldn't see the panel from where she was, she saw a green light move up and down the cyborg's chest as though the panel was scanning the surface of his palm. The energy field dropped, and she watched in terror as he stepped inside.

She stumbled to her feet. "Why are you here? What are you doing?"

"You will die at my hands. For the pain your people have caused. For the lives of my people. I will avenge them."

She tried to stall, looking for some kind of chance to slip around him. "But why? What will killing me accomplish? You beat us centuries ago! What would my death do for you?"

The cyborg paused, but only for a moment. He'd already made his choice.

"Your death will please me. That is enough."

Laina had imagined many times what she might do when this day came. The hows and whys played out in different ways, but the outcome was always the same. But what she never could be sure about was whether she would be as brave as she hoped she'd be. She couldn't fight him, but she could deny him the satisfaction of her trying.

She forced herself to relax and, standing perfectly still, unfolded her hands.

"What a glorious victory, to kill a defenseless woman who's at your mercy. I'm sure you'll tell this story with pride to your comrades."

She hadn't expected her words to change his mind. If anything, they only infuriated him more. He grabbed her and pinned her to the wall, locking his fingers around her throat, tightening his grip as he lifted her off the ground until her eyes were level with his.

"Your kind never changes. You took *everything* from me."

Black dots splattered across her vision as she gasped for air. She wondered if this was like being jettisoned into space, opening and closing one's mouth and finding nothing. Her lungs burned as though on fire, and soon her instincts took over, and a wild animal panic set in.

She clawed at his hands, screeching without sound because no breath could escape her lips. Her legs flailed as her body demanded air and life.

It happened so fast, the sudden rush of darkness, the fading sensations and sense of self. One last squeeze and she was gone.

"Report, Ronan." Commander Alaric Corvus leaned back in his chair in the central part of the *Orion's* command deck. He steepled his fingers and fixed a curious gaze on Ronan.

"The freeborn was taken to the sickbay, where Dr. Schedar performed an examination. She reported some kind of anomaly in her palm."

"What kind of anomaly?"

"Uncertain, but she will be investigating further once she's had a chance to recover."

"And where is the freeborn now?"

"She's been placed in the brig."

"You consider her a threat to the ship?"

"I prefer not to take chances," Ronan answered.

"With her, or yourself?"

Ronan almost protested the implication, but stopped himself short. The commander no doubt was referring to his anger toward the freeborn, but at this moment he was feeling something completely different.

Ronan had been doing everything he could not to think about her. Laina. Such a lovely name, unworthy of someone like her. He didn't like the way his body had responded when he had carried her from the Nubran ship. Or how there had been more at work than the safety of the ship when he had her pinned to the medical bed.

Something about her called out to him. He was conflicted, and that worried him. Laina was a freeborn human, she was a prisoner, and his people were determined not repeat the mistakes of their creators. He would not use her simply because he felt a raw attraction, no matter how strong it was. The cyborgs were not animals, which was more than he could say for the freeborn. He would simply have to control his fascination with her until it faded and passed with time.

"I sense your thoughts wandering," Alaric mused.

Ronan refused to rise to his commander's bait. "Apologies, sir. What are your orders?"

Alaric rose from his chair and strode to the large viewport at the front of the deck, which reached from floor to ceiling and extended out in a 120-degree arc. The rest of the bridge crew continued with their duties.

The *Orion*'s command deck was a concession to beauty over function that they'd added themselves, and the wide viewport was part of that design. Stars and galaxies stretched out in every direction, winking at them like a thousand tiny jewels tossed over black velvet. In times of battle, thick ablative plating would be raised and holographic projections with tactical information displayed in its place.

Alaric clasped his hands behind his back. "I was rereading the Ark Diary last night."

Ronan focused instantly, all thoughts of the soft human female forgotten.

The diary was the only sign the cyborgs had that the key to their salvation still existed somewhere. The commander had discovered a diary that had belonged to one of the key scientists behind Project N. It was the only information from that team he was aware of that had survived the Terran Disaster. And for the last three hundred years he'd tried to decrypt the diary, to no avail.

But then, a few months ago, he had succeeded. Exactly how was a matter he had been tight-lipped about, even to his second in command, but what it contained he'd been more open with. Much of it they already knew, a history of time before the Terran Disaster, back when the freeborn were in control. But it was incomplete and hinted toward more information that had survived the disaster. Information they needed if their species were to survive.

"And?"

"I'm beginning to wonder if the freeborns are more important in our quest than we thought."

"I can't imagine how. Their great-grandparents weren't even born when Earth was lost."

"True, but on more than one occasion the diary refers to the future belonging to their children, or their children's children."

"A common enough proverb, isn't it?"

His commander turned away from the window, his faced lined with shadows. "Also true. But the diary refers specifically to the children of the scientists who created us. You remember them?"

Ronan felt his blood boil. "How could I forget? Their names are branded on my soul." Wolfe. Maguire. Patel. Latimer. Nguyen. Brockman. Adams. Roberts. The lead scientists of Project N.

"I believe those men and women somehow passed the answers to their children, even if they themselves stayed behind on Earth."

"And you feel they somehow passed that information on for generations?"

"Yes, though not in the way you might think. I've contacted the fleet, asking them to do a scan on every registered freeborn, looking for any direct genetic match to those names."

"That might take a while."

"Yes," the commander agreed. "It is a large number to search." Guilt and frustration were evident on Alaric's face, as frown lines etched themselves more deeply. It was the only sign of his advanced age. That and the sorrow and loneliness of three centuries that haunted his light-brown eyes like storms swirling in the atmosphere over Jupiter.

"And when you find those matches? What makes you think they will know anything? Too much time has passed. Any whispered stories passed on from father to son will be less than useless to us now. Fables, nothing more. And if the information was being passed through data crystals, we'd have discovered them by now."

"Well, that's just it," said Alaric. "I don't believe they were passed down as stories or data crystals. I believe that before the loss of Earth and all that came from it, they were trying something new. Consider this, Ronan. What if they passed on what we need through their own *genes*?"

Ronan considered the possibility. "I suppose it's possible, rewriting DNA inside junk code to hide information. But it would never be passed on to their children. And even if it could be, the code would degrade after only a couple of generations."

"I don't believe the technique they'd use would be as simple as that. I also don't believe they worked on this alone."

That had a disturbing implication. "You think the Elysians were involved?" Of the five main Protectorate species, the Elysians had the most obvious history of genetic alteration behind them.

"It's possible. There have always been sympathizers for the freeborns from the other races. We stopped a number of ships trying to smuggle them out of Sol after the Protectorate's ruling. We also know that some succeeded."

Ronan nodded. "Then what should we be looking for?"

"I need to speak with Valeria, but I have some theories. It might use nanotech, not unlike what's in our own genetic makeup."

"Only that would show up in a gene scan," Ronan argued.

"True, which is why I need to speak to the doctor. She'll be able to think of more creative possibilities, I'm sure. It might even be organic, infused in some kind of symbiotic fashion. Honestly, it could be anything."

Ronan's heart jolted. Valeria said the human, Laina, had some kind of anomaly in her hand.

It was as if Alaric had read his mind. "I wish for Valeria to begin her tests on our prisoner immediately."

"She's not yet awakened."

"Then wake her."

"But—"

"*Now*, Sub-Commander. I'm eager for answers."

"Yes, Commander." He stalked from the bridge, unhappy with the situation. He would go to the brig and speak to the woman himself before he took her to the doctor. Every instinct in him said she was important, but he wasn't sure whether that was a good thing.

He was halfway to the lift when Julian stopped him.

"Hey, Ronan. Looking for dust on the bulkheads to complain about, or do you have a minute?"

Sometimes Julian could really test his patience. "What is it, Ensign?"

"Have you seen Erik? He didn't show up for his watch assignment."

Ronan froze in his tracks. He didn't trust freeborns, and generally thought the worst of them, but Erik Keid truly hated them. In the years leading up to the Terran Disaster, he'd been experimented on by a covert military faction. They were trying to understand the cause of the cyborgs' growing dissent, like it was a simple software malfunction. Then, after Earth was destroyed, they'd abandoned the facility, and him with it. It wasn't until the next year—after the cyborgs and synths reestablished stability in the solar system—that they'd found him, wild and starving.

And he had lost so much more since then. They'd nicknamed him the Berserker, and he certainly couldn't be trusted alone with a freeborn.

And apparently he was missing...

"Does he know we have a freeborn on board?" Ronan started to jog through the corridor.

"He was by the airlock when you brought her on board. He looked..." Julian paused as he ran to catch up with Ronan by the lift. The doors opened, and they stepped inside.

"He looked what?"

"Uh...pissed. Should we expect trouble?"

Ronan engaged the lift, and they dropped down toward the brig. "Lots of it. I knew this woman would be a problem."

The lift opened, and Ronan pulled his pulse gun from his holster. Julian nodded and pulled out his own. They both set their weapons to deliver a stun charge instead of a lethal blast.

They heard a scream, which was almost instantly silenced. Ronan's heart beat wildly, and he burst into a mad run, praying he'd get there in time.

"Erik!" Julian shouted. "Stay back! That's an order! We're coming your way."

Ronan and Julian ran into the brig, which was empty and unlit. What had happened here? Erik stood inside one of the cells, holding a limp Laina in his arms, a vicious snarl distorting his features. Ronan prepared to fire, but Julian stepped in front of him, blocking his shot.

"Erik, put her down," Julian said soothingly, holding his weapon to the side, his other hand raised. "Come on, buddy. You've subdued her. It's safe to put her down. The commander has ordered you to the command deck. He needs you there. Think about your duty."

Erik's growling ceased, and confusion softened his menace. He moved slowly and set Laina down. He backed up and exited the cell. Then he stopped and, as if recovering his wits, snapped to attention.

"She was a threat, sir," he said, looking to Ronan. "I...I have neutralized her."

Ronan glowered at him. "Dismissed."

He knelt next to Laina and placed two fingers under her chin to search for a pulse. It beat steadily, thumping with surprising strength. But she was hurt. Dark, angry bruises were already forming around her wrists, and a welt was visible around her throat. She had a swollen eye that would turn black in a few hours if left untreated.

"Julian, escort Ensign Keid to his quarters." He took Julian aside. "Do not inform the commander of what has happened. I will deal with it. But do not let him out of your sight until he is secured, understood?" Ronan fought to keep the disapproval out of his voice. They were supposed to be *better* than this. "I'll see to the woman."

"Come on, buddy," said Julian.

Erik seemed confused. "What about the commander?"

Julian patted Erik on the shoulder and led him out of the brig. "Later. First we need you to calm down."

Ronan lifted Laina's body up and carried her back to sickbay. He cradled her against his chest, trying to convince himself that it wasn't because he liked the feel of her so close, that it was simply easier to hold her that way.

CHAPTER 5

ARK CHRONICLE ENTRY 45-77

When the Protectorate first made contact, humanity was in the midst of a civil war. The inner systems and outer systems of Sol struggled for dominance or independence.

It is fair to say we did not provide the best first impression that day.

We soon learned just how vast the Protectorate was and how small our pocket of space was compared to it. And we worried.

This history of humanity is one full of civilizations that assumed dominion of whatever land they came across, regardless of who was already living there. Our greatest fear now was that it was our turn to be treated in this manner.

But we learned that the Protectorate had been around for about as long as human history itself, and though they had expanded slowly until the last five hundred years, they had rules for how to deal with young civilizations that were taking their first shaky steps into the galactic community.

And those rules would someday lead to our undoing.

. . .

"Back so soon?" Valeria glanced at Laina and
Ronan as they returned to the sickbay, then did a double
take. "What did you *do* to her?"

Ronan set her down on the examination table and
waited as the doctor looked her patient over. "I did
nothing."

Val touched the bruises around her neck and wrists.
"What happened?"

"Ensign Keid found out about her. He was strangling
her when we found him."

"How? Who was on duty in the brig?"

"No one, and I'd like to know why." Ronan sighed. "I
knew Erik had been suffering since we lost the *Rapier*, but I
didn't think he'd become this unstable."

Valeria closed her eyes for a moment, her expression
strained. "Erik's wounds go deeper than you know, Ronan.
But I fear he might have become a liability. One of us
should speak to the commander about him."

Ronan ran a hand through his hair. "It's my responsibility," he said. "But I will choose the time to bring it up. Erik
has suffered more than most of us. I want him to get the
help he needs, not be locked away and forgotten." He
looked back at Laina, who lay still on the exam table. "But
we are supposed to be *better* than this. What does it say
about us when we act like animals?"

"They made us too human," said Valeria.

Ronan almost laughed. "Perhaps they should have
removed our feelings entirely."

"Be thankful that they didn't," said Val. "Before Earth
was lost, one of the lead scientists, Roberts, was surprised by
how I would get upset whenever we failed to save a patient.
I still do, no matter the species. He asked me if they should

have removed those feelings completely, if it would have made things easier for me."

"And what did you say?"

"I told him I believed it was a virtue. Not knowing pain is not having a reason to do better."

Ronan grumbled, not happy with that answer at all. "So we should embrace these feelings?"

"And learn from them, yes. You have to understand what pain is if you are to understand compassion."

Valeria spent the next few minutes silently examining the patient. Ronan turned away while the doctor worked. For some reason he couldn't explain, he'd found it unsettling to see his friend's hands on the soft exposed skin of the freeborn. What had she done to deserve that? Nothing, other than the crime of being born. And yet, when he had first seen her, that had been enough.

He didn't like this train of thought. "Are you done yet?"

"Her injuries are minor. Erik bruised her throat. She may have some trouble speaking for a day or so. He cut off blood flow to her brain, but thankfully not long enough to cause any damage." Valeria turned his way, her face grave. "Do you want my medical opinion?"

Ronan nodded.

"She shouldn't be sent back to the brig. This event has proved that we are a greater threat to her than she is to us. Someone *arranged* for the brig to be empty, knowing that Erik had access."

That security issue concerned Ronan. "And where do you expect me to keep her?"

The doctor shrugged. "She could be secured in my room. I would be fine checking on her during my shift breaks. I can remove anything she might use as—"

A growl escaped Ronan, and before he knew what he was doing, he'd stepped between her and the exam table.

"*Ronan.*" Valeria's voice rose in warning. "Is this your idea of being better than them?"

His feelings had taken over. He felt possessive of the freeborn. Responsible for her condition. Yes, she was his responsibility. At that moment, nothing else mattered.

"If she cannot stay in the brig, then she will stay in my chamber."

"Don't you mean your *cave*?" Valeria asked, eyes narrowed.

"I can monitor her there from the bridge, and my quarters can only be accessed by you and the commander. I do not trust her with anyone else."

"Ronan, this is ridiculous. What has gotten into you?"

The sickbay door hissed open. Commander Corvus stepped inside, frowning, as if he'd heard everything.

"Any decision regarding the freeborn is *my* concern first and foremost, Sub-Commander. Is that clear?"

Ronan stood at attention. "Yes, Commander. I was only concerned with the safety of this ship."

Alaric raised a hand. "Yes, and quite vocally too, I noticed. Now, Valeria, perhaps you can explain what has my first officer ready to do battle over one frail human."

"I don't believe she is safe in the brig, nor is it healthy for her. It's designed for Draxon physiology. It's too cold and uncomfortable. Since Ronan doesn't feel safe keeping her here, I suggested putting her in my room and checking on her periodically. Ronan obviously objects to that." She made no mention of the situation with Erik.

"Obviously." Alaric turned to his first officer. "Explain yourself."

Shame and embarrassment filled him, but he didn't

allow it to show. "Any trouble she causes is my responsibility. It would be easier to prevent further complications if she was in my care."

Alaric stroked his chin, eyes fixed on Ronan. "Very well. Keep her secure in your chamber. If she leaves for any reason, she must be in your company and kept in restraints. Do whatever you see fit to keep her from being a risk to the ship or crew."

Valeria rolled her eyes at that last comment, but only Ronan saw it.

A soft moan drew everyone's gaze to the exam table. Laina raised a hand to her throat and coughed. Her head rolled to the side. When she saw them all staring, she curled into a fetal position and raised clenched fists around her head.

"Yes, how will *any* of us survive her reign of terror?" said Valeria.

"You will be able to manage her, then?" The commander's question wasn't actually a question.

"Yes, Commander," said Ronan.

"Very well. I'll leave you to it." Alaric turned and exited the sickbay, the matter closed.

Valeria moved in Laina's direction, but Ronan reached her first. He put a firm hand on Laina's shoulder.

"Be still. We have no plans to harm you."

"You said that before." She looked to Valeria as if she'd somehow betrayed her. Despite his feelings toward the freeborn as a whole, it hurt Ronan's pride to think that they could not be trusted.

"You have my word as an officer of the Silver Legion. No further harm will come to you on board this ship. The matter *will* be dealt with."

Valeria stepped back as Ronan helped Laina off the

table. Her legs buckled, and she fell into him. He sensed her body temperature spike, and his heartbeat quickened in response. He steadied her and set her farther from himself than he wanted. He silently cursed himself, wondering if the doctor's comments regarding his unusual behavior carried some merit.

Laina's eyes lifted to his, looking like a pair of crescent moons at the edge of a lonely galaxy. When he reached for her, she pulled away, as though she expected him to strike her.

He felt disappointment at this, but why? She ought to fear him; he should *want* her to fear him. Yet all he felt was a strange discomfort.

Ronan shoved these odd, unsettling thoughts aside and gripped her arm just above the elbow.

"Come along. I will secure you in my quarters, and you can recover from your..." He'd been about to say *injuries*, but the word seemed inadequate. "Ordeal."

The sickbay doors parted with a soft hiss, and they left. Laina fell into step beside him, struggling to keep up. Her labored breaths and the strain of her struggles under the grip of his arm forced him to slow his pace.

Thankfully, the route to his quarters was currently empty. At least, it was until they turned down the last passage and he found Julian waiting in front of his quarters. His shoulder was propped against the wall, legs crossed at the ankles, arms folded over his chest.

"Julian," he greeted softly. "Is Ensign Keid secured?"

"He's sleeping it off in his room," said Julian. "Gave him a drink that would knock out a Hopat. You owe me one."

With anyone else he'd give a stern reprimand for this clear lack of respect, but he'd known Julian Aquila for years and had been his first commander. He was incredibly skilled at dealing with people, gathering information, and manipulation. As Dr. Schedar had once put it, Julian was always working an angle. He could have been in command of his own ship by now, but Julian preferred to be where the action was—or the fun. Often the two were one and the same.

"Thank you. I will deal with him shortly."

Julian cocked a brow as he turned his gaze to the human. "The commander said you're going to keep her in your quarters. I thought I'd help you secure her."

"I will have no trouble securing her, Ensign." Julian's main problem was a lack of discipline. He could be a charmer, but he didn't hold to the ideals of the Legion the way Ronan did, and right now he didn't seem to be acting quite like himself. He seemed more intense somehow.

"Forgive me if I don't believe you. She's already proved violent and cunning. She could be fooling you."

Ronan cracked a smile. "Just because she caught you unawares does not make her a master assassin, Julian. But if it will put your mind at ease, you may assist." He had no intention of letting his friend linger more than a few minutes.

The ensign stepped back, allowing Ronan to place his palm on the door panel. A green light pulsed, and the door slid open. He shoved Laina inside, not wanting to appear soft on her, and she stumbled forward, landing at the foot of his bed a few feet from the door. She unintentionally presented a perfectly rounded backside, even in the loose-fitting uniform Valeria had given her.

Julian stepped inside. "For a vicious little creature, she has certain desirable...assets." Before Ronan could stop him, he had smacked his hand on Laina's bottom. She squeaked and tried to scramble away.

Ronan's hand shot out, fingers curling around Julian's arm. "Leave her be. She is not worth the trouble. We will reach Isla 55 station in a few days. If you're having trouble finding company on board, you can always purchase a female's time there to ease your needs."

"Perhaps I'd prefer a challenge and save my credits? Or would you prefer to have her to yourself?"

"Do not test me, Julian. Get out." His warning was barely above a growl.

"I've never known you to be protective of freeborns." Ronan didn't like the censure in Julian's tone, but he continued. "You probably think you're being noble, but I recognize that look in your eye, Ronan. I've seen it in others. It doesn't end well." He said nothing more as he left.

When they were alone, Ronan locked his door. Laina leaned against the bed facing him, looking like a cornered animal. He wanted to leave her there, give her a chance to recover her wits, but he couldn't trust her alone. Not until he had made his quarters secure and free of anything that could be used against him. He took a step toward her.

"If you think you can touch me, I'll rip your heart out or die trying."

"You're safe. I gave you my word. No harm will come to you on this ship. But I must restrain you for now. Wrists." He held out a hand expectantly, and she held out her wrists, the slaver cuffs still secured against them. Again, though the cuffs had no clear means of fastening, he had no problem locking them to the long metal pole that ran horizontally along the bed behind his pillows.

"This is a temporary measure. Only until the room is

secured," said Ronan. "Rest. Food will be brought here soon. I will see to it that no one else bothers you."

Something about the resigned, wounded expression on her face made him feel uncomfortable. Dealing with free-borns had always been easy before, yet this all felt terribly wrong. He didn't know what to do about her or how to deal with her. But whatever he was going to do, he wasn't going to hurt her. She had witnessed a dark side of his people that he wished didn't exist. Erik had almost killed her, and Julian had seen her as nothing more than an object to be used. Simply because of who she was.

We're supposed to be better than this. He kept saying it to himself because he truly believed it. But right now he wasn't so sure. The least he could do was minimize the damage to her as much as possible. He felt as though he owed her that much.

Why he felt that, however, he couldn't say.

Laina couldn't breathe, not until Ronan disappeared into the washroom and shut the door. As the sound of a shower started to hiss, she finally exhaled. Her muscles went limp, and she collapsed on the bed, cuffed arms still hanging above her head.

She was cold, hungry, and tired, and it felt like she hadn't slept in days. Her mind was muddled, and a headache throbbed behind her eyes. The ring of bruises around her neck twinged when she tried to relax. That cyborg in the brig had nearly killed her.

Between him and the one who'd just left, she wondered if she would make it off this ship alive. They confirmed everything she'd been told about these monsters, these abominations that the Protectorate's High Council had laughably ruled to be the dominant species of their shattered homeworld.

But then Ronan had surprised her. He'd sent the one called Julian packing and reaffirmed his promise that she wouldn't be harmed. This had come from the same cyborg who had demanded she be restrained during her medical examination and then sent her to the brig. Maybe he'd realized she wasn't a threat, that she was harmless. Why not? It was the truth.

But the truth didn't sit well with her. She wished she could fight them. She wished she could avenge her parents. But she wasn't a fighter and had lived a life of running, hiding, and avoiding violence. She tried to tell herself it was for moral reasons. That she had been taught to run since she was a child. That she wasn't a coward, not really.

The thought then crossed her mind: *What if I'm the last free human?* It had been more than a year since she'd even heard of other freeborns on the run. Rumors only, but it had been hopeful, hearing that others might still be out there. Now she wondered if it had been nothing more than that. Rumors.

Am I the last? A woman missed by no one, with little value or consequence, a speck of dust in the universe. And then she realized she was no longer free. She'd known it, of course, from the moment she'd been brought on board, but the reality of it hit her now harder than Ronan's pulse gun. It could be that all that was left of humanity was a race of slaves.

Tears welled up in her eyes. She might as well roll over and die, for all that she'd done to save herself. To keep that hope alive, if only in herself.

She remembered her father's words from when she'd

been a child. *"Humans are visionaries. We dream, fight, love, and die, but we endure. Somehow, we always endure. It is our strength. As a species, we cannot be broken. We can survive anything, and as long as we survive, we can continue to dream. And dreams are what set us free."*

What had she dreamed of? It had been years since she had dreamed of more than her next short-term job or planet to run to once someone figured out what she really was. Fear had clouded her mind and weighed her down in the minutiae of survival. She'd never lived in a time when there hadn't been fear.

Laina shut her eyes, stilling the tears there, and blew out another shaky breath. Was there any way to convince them to let her go? What was one silly freeborn to them, really? But if the behavior of those on board was any indication, even one was one too many.

She wasn't sure how long she lay there, half-asleep. At some point the sounds of the shower shut off. Laina clamped her eyes shut and forced herself to relax. Maybe if he thought she was asleep, he'd leave her alone.

The door opened, and she heard the sound of bare feet padding over. A warm palm cupped her cheek.

"No use hiding you're awake. Your resting heart rate is quicker than it would be if you were asleep."

Well, didn't that just suck. She knew cyborgs had heightened senses, but she hadn't realized they went *that* far. Reluctantly, Laina opened her eyes. He was staring down at her, his hand still on her cheek. The touch was oddly intimate, and she was both comforted and confused by it.

"When was the last time you ate?"

"I... I guess that depends on how long I've been here."

"No more than half a day." Ronan withdrew his hand

from her face and unlocked her cuffs from the pole. She got up slowly, sitting on the edge of the bed, rubbing her arms around the cuffs. They didn't hurt, but it was a relief to feel free, at least in a small way.

"Well, it must be a couple of days now..."

"That long?" His echo came out sharp, and she jumped. "Did your captain not feed you?" He crossed his arms over his chest and glowered as though her lack of food was somehow her fault.

"Captain Zore's crew only served stuff that tasted like fermented vegetables. I had to drown the stuff in protein paste just to make it palatable, and I didn't eat much last time before your ship... Never mind."

"I'll provide you some food." He went over to the door panel and entered some commands.

"Alanna is going to bring you something. I have to return to my post on deck and must leave you." She looked up at him as he approached her. "Against my better judgment, I'm going to trust you. I won't bind you. I want you to stay here and not leave this room unless you need to use the cleansing unit." He moved around the room, taking anything that looked remotely like it could be used as a weapon and placing it in a closet. He then placed a hand on its panel, which briefly glowed as the door locked.

"Cleansing unit?" Laina asked. His way of speaking never stopped sounding odd to her. He was like a spokesman for their propaganda videos. Next thing you knew, he'd be spouting off about honor and strength.

Ronan seemed puzzled by this, gesturing to the washroom. "Yes. You are familiar with cleansing units, are you not?"

Laina would have laughed, except there was really nothing

to laugh about given her situation. "Oh, I am familiar with them. Washroom, bathroom, lavatory, even 'the crapper.' But you're the first person I've come across to call it a *cleansing unit.*"

Ronan frowned. "The...crapper?" he said it like the word itself had made him dirty. He shook his head, not wanting to debate the point. "Whatever you wish to call it, you are to stay in this room unless you need to use it. Do you understand?" He pointed to the corners of the room. "I will be checking up on you at any time I choose."

"How long will you be gone?" Laina held very still on the bed, hoping it would convey her desire to obey.

"My shift is eight hours."

"What am I supposed to do?" It was a strange thing to ask. She should have simply been grateful that she wasn't in the cold, empty brig. But she wasn't as afraid of him as she was before. He seemed to be sincere about making her comfortable, and it seemed natural to risk asking the question. If she was going to be stuck here, she'd have to find a way to occupy her time.

However, the question went over about as well as she should have expected. "I'm not here to provide you with entertainment. You're here as a captive of the Silver Legion until you can be turned over to the Terran Colony Fleet. If you grow bored, you may sleep."

She wrinkled her nose and tried to refrain from speaking out. His answering smirk only flamed her irritation.

"It's nice see some of that fiery spirit return. I find your irritation more interesting than your resignation. It is beneath you."

"I'm not here to provide *you* with entertainment, either," she said and scooted away from him on the bed.

Ronan didn't say anything more as he pulled on his uniform jacket, which had an insignia on the left breast.

"What is that?" she asked suddenly, pointing to the symbol, wanting a closer look. He turned to face her, coming a few steps closer.

"What?"

"Your insignia." She pointed at it. Now he was close enough she could see clearly. A crescent moon with three stars curved around it, completing the other side in a matching circular pattern. The hairs on the back of her neck rose. She'd seen it before, of course. Anytime there was a news broadcast involving the Legion it would be shown, and anytime she saw it on a ship she knew it was time to leave.

Yet there was something so familiar about the symbol now, raised and embossed, catching the light just so, but she couldn't quite remember why. It was like the way she thought she sometimes had dreams about a planet she had never been to before, let alone seen. Earth.

This symbol, the moon and the three stars, had stirred something just as strong, just as powerful in her mind.

"It is the emblem of the Silver Legion," Ronan answered. "The three stars represent humanity in all its forms." She saw that he was studying her with a frown. "You act as though you've never seen it before."

"No, I have. It's just..." What could she say? She didn't even understand the feeling herself. Déjà vu?

Ronan zipped up his uniform and headed for the door. She watched him, still perplexed. He paused as the door slid open, looking over his shoulder at her.

"If anyone comes here and it's not Alanna, or if she is not alone, say my name. *Ronan.* Say it loud and clear. The comm will connect directly to whatever station I am at. I will not risk a repeat of what happened to you in the brig."

Ronan waited for a response, and though she was reluctant to say what he was waiting to hear, she said it anyway. "Thank you."

"We are doing our duty here, freeborn. Maybe someday you'll see that."

"I really doubt it."

The two stared at one another, with her wishing that he could see things from her perspective. Was he thinking the same thing? Ronan turned to leave.

"Wait."

He stopped before the door shut, leaving Laina wondering what to say next. It had been an impulse on her part, brought partly out of fear. Somehow being alone was more frightening than being with him. But what if she was right about what he was thinking? What if he wanted her to understand his perspective? Maybe if she tried to understand him, he'd try to understand her.

"What is it?"

"I... The truth is, I've never met a cyborg before. I was born long after Earth was gone. None of our family liked talking about you. The kids I grew up with all assumed you were...well...mostly machine or something."

"Machine?" Ronan came toward her. She retreated until he'd backed her against the wall.

"Well, yes... A machine wearing a skin suit. That's what I always heard. That you guys had metal inside you and weren't really..."

"Alive? Sapient? *Human?*"

Laina nodded, feeling more nervous than ever. Ronan's anger was growing. Instead of creating a bridge between them, it felt like she was burning one.

"Those who created us would have liked to believe that as well," Ronan growled. "Even the names they gave us were meant to strip us of our humanity. Synth. Cyborg. But we are flesh and blood, just like you." He spoke softly, yet his tone turned dangerously silky. "But we are better in every way. There is nothing stopping me from killing you or doing whatever I please with you." His blue eyes burned like the heart of a ship's power core, an electric blue. "*Never* forget that."

"But you said you won't hurt me, right?"

"No. There is no honor in harming those who pose no threat. And I made a promise." His reply was reassuring, but the way he had backed her against the wall seemed to imply he was dangerous in a way she hadn't expected. It was the look the other cyborg, Julian, had given her. That she was just interesting enough to him that he'd consider taking what he wanted from her...

Did cyborgs have the same sexual urges as other humans? Did they form emotional attachments? If they did, then perhaps...

She'd once been told of something called Stockholm syndrome, though she didn't know what a Stockholm was. It was the idea that a prisoner might empathize and bond with their captor over time. It had been something she'd been warned about happening if she ever found herself captured.

But she wondered if it worked both ways. Could the captor bond with the prisoner? She could never fight someone like Ronan, but perhaps there were other ways to find opportunities for freedom...

Biting her lip, she raised a palm slowly to his chest. He was warm. Heat radiated beneath the red-and-silver jacket he wore. For a second neither of them moved, but then, with a slow exhalation, he stepped back, dropping his hands to his sides. His fingers curled into fists, and he paced away from her back toward the door.

He does feel...doesn't he? She was sure that he could lose control, like a human could. Knowing this somehow made her feel better. It seemed crazy to think a cyborg losing control like that was a good thing, but to her it was. She might get him to understand her and not want to send her back to the Colony Fleet or whatever was left of Sol. Perhaps she could get him to let her go, or at least wait until he let his guard down when she saw an opportunity for escape. She smiled again, brightly, feeling hope for the first time in a long while.

"Why do you smile?" he asked.

"Why do I smile?" She cocked her head, contemplating how best to answer him. "I suppose I enjoy learning new things. It makes me happy. Ergo, I smile." It was the truth. Her father and mother had taught her as best they could, given their ways and means. She'd craved each new lesson, thrilled by the historical stories, scientific theories, even just the expressions of human thought on the page. There was an undeniable pull toward one's culture there, an intrinsic connection that spanned thousands of years. To remember the past, to understand the journeys of the great men and women who came before, that was the key to growth and prosperity.

Perhaps she was a dreamer after all.

"And now you frown?" Ronan observed. This time his tone was the one that held curiosity.

"You're frowning too," she pointed out.

Ronan shook himself, as if coming to his senses. "I must report to my station. As I said before, call if you are in danger, but for no other reason."

"Okay, sure." She flopped back on the bed and stared up at the ceiling.

"Do not make yourself too comfortable. I will arrange for a more secure location as soon as possible."

Laina didn't move or even look in his direction, but she heard the door shut. She was alone, trapped on a starship with a species hell-bent on enslaving her kind. She had no idea how she was going to cope.

CHAPTER 6

Ark Chronicle Entry 45-78

It is ironic, perhaps, given what we have done, that our solar system is located within the only territory of the Protectorate that tolerates slavery, that of the Draxon Collective.

The Draxon are an unusual species within the five elder races. Despite their humanoid appearance, they exhibit qualities that we would attribute to insects. They have four castes, the most numerous of which are referred to as workers, or drones. These have little or no sense of personal identity, even referring to themselves in the plural. The other castes also exhibit this to some degree, though they are able to see themselves as individuals as well.

It is because of this that slavery is not seen as something that should be illegal within their borders. With little concept of individuality, how can they conceive of individual rights? The group is what matters, and all units work toward the greater good of the collective.

This has caused some problems for the Protectorate as a whole. Not all younger species that achieve interstellar travel within Draxon space share these beliefs. Yet the Protectorate must respect the governance of the dominant species within its territory. The best they can do, under these circumstances, is to ensure that slaves are treated as fairly as possible.

I do not say it is ironic because we bred the synthetics to be little more than slaves, of course. I say it because we now find ourselves the slaves, and there is no authority that we can appeal to for clemency.

RONAN PAUSED OUTSIDE HIS CLOSED DOOR, CHECKING the hall for any curious crewmembers. He exhaled and focused on regaining his self-control. He should have been able to maintain a steady heart rate, but at that moment his heart pounded like it had before his first real battle.

All because she'd smiled.

It'd been decades, perhaps even a century since he'd seen a smile quite like that. One full of genuine joy, simply because she had expressed an interest in learning.

He'd never had the benefit of a childhood, not the way humans understood it. He'd been born an adolescent with a basic education imprinted into him, and he'd matured rapidly as he trained, until his body stabilized. The process had been efficient, but it had denied him whatever joy he might have had if he had been born a regular human.

He had experienced the mysterious inner workings of the heart before, but Laina had affected him like no other. His senses seemed to heighten around her to the point of distraction. Even now he was haunted by the memory of her silky hair, satin skin, and the sweet faintly earthy scent of her that enveloped him when he was close to her.

It was maddening to have no sense of control over his own body, but at least he had regained his sanity.

The corridor was still empty as he headed toward the

lift. But instead of going to the command deck, he dropped down one floor to the secondary crew deck. He found Ensign Keid's room, overrode the lock, and entered.

Erik was sitting on his bed, looking groggy. The drink Julian gave him might have been strong enough to knock out a Hopat, but Ronan had seen Erik drink a Hopat under the table.

Erik looked to him, then quickly away, shame upon his face. Ronan decided to drop the formalities. Instead of addressing him as his senior officer, he simply said, "Erik."

Erik said nothing, staring off at the wall across from him. Ronan took a chair and pulled it up so he was sitting eye level with him.

"At some point I'm going to have to tell the commander about this."

Erik nodded slowly. "I know."

"So help me understand. What happened?"

It took a moment for Erik to speak. "I do not know. I heard about the freeborn, and... It was ten years ago this month."

Ronan nodded. "I know."

"I still miss her."

"I know."

"Those cowards took her from me."

Ronan closed his eyes. They'd both lost much aboard the *Rapier*. Ronan had lost most of his crew, but Erik had lost both them and the woman he loved. There was no doubt in his mind whose pain was greater.

"When I saw the brig was empty, something came over me. A red haze."

"Wait. Empty? How did you know it was empty?"

"The doors were open. No one was inside. Except for her."

That shouldn't have been possible. Ronan had assumed Erik had sent the guard on duty away with some kind of deception. He hadn't had time yet to pursue that line of inquiry. And why would the doors be open unless...?

"Erik, would you say you've been feeling more emotional today? Angrier? Sadder?"

Erik's eyes started to glisten. "It has been ten years..."

Something about this did not sit well with Ronan at all. Grief was normal. *This* was not.

"Ensign, you are to stay here for the remainder of the day. Rest. I will have the doctor check on you later. Understood?"

Erik sniffed, but nodded.

Ronan left and took the lift to the command deck. He had an unsettling hunch about recent events and would have to investigate further when his duties allowed. Right now, getting into a productive state of mind was what he needed. He wouldn't have to worry about the freeborn for the moment. She was safe in his room, sitting on his bed...

The image that followed, Laina with her arms cuffed over her head to the bed, cut his breath short.

"Hell." He tried doubly hard to focus on his duties instead.

The command deck was his favorite part of the ship. Though the *Orion* had begun life as a Draxon heavy cruiser, most of it had been overhauled to suit the needs of the Legion. This included the aesthetics of the ship, which had been functional, but without warmth or individuality. They borrowed heavily from colorful Elysian designs and inter-faces, though their more flamboyant looks were scaled back a bit. The result was, in his opinion, a thing of beauty.

A number of holographic screens and a thousand colored lights filled the bridge. It was manned by nearly a dozen officers, with key stations located in the center and auxiliary stations around the edges.

The *Orion* had only recently returned from an eight-year-long expedition on behalf of the High Council, and was currently outfitted as an exploratory vessel, capable of analyzing systems and conducting detailed surveys of planets and moons, without losing any of its combat capability. After a routine refit, they'd been called upon to monitor smuggling activity along the edge of the Void, waiting for their next long-term assignment.

But these expeditions also served a secondary purpose: the hope of finding an uninhabited Earth-like world not yet claimed by any of the major or minor races within the Protectorate, or within the influence bubble of another sapient race. Should they find one, they hoped to petition the High Council for permission to colonize it, despite their unique and complicated status within the Protectorate.

Sometimes politics could be more brutal than battles.

"I heard your little human is giving you trouble?" Lieutenant Hawking, or Hawk as everyone called him, asked this without looking away from his navigation station. Normally a seated station like the others, right now it had extended from floor to ceiling as a large hologram, providing an easy virtual representation of their current system to interact with.

At the moment, Hawk's cybernetic eyes scanned the star charts, mapping their current progress. The honey-gold prosthetics could see far more than Ronan's naturally enhanced vision, even beyond the visible light spectrum.

Julian scowled. "If you'd given her to me, I could give her what she needs. A good, hard—"

"That's *enough*," Ronan growled. He had the sudden urge to punch his friend's jaw. It was bad enough when he spoke this way while off duty. His lack of discipline could be a source of deep frustration at times.

"Is it true? Is she attractive?" Hawk queried. His eyes shifted away from the holographic projection toward Ronan.

Ronan walked over to his station, close to the commander's chair, currently unoccupied.

"Well?" Hawk pressed.

"She's attractive enough. What does it matter?"

Hawk and Julian shared a smirk, as if some kind of bet had been won or lost. Ronan turned his gaze to Julian.

"Ensign, you continue to be a bad influence on the crew. I remind you that this is a Legion ship, and I am the ranking officer on deck. Return to your duties and save your gossip for when you are off duty."

The ship recognized his authorization, and the chair's armrest lit up with controls. Ronan brought up diagnostics from the other parts of the ship. He scanned the various stations, ensuring that all was well and the crew was having no trouble.

When he had finished, he viewed the video feed from his cabin. When he saw where his little freeborn was, he smiled. She'd disobeyed him, as he'd expected. She was exploring every room in his quarters. He should have been angry, but he'd made sure she wouldn't find anything she could use against him. She had to know it was foolish to even try, but he supposed he couldn't fault her for checking every possibility available to her. Especially after what had happened with Erik.

He frowned and checked the duty roster for the brig. It showed a shift change occurring as usual before the incident with Erik. Only clearly it hadn't. He would look deeper into this later, but for now he kept his eye on Laina.

She was now examining the contents of his closet, the one he hadn't locked. Her hands were sliding over his shirts on the rack, touching the various fabrics. He wondered what she was looking for. He had an assortment of uniforms and casual wear, depending on what his job required, but she seemed more interested in the Silver Legion emblem on his jackets, as if they held some other meaning for her.

Some of his non-uniform clothes were quite expensive. Perhaps that was what confused her. Why would he need such clothes? He rarely ever wore them, except when visiting the dignitaries of other planets to negotiate a service contract. Or for the occasional Senate meeting. Though the Terrans held no vote there, that did not mean they held no influence. It allowed them the chance to bargain with other nations regarding the Legion's services, and to garner their good will and support for the Colony Fleet in the process. Making a good impression was crucial to his people's cause. And he had all the time in the world in which to achieve it.

Back on the video feed, Laina had abandoned searching his closet and turned her attention to the display terminal in his chamber. He had left it off, but now he wondered why. It would have been harmless enough to let her be entertained by it.

The *Orion* databanks contained a wide variety of recordings, ranging from whatever had survived the Terran Disaster to their more modern productions. Some were bizarre documentaries that took rudimentary parts of human life—such as dating, or wilderness survival, or living with a number of companions in a small house—and turned it into a competition, where people were steadily eliminated until there was a single victor. Others were old movies full of action, set on Earth or in space, using either obsolete or unrealistic technology. Nubrans loved these for some reason, but he found them tedious. And, of course, there were the shows the Terran Colony Fleet produced themselves, generally set upon a massive colony ship or one of the Silver Legion's cruisers. He mostly enjoyed watching those with his crewmates, where they made a game of pointing out any details they got wrong.

But the programs Ronan watched most often didn't feature humans at all. His favorites were recordings of nature and animals that no longer existed. He'd seen amazing creatures across a thousand different worlds, yet the tragedy that these creatures of Earth no longer existed only made them more precious to him.

Mischievousness filled Ronan for a moment, and he tapped into the controls tied to his cabin, turning on the display. It bathed the woman in white light, and she shrieked and fell back on the bed. He selected one of his favorite videos and played it.

A family of humpback whales filled the screen, the underwater shot capturing their massive bodies gliding through the dark blue depths of the Atlantic Ocean. He'd seen that ocean once before being shipped off-world, but he'd never seen a whale in person.

Laina blinked as she studied the creatures. Ronan changed cameras so he could see her face better. She leaned forward, watching in fascination as light cut through the surface of the ocean, rippling down over the backs of the water mammals. One whale let out a soft, keening cry.

Her face softened, the lines of fear and worry smoothing into curiosity and wonder. She reached behind her and grabbed his pillow, then stretched out her feet toward the head of his bed. She propped her elbows on his pillow and gazed at the screen, enraptured.

It occurred to him that she'd never seen a sunrise on

Earth or run into the shallows of the Atlantic like he once had. She'd been born centuries after that world was dust, and she'd lived on the run, hiding from his people. There was a rough justice to it, perhaps, yet he couldn't shake the sense of sorrow he felt knowing Laina had never seen Earth. It was possible she didn't even know what a whale was.

"What are you doing, Ronan?" Hawk leaned over his shoulder, eyeing the small display.

"Checking on the prisoner, making sure she isn't trying to escape." He attempted to deactivate the display, but Hawk was too quick with his next question.

"So, is that her?" His voice was colored with interest. "Rather pretty. For a freeborn, that is."

"She is a prisoner of the Legion until she can be turned over to the Colony Fleet. You will not treat her like some pleasure worker." Ronan didn't like the way Hawk stared at the woman. He had *definitely* been spending too much time with Julian.

But his intrigued tone had made Ronan look at Laina through his eyes, if only for a moment. Val had said she was still a little malnourished and dehydrated, yet there was no denying she was beautiful. And perhaps after she'd recovered more she wouldn't be so afraid. Maybe they could talk some more. She might have questions about Earth, questions only he could answer. He could already picture her smiling at him as he told her—

He had to stop thinking about that. She was a prisoner. He could not allow himself to get caught up in fantasies about her, or the way she made him feel strangely homesick for Earth.

Hawk's tawny eyes narrowed as the cybernetics zoomed in for a better look. "With a face and body like that, she might end up a pleasure worker on the Colony anyway."

Ronan slapped his hand on the control panel, and the display shut off. He stood, glowering at his subordinate.

"You will refrain from speaking of her in that way. Is that understood, Lieutenant?"

Hawk exchanged glances with Julian. The ensign's brows lowered as he shared a look with the officer.

"I never thought I'd see the day where you'd defend a freeborn." Hawk's tone was soft, but no less dangerous.

"And I never thought I'd see the day a member of the Silver Legion would stoop to the level of their enemies."

Hawk's eyes narrowed, but he let the challenge pass. He returned to his station. Julian also returned to work. Ronan slumped back into his chair.

This was going to be a long shift.

IT WAS THE MOST BEAUTIFUL SIGHT SHE'D EVER SEEN. Laina gazed at the beasts on the screen. Their bodies moved slowly through the water, but their fins were muscled and powerful. Light shimmered on the surface far above the creatures. Something deep inside her stirred, like a memory that had never existed before yet was trying to will itself into creation. Her hand with the anomaly, as the doctor had called it, began to tingle. She rubbed the spot with her fingers, still watching the creatures on the screen.

Whales... Where the word came from she couldn't say. The memory of learning it was perhaps too distant, or buried too deep. But she knew with certainty that these were whales from Earth.

Home.

She gasped as one of the creatures suddenly shot up toward the ocean's surface. The camera angle changed, and now she was eye level with the surface as the creature leapt into the air and came crashing down, creating a mighty wave. Her breath caught and held as she let the image burn into her memory. She never wanted to forget this incredible sight.

There was something deeply magical about seeing a beast so large and strong defiantly breach its world of water into another, that of the air. Was it so different from her situation? A lonely human struggling to escape one world for another. And for a moment she had. For a moment, she had tasted the air.

Now she was crashing back down.

The screen faded to darkness. How had it turned on in the first place? Ronan must have been watching her and turned it on remotely. But why? To remind her that he was watching? She was angry that he would stoop to observing her like some caged animal, but at the same time she was happy that she'd seen the whales. He seemed to create conflicting feelings in her at every turn, and it caused a knot to form in her stomach.

A soft chime from the door made her sit up. The door opened, and a tall woman entered. She'd seen her before, back on the *Beautiful Star Chaser*. She was beautiful, the kind of effortless beauty she'd expected from the cyborgs, making her feel inferior even in that regard. Laina plucked at the loose-fitting outfit she wore, wishing she had something more appropriate like the formfitting uniform the woman wore. It at least complemented her form, rather than hiding it like a loose sack.

"Are you Alanna?" she asked.

The cyborg entered and set down the tray of food she carried. Slung over one of her shoulders was a backpack. Laina gasped, surging to her feet and reaching for the bag.

Alanna reacted instantly, grabbing her wrist in a viselike grip.

"Are you trying to attack an officer of the Legion?"

Laina winced as the grip tightened. "I wasn't...attacking..."

"It's bad enough I've been relegated to a crewman's role, bringing you food..."

"I was...excited."

"To say the least, this is beneath my position."

"My...pack." Her wrist burned, and for a moment she worried Alanna might snap it without even meaning to.

Alanna released her wrist with as little concern as when she had grabbed it.

"Your pack? *This* excites you?" Alanna shut the door, sealing them inside. Laina didn't dare move. She realized her mistake. She'd allowed herself to get comfortable. She'd forgotten where she was. Who she was among.

Laina watched as Alanna unceremoniously dropped the pack's contents onto the bed. Laina's entire life was in that backpack, and the woman treated it like garbage.

Alanna sorted through the items on the bed as if expecting to find something hidden among them. A reading pad with thousands of books stored on it, a data crystal, some protein tubes, a few shirts, and some underclothes. The cyborg studied the reading device, scanning the covers on the flat screen as she flipped through them curiously. Then she picked up the data crystal.

"What's on this?" Alanna asked.

"Nothing," she replied instantly. What was on that was hers and hers alone.

"Our scans showed nothing unusual, yet you show deep concern for it. There is something important here. Tell me or I will destroy it." Alanna held the crystal in her hands, and Laina wondered if she could crush it with her bare hand.

"No, please!" She stumbled to her feet, hands up in surrender. "It's my parents. The crystal has a few memories of them I recorded. It's all I have left besides my dad's jacket."

Alanna eyed the crystal, and then she turned to the large screen. She accessed the small keypad and inserted the crystal. The reader shifted in size to fit and glowed green as it scanned the data within.

"I'll have to confirm the contents before I can let you have it."

Laina fell back onto the bed and tried not to let her emotions get the best of her. She hadn't wanted to watch this, not now.

A hologram projected out. Alanna stepped back and sat down next to Laina on the bed. The hologram changed from a blurry orb of light to the shapes of three people. Laina as a child and her parents. It was from when they'd lived on a planet called Allasant. It was a Nubran colony near the Void. The locals had been sympathetic to the free-born refugees and allowed them to stay on the outskirts of the settlement for a time, but they were too afraid of the High Council's mandate regarding Terran freeborns to directly aid them.

The projector showed her at eight years old, splashing in the shallows of a lake. Her father was chasing her, pretending to be a monster. Her mother stood at the lake's edge, arms banded around her waist as she laughed.

"That is you, as a child?" Alanna asked.

"Yes. With my parents."

"You freeborns start life very small."

"It's the only way we know how."

"And where are you?"

"A place called Allasant."

Alanna's brows rose. "Allasant? I know that planet..." Her voice trailed off.

"You've been there?" Laina hoped to get her to talk more, but the woman didn't say anything else.

The hologram drew their focus again. She could remember everything about that day, the feel of the sand between her toes, the crisp, cool water clinging to her skin, her parents' laughter. Feeling safe, at home. It had been the closest thing to Earth she supposed she'd ever experience. A pang in her chest made her shut her eyes, but she soon opened them again. The projection started flickering, then vanished.

Laina's throat hurt, like she'd swallowed broken glass. Neither of them spoke for a moment.

"What was it like?" Alanna finally asked.

"What was what like? Allasant?"

"Being a child."

It was hard to imagine anyone not having been a child, starting life at adolescence with the basics of education already imprinted on their brain. But then, she supposed the cyborgs had a hard time imagining anyone starting off so small and fragile, knowing absolutely nothing, yet somehow growing into an adult.

Laina wanted to give her an answer, to find a way to keep their conversation going, but realized she didn't even know where to begin. "It's hard to put into words, really," she said. "I'm sorry. I'm still tired and hungry."

Alanna removed the crystal from the projector and set it on the bed before she pointed at the tray.

"Eat and rest. You may keep the items in your pack. I do not see any danger in you having them."

"Thank you...Alanna." She smiled at the woman. "I'd like to talk with you more when I feel better...if you don't mind." She hoped the woman would want to come back and talk to her. She needed an ally, but she also needed a friend. If only for a little while.

"I... It isn't really part of my duties. But perhaps later." Alanna looked as though she was tempted to smile.

"Great, I look forward to it." Laina meant it.

Alanna said nothing else before she left the room. When Laina was positive she was alone, she collected her belongings and tucked them back into the pack, then clutched the bundle to her chest. She would never get used to this, being frightened and threatened from all sides. But by this point she was exhausted, and her eyelids kept drooping despite the need to stay awake and alert.

Just because Ronan said she was safe didn't mean it was true. Just about everyone she'd met so far had hurt her or threatened to do so. If any of the crew really wanted to get to her, she was sure they'd find a way. What she wouldn't give to have just one person to talk to she could trust, someone who didn't despise her very existence. The doctor, maybe?

She stretched out on the bed, taking Ronan's pillow and putting it beneath her head. His scent was there, both enticing and somehow comforting. Food, she decided, could wait. Instead, she kept her arms locked around her backpack and finally surrendered to sleep.

Commander Alaric Corvus entered the sickbay and spotted Dr. Schedar at her desk. The doctor's head was bent, her eye pressed against the molded eyepiece of a microscanner. Alaric chuckled. Valeria had the best display tools the Legion could buy at her disposal, yet she preferred more classical old-school instruments. Said it was more "hands on" and personal.

"Doctor, do you have a moment?" Alaric asked.

Valeria raised her head. "Commander, what can I do for you?"

Alaric looked around the sickbay. It had been months since he'd needed to be down here. They hadn't seen combat in years, and until recently their time had been spent on deep-space expeditions. Even after the refit it looked the same. Five exam tables pointed inward like a star, and Valeria's lab station was at the center. The surface of her desk was littered with samples, and several displays were lit up, running various analysis programs.

Alaric gestured to the doorway. "Can you lock that for a minute?"

Valeria returned to her desk and activated the door lock. Most doors on the ship could be opened by any of the crew, personal rooms excluded. But the sickbay was an exception. If any patient needed to be contained due to fears of contamination, Valeria had the ability to put the sickbay in full lockdown, something even the commander couldn't override.

A red light on the door panel flashed twice and held at a steady glow. Assured they were alone, Alaric produced an old Earth holodisk and inserted it into the computer system at the desk. Once the computer recognized the formatting and was able to read the information, a light spun out from the station's display. It projected the fuzzy outline of a man. Alaric turned to the doctor.

"What you are about to see is confidential. Only Ronan

knows this disk exists, and even he has not seen all of its contents."

"Not even Legion Commander Leonis knows?"

Alaric shook his head. "You'll have to trust me that I have my reasons for this."

Valeria crossed her arms over her chest, ready for whatever came next. The image's blurry shape transformed more clearly into a man they both knew. Tobias Wolfe. One of the heads of Project N. A three-hundred-year-old ghost. He began to speak. The damaged recording made his voice thin and reedy, but it still carried the weight of the authority the man once held.

"Project update. Entry number 215. We have isolated the sequence that affects the cyborgs' reproduction. After some debate, we have decided that, as with previous generations of synthetics, the fertility of the cyborgs must be rendered dormant. This was not taken lightly, especially among those who felt that the current synths were being denied a fundamental human right.

"But there is a concern that their enhanced capabilities might lead them to seek to replace us someday unless we take steps now. Therefore, all production chambers and databanks will contain only the final altered sequences, to a point where we have been assured no reverse engineering can take place. We have trusted Dr. Roberts with protecting the only copy of the unaltered sequences of all synthetics, along with details for the Ark program from Norway that we've been asked to assist with. It seemed fitting under the circumstances to link these two projects. Ensuring the survival of this information is an awesome responsibility.

"Our recent contact with extraterrestrial life and the realization that we are not only not alone in the universe, but mere children within a vast nation of adults, has been

humbling, to say the least. But it also reminds us of just how easily we could lose everything.”

Commander Corvus stopped the disk. The doctor looked at him quizzically.

“Well, we suspected they had to know how to reactivate the dormant genes within us. This does seem hopeful that they held on to such information. The genetic sequence wouldn’t be enough, however. The deadlocks in the nanotech, for example. But still, it would be a start…” She paused to consider the information. “But if the information was on Earth when it was—”

Alaric sometimes had a flare for the dramatic, and he’d waited patiently for the doctor to raise this very point. He raised a hand to silence her, then skipped ahead to the next bookmarked entry. The projection changed to that of another man, seated, who was looking at unseen displays off to the side in horror. He then looked at the camera.

“This is Dr. John Roberts. Division head, Project… You know, it doesn’t even matter anymore.” He looked back at the displays, then the camera, then the displays. “They did it. They actually did it. My God…” He said nothing for a while, then pulled his eyes away from the displays and addressed the screen.

“Earth is gone. I don’t know what weapon they used, but…there’s nothing left. There can’t be. The human fleet, the cyborg fleet… Nothing could have… Earth is…” Roberts searched for words that wouldn’t come. “If…if there are any survivors on the surface, there won’t be for long. The shock- wave alone would… Thank God Lisa is on Europa…”

He closed his eyes, and tears beaded up and coated his eyelids in the zero gravity. He wiped his eyes with his sleeve.

“We were en route to Armstrong Colony on Mars. I was supposed to meet with a representative of Nubra. She spoke

of a group who might be able to help us, but now... I don't know what anyone can do anymore."

Again Alaric stopped the recording. The doctor nodded as if she knew where this was going. "So if Dr. Roberts lived, and if he left with the Nubran woman, there's a chance he took the information with him."

Alaric nodded, then forwarded to the next entry on his list. Dr. Roberts appeared again, this time clearly in an alien home somewhere. He looked older now, though the years might have been piled on from stress instead of time.

"I'm being told that things don't look good for us from a legal standpoint. Honestly, I don't even understand how this is possible, but the High Council have laid the blame for the destruction of Earth squarely at our own feet, despite the fact they can't even explain how it happened. Word is their next ruling will approve the cyborgs' demands to be considered the dominant species of our system...what's left of it. I... I don't even know what to say. I fear the worst nightmare for humanity might be yet to come.

"The Ark, however, is safe. My Nubran friend, Sister Wazeru, has promised me and my family safe passage no matter the outcome. I am working closely with her people to incorporate every last bit of data we can find, but they have minds that are light-years ahead of my own. I feel like they are simply humoring me by allowing me to assist them, like a child trying to help their parents bake.

"They have come up with a unique way to preserve the Ark under any circumstances. After all, you can't lose something that's become part of you, and I will be able to continue this chronicle using it instead of a disk. No matter what happens next, the Ark will survive, so long as we survive. Our light will not go out, no matter how dark the years ahead might be."

Dr. Roberts's image flickered and then winked out.

For several long seconds neither Alaric nor Valeria spoke.

"Sister?" Valeria asked at last.

Alaric nodded. It stood out to him as odd as well. "A mistranslation, I assume. Though the Nubrans do have many religions."

"So the Nubrans were working with the freeborns behind our backs, even then."

Alaric frowned. "Actually, it's not as simple as that. Roberts was always sparse on details and rarely referred to anyone by name, but it seems the group helping him was made up of many different species."

"Were they working for the Protectorate?"

The commander shook his head. "Unlikely. We'd have heard something about that. It's just one more mystery to add to the pile. For now, I suggest we stick to the points I have just shown you."

The doctor nodded. "And what have you just shown me?"

"Hope," said Alaric. "Let's go over what we know. Everything we need to ensure our survival was carried in something called the Ark, held in the trust of Dr. John Roberts. Roberts escaped Earth's destruction and still had possession of the Ark when he left. We have every reason to assume it still exists today."

"What is this Ark, though?" asked Valeria.

"I believe it is a database of knowledge. To preserve our knowledge in case relations with their newfound neighbors went poorly. To ensure that something of humanity survived. But within that Ark also lies the key to our survival.

"When I came into possession of this disk, the data was encrypted. I've dedicated our computer's surplus runtime to trying to crack the encryption for years now." He hesitated a moment, choosing his next words more carefully. "I was recently able to break the encryption, and I've been reading the entries here for the last year. Most of the information is trivial, common knowledge, or otherwise unenlightening. But once I saw the connection between these recordings..." Alaric leaned against the doctor's desk and waited for her to respond. The doctor pulled back the chair at her desk and sank into it.

"Tell me if I understand what I just heard. Dr. Roberts has this Ark, and his collaborators found a way to preserve it...on his body?"

Alaric gave a quick nod. Valeria blew out a breath and twirled her ponytail in a nervous habit. "He's long dead by now, but it sounds as if it was designed to pass itself on. Self-replicate, perhaps. Yes, that would work...but the process, what would the process be?"

The commander saw he was beginning to lose the doctor in a whirlwind of puzzle solving.

"The important thing is that we have every reason to believe that it has passed itself on, generation after generation."

"Reminds me of the ancient city of Alexandria on Earth," said Val. "It had a backup library, as I recall. So anyone could be carrying a copy?"

The commander shook his head. "Not just anyone. I remember Roberts, and I've studied him extensively ever since I began this line of inquiry. He would be too afraid of this information falling into our hands to pass on too many copies. It is more likely he would pass it on to one or two wards he trusted, along with the means to pass it on again.

Trusted guardians of lost information, from generation to generation. Probably his own children."

"The anomaly I found in the prisoner's hand," the doctor said.

Alaric nodded. "It's a possibility. I want you to examine her again immediately and report back on what you find. But do not share this with the others. I am not ready to discuss this with the crew, and if they were to learn we have one of the descendants from Project N on board her life might be in danger. Anger has a way of overcoming reason."

The doctor seemed to react to that comment. "What about Ronan? I'm concerned about his behavior recently. He's grown possessive toward the woman, and his insistence of locking her in his quarters? Highly unusual."

"Leave him to me. He is an officer of the Legion. I will remind him where his loyalties lie."

CHAPTER 7

Ark Chronicle Entry 45-81

The Protectorate's solution regarding the younger races was two-fold. First, they would be afforded a region of space around their homeworld that would be completely under their control. This resource "bubble" extended approximately forty-three light-years (by Earth standards) in every direction and would provide any species more than enough in terms of resources and room for expansion as they developed, all the while being aided and guided by the Protectorate.

Their belief was, once they needed to expand beyond this bubble, they would be able to fully integrate with the Protectorate species whose borders they were located within.

The second part of the solution was to give them a voice within the Protectorate. The Senate was divided into two branches, the High Council, made up of the five founding species, and the Low Council, made up of the younger races. If new species were discovered later on, they would be given the same treatment.

This all occurred nearly two thousand years ago, and it

worked well for the most part. But around the time Earth was first going to war with tanks and airplanes, that all changed.

ALARIC RETRIEVED THE ARK HOLODISK AND SLID IT back into a pocket in his uniform. Valeria unlocked the sickbay doors. A silent nod passed between them as he left.

He passed a couple of the synth crew en route to the lift and exchanged a casual salute, fist to heart. But his mind was weighed down with other matters. He tried to temper his expectations, but it was difficult. First he'd unlocked the diary, and now they had captured someone with an anomaly that might fit what was alluded to in the recordings. It gave one hope, but he'd had hundreds of years to learn that hope could quickly evaporate into nothing at all.

Once on the bridge, Alaric found Ronan seated in his chair, scanning reports from various stations. He didn't appear to be in the middle of anything important.

"Ronan, a word, please." Alaric waved his first officer into the hall.

"What is it?"

"It's about the freeborn—"

"Laina? What's wrong? Did something happen?" Ronan's tone surprised Alaric. And using her name? Perhaps the doctor was right. The question now was whether or not this behavior would interfere with his duties.

"Nothing has happened. I want you to escort her to sickbay and leave her in Valeria's care for now."

Ronan paled. "Why?"

"I want her to run those tests on the anomaly in her hand immediately."

Ronan stood more to attention, something he did whenever he felt uncomfortable having to explain himself. "The doctor herself said that she requires rest. I don't see why the doctor cannot wait a day or two."

Alaric studied his friend. "One minute you don't trust her, the next you fear for her health?"

Ronan's back got straighter still. "She would be more inclined to cooperate with us if she felt secure. The unclaimed freeborn exaggerate our treatment of them amongst themselves, turning us into monsters. When we find them, they lash out, resist. Some have even chosen death over capture."

This was true. While there were laws laid down by the High Council ensuring that slaves were treated fairly, many freeborn they'd captured reacted as if they were being rounded up for extermination.

"Has she tried to attack you?" Alaric asked.

"Well, she hasn't been trained. I wouldn't expect her to. But her treatment so far here has..." Here he wavered, unsure of what to say next. "We have not given her reason to trust us."

Alaric suspected there was far more to that statement than he was aware of. "Is there a problem, Ronan?"

"No, sir. She's...well she's not weak. She is a survivor."

Alaric agreed. "She would have to be to be on her own for so long." He sensed admiration in Ronan's tone. It was unusual. Alaric had never been harsh toward the humans they'd captured over the years, but until now Ronan had acted as though he had a personal score to settle with them. Whatever compassion Ronan might have once possessed had been lost with his patrol ship and its crew. Or so the commander had thought.

"What happens to the human is my decision," Alaric reminded him. "I can't have you becoming insubordinate if my orders somehow conflict with your feelings for her." He let that point sink in before he continued. "Since we established the Colony Fleet, we have tried to help our people believe in something greater than themselves. You were with me when the Silver Legion was formed. You swore the oath that I helped write, an oath that was meant to bond us all to a common cause. One I know you believe in. Would you throw that all away?" His words struck a blow, and Ronan stepped back before returning to attention.

The stony expression returned to Ronan's face. "I serve only the Legion. When should I deliver her to the doctor?"

"Immediately. The doctor has assured me that the freeborn will be no threat, and I am inclined to agree. Val will be safe with her while you return to your post." Alaric paused, debating whether to allow his subordinate to keep the female in his quarters once the doctor's exam was finished. If his hunch was right about her, then treating her well was in their best interests, and the brig was no place for such a person.

"Sir?" Ronan waited to be dismissed.

"When Valeria is finished with her tests, you may return her to your quarters. You are dismissed." The flicker of relief on Ronan's face didn't go unnoticed, but he quickly masked it. He saluted and left.

Alaric returned to the command deck. The rest of the bridge crew were pointedly looking toward him, rather than at their stations. Their prisoner was breeding far too much curiosity. More so than any who had come before her. He was puzzled as to why this was the case.

He'd had his fill of the species *Homo sapiens*, which in his opinion had failed spectacularly at living up to their name. They were to be pitied, though not hated. Not anymore. He'd known them longer than any other of his kind. He was one of the first successful cyborgs to be created, and the oldest still alive after the Terran Disaster.

The centuries weighed heavily upon him, and he often felt far closer to his true age as a result. He had been the deciding vote to send the cyborg fleet to Earth, to force the surrender of their birthing chambers.

He should have been there with them. Instead, he had been ordered to stay behind with the colony ships, to prepare for their exodus. That was where he'd learned that the cyborg fleet, the human fleet, and Earth itself had been lost.

The damned fools.

To this day it remained a mystery as to what insane weapon the humans had unleashed and how it had back-fired so horribly.

As the oldest left among them, Alaric had been offered the post of Legion commander several times. But his place was out here, working hands-on side by side with his people for the betterment of the Colony Fleet. He was often looked up to for guidance by his crew. Not just as a commander, but almost as a father.

But no one understood the burden he bore. Because of him, the future of his race was uncertain, and he often felt as though he was spiraling toward the event horizon of a black hole. He needed answers. He needed hope. He needed redemption. And it might just be that their prisoner was the key to it all.

RONAN ENTERED HIS QUARTERS, PLEASED TO SEE THE empty tray of food, not even a crumb left. Laina was curled up on his bed, asleep.

She looked so at peace where she lay, one arm curled around her small bag. Alanna had contacted him earlier, explaining what had happened and that the items in the pack were harmless but emotionally crucial for the woman. Ronan was curious as to what the items were, but he would have time to find out later, since it seemed Laina would be with him a while longer.

Why did that thought please him?

He approached the bed, loath to wake her but knowing he had to. But first he gave in to the urge he felt to touch her. Nothing inappropriate. At least, he hoped not. Judging from her reactions earlier, he could not be certain what was taboo in her mind. Stroking her hair back, he let the silken strands tease his fingertips. Why did this simple act seem so satisfying?

He traced her lips with one fingertip, imagined leaning over her and kissing her, and realized he was crossing a line. But would it be so bad...to have a small taste of her?

Of course it was. He'd be no better than Julian, that scoundrel. But still, one could imagine. Imagination harmed no one...

Ronan stood there for a long moment, losing himself in his thoughts, imagining how he'd possess her body if given the chance. Gently at first, then hard and hungry. But only if she trusted him. Wanted him. Once they—

He jerked the trailing thoughts to a stop and banished them. This was wrong. He had his orders. Ronan placed a hand on her shoulder and gently jostled her awake. Or, at least he thought it had been gentle. She jerked awake, hands raised to cover her head.

"Easy, it is only me," he said, hand still on her shoulder. Perhaps Alaric and the doctor were right. He was feeling too much for this woman. There was no other way he could explain his need to calm and reassure her. It wasn't logical. And there was certainly a danger in wanting to take her to bed, to claim her body for his own.

She blinked a few times and lowered her arms. "What's going on?"

"The commander has ordered you to the sickbay."

She rubbed her eyes and then covered her mouth as she struggled to hide a yawn. "What for?" Her brown hair hung about her shoulders in a wild tumble. Ronan's hands twitched as he fought the urge to reach out and touch her. "Is something wrong?"

"Dr. Valeria wishes to run some tests on the anomaly in your hand." After he said it, he realized he should not have discussed the details of his commander's orders, but talking to her was so easy.

"The anomaly?" She looked at her hand, puzzled. "Oh, right. Have they figured out what it is?" Laina straightened the baggy outfit she wore and stood up.

Ronan couldn't help but smile. "If we knew that, then it wouldn't be an anomaly."

In a move that seemed born more out of instinct than intention, she looked around the room, then tucked her backpack under Ronan's bed. She blushed when she caught him looking but didn't explain herself. She planted her hands on her hips. "The least you can do for someone you're going to start scanning and jabbing is explain why you're doing it."

It amused him that she seemed secure enough to challenge him, given that her natural reaction to conflict was to duck and hide to seek safety. It should have upset him, being defied by a prisoner, but he found her determination amusing.

"You'll be lucky if we don't do more than a few tests," he

said, though he regretted it when he saw her face pale. Still, it was important that neither of them forget their places. She was a captive, not a guest.

Laina's eyes, which had dropped to the floor, slowly moved back up to his face.

"Will you be there? During the tests, I mean? I'd like it if you could stay."

Her words surprised him. She must have at least somewhat trusted him now to ask such a question. He wasn't sure how to take that.

"No." He shifted on his feet before straightening himself. "I have to return to my post and finish my shift. Please, place your wrists together." He tapped the controls for the slaver cuffs on his wrist computer.

She tapped the slaver cuffs together so he could lock them. "Is this really necessary?"

Ronan was about to insist, but then thought better of it. She was cooperating, and it was true she didn't pose any kind of threat that he could perceive. That should be rewarded, albeit cautiously.

"Perhaps not." He held the door open for her. "Come. We've wasted enough time. I must take you to Dr. Schedar."

Ronan led her out of his room and down the winding halls of the ship. Every now and again they'd pass by an open doorway and a cyborg or synth would eye them with open curiosity. Not that she could tell the two types apart—they all looked human to her.

Laina met their stares with her own. Her safety had been guaranteed, at least for the moment, and that had put her in a curious mood. She was less afraid now. She could always panic later, but for now she was caught up in learning about her new environment. Here she was surrounded by the creatures of her childhood nightmares, yet all she could do was watch in wonder and awe.

Their ship was a thing of beauty, both inside and out. It looked as though it had been designed for luxury as well as practicality. It wasn't at all what Laina thought cyborgs would care about, given their close ties with the Draxon. Clearly they had a creative side, unlike their patrons.

Laina was drawn out of her silent ponderings as Valeria greeted her in the sickbay. She looked pleased to see her again.

"Hello, Laina. How you feeling? Better, I hope?" Valeria pulled out a small handheld scanner and ran it over her face and chest.

"I'm fine, I think."

The doctor dropped the scanner lower, sweeping it over Laina's abdomen.

"You're still a bit malnourished. Biocompatible or not, Nubran food doesn't really agree with you. I'll have something brought up. You can eat while I run my tests." She pocketed the scanner and turned to Laina's escort. "You can leave her, Ronan. She'll be safe with me."

Ronan hesitated. A flash of worry showed in his eyes. Laina wondered if she was already having an effect on him, creating some kind of emotional bond. He'd stopped treating her like a war criminal, and that, at least, was progress.

"I'll inform you once the tests are complete, and you can return her to your quarters," said the doctor, suggesting it was time for Ronan to leave.

Ronan nodded to Laina reassuringly, then looked to the doctor.

"I trust her safety to your hands," Ronan said as he left. The tone suggested there would be consequences for betraying that trust.

"Men," said Valeria. "I wonder if they are the same across *every* species?"

Laina smiled. If he'd left her with anyone besides the doctor she might have been worried, but Valeria seemed to understand her.

"Make yourself comfortable," the doctor said. "I still need a few minutes to prepare my tests."

Instead of sitting down, Laina took her time examining the room again, trying to focus on things she hadn't noticed before. One of the walls had tiny compartments fitted into it where plant life and small creatures were apparently living. She walked over to a plant that was completely submerged in water, its fuzzy top billowing with the shifting water around it, making the red strands look like hair.

She turned to look at Valeria. "What are all of these?"

The doctor smiled and joined her. "Do you like my collection?"

"Collection?"

Valeria gestured to the wall, encouraging her to keep looking. "These are species of flora and fauna we encountered on our most recent expedition, looking for planets that share similarities with Earth. Carbon-based life, nitrogen-oxygen atmosphere, and so forth. I've been conducting studies on them to see if I can find genetic similarities to other worlds, including old Earth." Valeria gestured to the red fuzzy plant. "That's extremely close to a sea anemone found on Earth." She tapped the glass, and the red strands of the plant disappeared, sucked deep into the dark-ruby base of the plant.

Laina leapt back, her heart lodged in her throat as she

crashed into the doctor behind her. Valeria steadied her with a light chuckle.

"Sorry, I should have warned you. It's not a plant, you see. I startled it, and it pulled its feelers back as a way of protecting itself, just like an anemone. But that's just external appearances. Convergent evolution, where vastly different species take on similar traits simply because they are best suited for a given environment. Genetically, however, there are very few similarities."

Laina moved closer to the glass again, giving it an experimental tap as one of the tentacles had started to slither out of the base. It shot back inside. She grinned. It was kind of fun to do that, though it was probably mean to taunt the creature.

"Why are you collecting all of these things?" she asked.

Valeria, who had returned to her desk, paused and looked at her thoughtfully.

"We are explorers, amongst other things. Believe me, despite what you might see on the vids, we don't spend all our time waging war or rounding up stray humans. Our most recent expedition was on the farthest edges of Draxon space. We were surveying the region for the better part of eight years."

"What are you hoping to find?" Laina asked.

The doctor smiled. "The unknown, for one thing. Every new discovery tells us something more about the galaxy we live in. I also have some pet theories I'm trying to prove."

"About what?"

Valeria leaned back in her chair. "Life, the universe, everything. The usual."

"Is that all?"

"I've been around a long time. I need a hobby." Valeria

chuckled. The sound made Laina relax. It was a human sound, one of comfort and companionship.

"But you don't need to *collect* all these things to do that, do you?"

"I..." Valeria looked to the wall, then shook her head. "I miss Earth, to be honest. It helps comfort me on long voyages to seek out creatures and plants that remind me of home."

Home. The word always made Laina's heart ache. She'd never really had one, but every day it felt as if she'd lost one all the same. Once again she was overtaken by a swell of panic mixed with sadness. She wanted to be back on the ground, to leave the void of space behind and breathe in air, *fresh* air, not recycled oxygen.

"Laina? Are you all right?" Valeria moved next to her and started another scan.

"Sorry," she gasped. "I get these attacks sometimes. It's just...sometimes I hate space. Like, *really* hate it," she confessed. "I guess it's like claustrophobia or something. I have this crazy need to be on a planet, feet on the ground, real air, you know."

The doctor's eyes lit up. "I suppose I do, but in reverse. I spent much of my early life on Earth, long ago, and all I could do then was long for the long dark of space in which to escape, to move freely. Instead I was confined to the ground. A prisoner of gravity, if you will."

"I can't believe you were actually on Earth," Laina said. Earth to her had always been closer to a legend than a reality.

"Oh yes. Every cyborg was created there. Some stayed there longer than others. Most were shipped off to Mars or the Outer Colonies as soon as they were trained."

Laina wanted to ask about what Earth was like, but

couldn't. If she did, she wouldn't be able to resist asking the next obvious question: Why did they destroy it?

Valeria went back to her desk and bent over one of the transparent screens. Colored symbols lit up the display, and the screen went dark after she tapped one. She turned back to Laina.

"I've ordered you something to eat. Come over to the examination table and we'll get started." She gestured to one of the tables, and Laina hopped up on it.

She complied, hoping whatever tests Valeria needed to run wouldn't hurt. She wasn't a fan of needles or deep scanners or probes. *Especially* probes...

When the doctor lifted the largest needle she'd ever seen in her life, her muscles tensed and she eyed the exit. The doctor studied her for a moment, then set the needle aside and retrieved a small and unthreatening black box. "I'm joking."

Laina laughed, even if it was a little forced. "Well that's a relief."

Valeria smiled. "The needle inside this is coated with an anesthetic, but you'll still feel a tiny sting and possibly a tugging sensation," the doctor cautioned as she gently took hold of her hand and placed the box into the center of her palm where the anomaly was.

She felt a pinch as the needle broke through her skin, then could swear she felt it run up against something. A bone? She didn't think so. The probe pinched harder as it started to extract a sample. A few seconds later the probe retracted, and Valeria removed the box from her hand. She took a small dab of some pale cream and rubbed it over the pinprick. Her skin tingled, and then the ache receded.

"I'm not used to healing people this way," Valeria admitted.

"But you *are* a doctor, right?" she asked.

"Well," she said with another smile, "I'm more of what you might call a big-picture doctor. Pulse gun wounds, plasma burns, missing limbs..." She wondered if Valeria was just trying to make small talk, to keep her relaxed and let her know it was okay to ask questions.

Laina shook her head. "Honestly, my only knowledge of you is more or less rooted in childhood stories." She hesitated, afraid to really question the doctor, but her need to understand them was greater. "I'd like to know more about you. What you're really like, I mean."

The doctor nodded. "I'd be happy to tell you."

"How do the machines in you actually work? It's nanotechnology, right?"

Valeria nodded. "Yes, but it's more complex than that. It's a special kind of bond, designed to be unique to each individual. It aided in our accelerated growth, far more rapid than the synths that came before us, and after that keeps our bodies in perfect shape and virtually ageless."

Laina looked at the doctor's lean, strong, and yet feminine body. "Whoa..." A thought occurred to her. "How awful."

Valeria looked puzzled. "Awful?"

"Sorry, I didn't mean it like that. I meant..." How could she explain it? She was reminded of what Alanna had said before in Ronan's room. These people had missed out on having a childhood, something that made up half her own life. "You had even less time to be young. A childhood is sacred. Everyone deserves to be a kid."

"I've sometimes thought that myself. But have you considered how odd and tragic I find you? You waste a quarter of your brief lives simply maturing, and another quarter is spent deteriorating and breaking down. How awful."

Laina was shocked by the sudden shift in perspective. She supposed Valeria had a point.

"But if it's so great, why didn't we ever use the nanotech on ourselves?"

"You tried. But this isn't simple gene modification we're talking about. You'd perfected that decades before. No doubt you've inherited genes from your ancestors who'd had gene therapy done to them before Earth was lost. Greater radiation resistance, increased lifespan, better bone density, the sorts of things they needed if they were to thrive outside of Earth.

"Cyborgs, however, use something entirely different. The process required the bond to exist from the moment of conception. Attempts to adapt it to human use were...well, disastrous." The tone of regret in her voice suggested she knew this from personal experience. "And to be honest, I never fully understood how the process worked. It was a closely guarded secret."

"Can I ask you something else?" Laina asked.

"By all means."

"Well, this isn't about you as a whole. I had a question about Ronan."

Valeria raised an eyebrow. "Oh?"

"Why does he talk so strange?"

It took a moment for the doctor to understand her meaning, but when she did she actually laughed. "Call it a quest for identity. After the Terran Disaster, we were a lost people. All of us. As we rebuilt our society, we forged a new identity for ourselves, and language is part of that identity."

"But you don't talk like he does. You talk more, well..."

"Normal?"

"Compared to him, anyway."

"Not everyone buys into the Silver Legion *rah-rah* propaganda the same way. I've seen far too much of the universe to care. I am who I've always been. I've never needed to reinvent myself. You'll find the synths on board talk more like you do as well. But then, there's always been a bit of a divide between us and the synths."

She wondered what Valeria meant by that. Laina was about to ask when the screen next to the doctor began to beep. She turned in her chair, scanning the information that was scrolling by in a blur. It was too fast for Laina to read, but she did glimpse one word repeated over and over: *match*.

"What is it?" She tried to move closer, but Valeria tapped the screen and it went dark, all the information vanishing. The doctor lowered her head, rubbing her eyes with her thumb and forefinger.

"What is your surname?"

"My surname? I—I don't have one." She'd always kept it a secret. She wasn't even supposed to know it, but when she'd accidentally found out, her parents had told her to take that secret to her grave.

"Laina. Don't lie to me. Not now." Valeria looked at her again, her eyes hard, the sympathy dropping away. "What. Is. Your. Surname?"

When she refused to answer, the doctor simply stated, "You are a Roberts."

She slowly nodded. There was no point in hiding now. The truth was out.

"Yes. I'm Laina Roberts."

CHAPTER 8

Ark Chronicle Entry 45-93

They called it the Great Leap Forward.

Around the twentieth century on Earth, advances in transit-drive technology within the Protectorate increased exponentially. Before this, the fastest anyone had traveled was one hundred times the speed of light. But even at these great speeds, it could take decades to travel from one end of a Protectorate species' territory to another.

These slow speeds greatly influenced the borders initially established by the Protectorate, with all but the Ugaro restricting themselves to the arms of the galaxy, where the stars were more densely clustered together. Cryotech was used extensively by those going on long journeys, and it wasn't unusual for the lifespan of an explorer to extend several hundred years, though the vast majority of that was spent in stasis.

In short, there was no such thing as "casual" space travel, unless it was to a neighboring star system.

Then this speed cap wasn't just broken, it was shattered, with a new theoretical top speed of ten thousand times the speed of light. One could cross the entire galaxy in less than ten years, and the Protectorate could be crossed in about one. Quantum entanglement breakthroughs allowed for reliable instantaneous communications, regardless of distance.

Politically, rather than creating a rush to expand their borders, this resulted in the five Protectorate species increasingly colonizing and exploring worlds within their borders, in part to strengthen and secure their positions.

This led to a new discovery—and a new problem.

Laina wondered what the doctor would do next. She didn't seem angry, but the lightness in her eyes had vanished. All at once she'd become deadly serious.

"I apologize." The doctor had no doubt sensed the unease she'd caused. "It's just that this news is rather significant. More than you realize."

The tests she'd conducted had recognized Laina's DNA and its lineage, but she was uncertain why it was such a big deal. For most of her life she had simply been Laina, and when she'd learned her father's family name he'd acted as if that name could doom her. But why? Had a Roberts in the past done something horrible?

Judging from the doctor's expression, it was at least a possibility.

"Is this bad?" she asked. "I mean, if someone related to me did something... I'm not that person. I shouldn't be punished because—"

The doctor actually laughed, which didn't make her feel any better.

"Actually, it's quite the opposite. From now on, you are going to be heavily protected. You're more important than you realize."

Her heart kicked. Important? How was that possible? She was just a human refugee who'd been on the run her whole adult life. "Why?"

"The commander has ordered my silence on the matter, but I assure you, keeping you alive is now our top priority. Cheer up. Things are going to get a lot better for you. I promise."

What was she supposed to think about that?

The medical bay's doors opened, and a tall man with gold hair entered, carrying a tray of food and a drink. He wore an officer's uniform, so he was most likely a cyborg, and he was just as handsome as the others. His gaze settled on her, and she was struck by the tawny glow of his eyes. They were an unusual color, almost a light topaz. Even from here she could see them dilate and spin a little. Implants? Danger shadowed the harsh lines of his jaw and cheekbones. Yet again Laina had encountered the glare of a cyborg who looked at her like she was a bug.

First impressions were really hard on this ship.

"We've just docked at the station. I brought some food." He placed the tray near Laina on the desk. Valeria flicked her display back on and resumed scanning the results. "For some reason, the commander thinks only a bridge officer can be trusted with this vital task."

"Thank you, Hawk." She nodded in the officer's direction but kept her focus on Laina.

Hawk, however, didn't spare Laina a second look. "The commander allowed us to open the last bottle of Talorian wine."

Valeria abandoned her work and turned toward the food with an eager smile. "Really? He must have been listening in on our conversation." She reached for the glass nearest her, tipping back the golden liquid and setting it down with a satisfied smile.

The sudden curve of Hawk's lips set off alarms in Laina's head.

"Thank you, Hawk. We have a lot to cele...oh no..." Valeria got up, but her legs were already unsteady.

"What's wrong, doc?" asked Hawk.

Valeria staggered toward her medical supplies. "Hawk... listen...you can't..." She crumpled to the ground, her face smacking into the floor with a soft thud. "You...don't..." was all she managed to say after that before her body went still.

"Oh my God, Valeria!" Laina gasped. She moved toward her, fearing the doctor was dead. But she never got a chance to check.

Hawk was already in front of her, a pulse gun in one hand and the second glass in the other.

"Drink up. You won't like the alternative."

***

Lieutenant Hawking stared down at the unconscious freeborn. He should have had her drink the drugged wine first, but he couldn't chance the doctor figuring out what his intentions were.

A thread of guilt and shame rippled underneath his skin. This would most likely be construed as mutiny. But to him it was about justice.

Hawk was one of the newest members of the crew, joining the *Orion* during their refit, right after their recent exploration mission. Before that he had been serving at the Colony Fleet, navigating a rusty old cruiser between the fleet and the mining operation it was currently running. An operation that relied heavily on freeborn labor.

Every time his ship docked there, he saw the freeborn and synths working together like they were one and the same. Without his enhanced vision, he wouldn't have been able to tell the two apart.

It frustrated him beyond words. To his eyes they were being treated the same, and that was not right. The High Council's ruling was clear—the creators were under the care and ownership of the creations. They were subordinate. They were *less than*. And they had earned that place in history.

He'd lost everyone when Earth was destroyed. His entire division, friends who had been more like family had been with the fleet that day, and he'd been stuck in a brig on Europa for insubordination.

He should have been there with them. He should have died with them. Instead he'd lived, rewarded for being a hothead who had trouble following orders. Where was the justice in that? Right now, the only justice that was left was the kind he felt when he saw the freeborn put in their rightful place—in chains.

But the woman on the floor beneath him hadn't done anything to him. She hadn't even been born when Earth was lost. She'd even shown concern for Valeria. For a moment he had doubt. Who was he to visit the sins of the fathers onto the children?

But the die was cast. Blood called out for blood. There was no turning back.

The sickbay doors swished open. Ensign Aquila stood there, grinning.

"Jackpot." Julian walked over to Hawk. "Told you it would work." When he noticed the woman's condition, he raised an eyebrow. "How much did you give her? She's not worth anything damaged."

"She only took a sip. And this isn't about money, Julian."

"Doesn't mean it can't be part of it." Hawk's friend knelt down and threaded his fingers through the woman's hair. "I forgot how silky their hair could be...freeborns, I mean." Julian's face softened, as if remembering something from his past. They'd been stationed on Europa at the same time, even sharing a cell that fateful day. But while Hawk had been locked up for insubordination, Julian had been there for less conventional reasons, namely involving two married human women, and a couple of jealous husbands who happened to be high-ranking officers.

"Maybe we should abort," said Hawking. "Ronan will be furious when he finds her missing."

Julian scoffed. "Ronan is blinded by his hormones and the novelty of keeping her for a pet. The sooner she's off this ship, the better. We just docked at Isla 55. I checked the logs there. There is a Charon delegation on board looking for a gift for their king. It's perfect."

The Charons were a humanoid species known for their voracious sensual appetites. While they were capable enough warriors, they were also a peaceful race. For the most part. Their palaces and cities were among the finest in the Protectorate after the Elysians.

"You would give her to the Charon?"

"Give, no. Sell, yes."

"They demand much of their slaves, from what I understand."

Julian raised a brow at him. "Your point?"

Hawk said nothing.

"Come on, let's get her into the station. She's just one freeborn. It's a month in the brig, tops, if we're caught. I can do that standing on my head. And the sooner she's out of our hair, the sooner things can get back to normal." Julian helped Hawk lift the woman up, and together they carried her out the door. "We've only got a five-minute window before the security feed is back online. Let's move."

"Put her down, Hawk. Let them see the merchandise," a voice said.

Laina gradually became aware of herself and her surroundings. She felt herself being placed on a cold, hard surface. Her head lolled, and she tried to make out those around her.

"Gentlemen, I present the Earth female. Freeborn." She recognized that voice from before. The one called Julian.

"What's happening?" Her question came out in a hoarse croak.

"We're dealing with you," said Julian, leaving her on the table to speak to someone else in the room. "Now shut up."

It was then that she got a good look at the two other beings present. They almost looked human, but their skin was golden. It actually seemed to glow in this light. Their eyes seemed to spark with electricity. Their hair was shoulder length and looked so pale it was almost white.

She sat up, remembering Julian's words earlier. *Merchandise? Are they selling me? But the doctor said...* Then she remembered Valeria falling unconscious, or dead, and the one called Hawk forcing her to drink some drugged wine. She saw him standing off to the side, looking around somewhat nervously. This couldn't have been under orders.

Ronan. Why hadn't she called out for Ronan? He'd arranged it so she could call him for help and when she actually needed to use it she'd completely blanked.

One of the aliens spoke to Julian in a language she couldn't understand. He laughed and pointed welcomingly at Laina. The other stepped toward her and held out a hand. It didn't seem like a threatening gesture, so she cautiously took it. Without warning, he leaned in and kissed her.

Laina's entire body went rigid, and she balled her fists, striking him in the chest, though it barely seemed to deter him. His body was rock-hard. Summoning all her strength, she pulled back her arm and socked the alien right in the face...and hurt her hand in the process. But at least he broke the kiss.

She rubbed her sore knuckles. "What are you made of, stone?"

Rather than release her or strike her back, he seemed to find her resistance amusing. He turned to Julian and spoke again. His words, although incomprehensible to Laina, were soft and full of mirth. He patted Laina's cheek and tapped her nose with an index finger. He then tossed Julian a large pouch that jangled when it landed in his hands.

"Julian, what's happening?" She didn't miss the clench of his jaw when she spoke his name.

"He thinks your resistance is 'delightful,' freeborn," he replied with a cold smile. "Charons love a challenge. Don't worry, you'll probably live better with him than you would have with us. We're doing you a favor."

Laina spat at him. "*Live?* Being a slave isn't living! Especially a pleasure slave. You're a monster!"

Julian made a move for her, but the Charon stood between them. Chivalrous but irritating, Laina noticed. She would have been happy to hit Julian in the groin again. She noticed Hawking's conflicted gaze. Was he having second thoughts?

"Please...please don't let them take me!" When she reached for him, the Charon gently but firmly caught her wrist and pulled her away.

Hawk shook his head. "The Charons follow all laws regarding slave treatment. This is better for you. More importantly, it's better for us."

"You don't understand! The doctor said things were going to get better! That keeping me alive was your top priority now!" She didn't know what else she could say. "Val said I was more important than I realized!"

She couldn't explain why, but she wanted to go back. No matter how well the Charon might treat her, she was still going to be a slave. And she'd felt like the doctor hadn't just been trying to make her feel better with her words. There was something bigger going on, and these two couldn't have known what she'd learned before they'd taken her.

And then there was Ronan.

She didn't know why she'd thought about him just now. It made no sense. He didn't like her, he barely tolerated her, yet she felt drawn to him.

The Charon who held her started to pull her away down the corridor. "No, please!" She struggled to slow down the man as he dragged her away. "The doctor said I was important!"

They stopped, and the one who seemed to be in charge said something to her in his tongue. He held up a device and pressed a button. A warning beep went off on the silver cuffs wrapped around her forearms. His meaning was clear. *Cooperate, or we will use this.* Getting hurt wouldn't help her, and she knew she should preserve her strength for whatever might come next.

There was nothing worse than realizing you had no

control over your own destiny, but Laina had had plenty of practice. The Charons led her down a series of halls on the space station, down toward the market area.

It seemed she would never be free. Her life wasn't her own and never would be again. The truth of this stung, and tears blurred her eyes. She stumbled, and one of the Charons caught her arm, gently lending her strength. She was still tired from the drug. Her body was ready to collapse. Maybe after she rested, she could find her way out of this mess. Find a way to escape. She didn't know where she would go next, but when had that ever stopped her before?

This station bore all the marks of a standard trade hub. She'd been on dozens of them before. Animated advertisements covered the walls, most of them written in Galactic Common, while the storefronts tended to show two languages, GalCom and whatever their usual clientele used.

The Charons led her through another maze of corridors, away from the shopping district. Other creatures passing them in the halls gave them curious looks, especially her. She kept her head down and tried not to meet anyone's eyes. She didn't want to be noticed or remembered. There were plenty of humanoid species she could be mistaken for with a bit of makeup or prosthetics. She'd masqueraded as a number of them at one point or another.

Eventually they reached a docking station, and a small porthole window from the station's wall revealed a sleek-looking ship waiting just behind the sliding doors. It was much smaller than the *Orion*, some kind of pleasure yacht, perhaps.

A large blue-skinned Draxon drone stood guard, which made Laina nervous. At first glance he could have been mistaken for a much larger, darker, and hairless Nubran, but the two species were nothing alike. The whole Perseus Arm was controlled by the Draxon, though this was the first one she'd seen in several weeks. She stayed away from them whenever she could. They were the staunch allies of the cyborgs and had been strong advocates for their current status within the Protectorate. When it came to collecting freeborns and returning them to the Terran Colony Fleet, they were all too eager to assist.

This Draxon worker, however, stepped back when the Charon holding her arm raised a medallion about his neck, something she hadn't noticed before. It looked like a flat milky stone, but there were iridescent shimmers of gold and purple playing on its surface. Something like a pearl.

Laina had seen a pearl once. Her mother had worn a pendant necklace with one on it. Laina had loved feeling the silky texture of the odd jewelry, marveling when her mother had explained that it came from an animal called an oyster, and that it had formed the pearl from a single grain of sand over time, adding layer upon layer to it. It was one more fascinating mystery from a planet that no longer existed.

The sliding doors of the airlock parted, and the two Charons led her onto their ship. The one she'd punched ushered her to a chamber not far inside the door. The other moved on ahead purposefully toward the front of the ship. It was then she noticed the subtle differences in their dress. The one who was leaving them was dressed in more...well, if she had to guess, she'd say he looked like an officer, whereas the one still with her wore finer clothes, with embroidered patterns on his tunic shirt. The medallion around his neck added a regal look to him. Perhaps he was some kind of noble or government official?

He spoke a few words to the other male, the one she

assumed was the pilot. The man stopped and waved a hand above his head in answer, then left, disappearing around a corner.

The Charon next to her nudged her into the open doorway of the nearest room, a richly decorated bedchamber with a massive bed. Far bigger than the one Ronan had. With another little push, she fell onto the bed.

Was he going to try to force himself upon her so soon? She panicked and flipped onto her back, arms raised in defense. Nothing happened, and she saw him stare down at her, an exasperated look in his eyes. He shook his head and went over to one of the drawers by the bed, which opened itself with a wave of his hand. He pulled out an earpiece, handed it to her, and mimed for her to put it on. She did so.

"Stay here. You will not be harmed."

She heard his words in his native tongue in one ear, but the other translated his words into Galactic Common, with only a slight delay. She'd used these adaptive translators before but had lost hers some time ago. Fortunately, she had learned Nubran and GalCom, which was usually enough to get by.

She nodded her understanding, and the man left her alone, shutting the door behind him. After a few seconds, when he didn't return, she sat up and rubbed her hand. The spot where Valeria had pricked her with the needle itched.

A wave of fatigue swept through her. Every time she thought things might get better, they ended up getting worse. She realized now that her backpack was still in Ronan's room and she'd probably never see it again. Or him.

Tears burned her eyes. She couldn't hold back the exhaustion she felt or the need to just let go. She wept into the pillows on the Charon's bed and tried not to think about what tomorrow would bring.

CHAPTER 9

Ark Chronicle Entry 45-98

After the Great Leap Forward, the Nubran found the first new spacefaring species in more than a thousand years. This would not be an isolated incident. Soon all five Protectorate species had encountered a new generation of younger races reaching for the stars, with no end in sight.

This created a number of political problems. The number of members sitting on the Low Council increased ever further, which meant each individual member's voice was increasingly diminished, and the voice of the High Council became increasingly important.

A bureaucratic solution was attempted, introducing a lengthy "Applicant" status for new races. Criteria was added that had to be met before they could become full members. But this led to only more problems and an ongoing state of bureaucratic stagnation.

Xenobiologists still can't explain why so many new spacefaring species have been found in such a short period of time, but it has strengthened the argument for those who

RONAN'S SHIFT WAS FINALLY OVER. NORMALLY HE surrendered his duties reluctantly, but right now all he wanted was to see Laina down in sickbay. There hadn't been any opportunities to check on her because he'd been far too busy with his duties, and once they'd docked at Isla 55 he'd had to oversee the resupply process with Erik and Alanna. They'd obtained a few crates of fresh fruit, and he'd hoped to offer Laina some. There were plenty of fruits that were similar to the ones on Earth, something he thought she'd appreciate.

He was worried about her, though he didn't want to admit it. But the doctor hadn't contacted him, and that only worried him more. Tests or no tests, he expected regular updates.

The sickbay door opened and he glanced about, surprised by the silence. He didn't see anyone. No, there was someone—on the floor. Valeria's black boots stuck out from behind her desk. She was lying facedown.

But there was no sign of Laina.

He ran to his friend and turned her over. "Valeria!"

The doctor stirred with a low groan. "What happened?" Valeria gripped the hand Ronan offered and sat up, holding her head with her other hand.

"Val, where is Laina?"

The doctor blinked, as if trying to remember. Her eyes widened and she cursed.

"Hawk! Damn his eyes. He must have drugged me, and...he's taken Laina!"

Ronan snarled. "Taken?"

"Yes, but why?"

"The *why* can wait. What we need to know is *where*." He pulled Valeria to her feet, and they both ran into the hall. As they cleared the doorway, they caught sight of Julian walking toward them, a pouch in his hand. He saw Ronan and Valeria, then tried to hide the pouch. But when he realized it was too late and he'd only drawn attention to it, he spun on his heel and made a run for it.

"Ensign! Halt!" Ronan bellowed. When he refused to stop, Ronan chased him down and tackled him from behind. He pressed Julian's face against the floor and locked his arms behind his back. The bag he'd been holding fell to the ground.

"What are you up to, Ensign?"

"Nothing!"

"Then why did you run?"

"I could tell you were in a bad mood!" Julian snapped. "I was right!"

"Where is Hawking?"

"How the hell should I know?"

"Laina is missing, and Valeria said Hawk drugged her. Now I find you with this—" He grabbed the bag on the ground with his free hand and threw it against the wall. The credits inside spilled out. "I know one of your schemes when I see it. Talk!"

"Hawk and I sold her. She's gone."

Ronan sucked in a breath and released Julian, standing up and towering over the ensign.

"On whose orders?" Ronan yelled as Dr. Schedar caught up to them.

Julian got to his feet, only to get slammed against the wall, facing Ronan. "*No one's* orders," Julian spat. "She was causing nothing but trouble, and if you and the commander weren't going to do anything about it, I was."

Ronan's grip loosened, but only a little. "What are you talking about?"

"I was there with you when we stopped Erik, remember? He's been unstable ever since you lost the *Rapier*. And you put a *freeborn* right under his nose? What, did you expect him to give her a hug?"

Ronan's eyes narrowed. "And just how did Erik get in the brig, Julian?"

"What?"

"I have checked the duty roster. It shows no gap between shifts, but when I spoke to the crew, I found there was a full twenty minutes when no one was present. At that same time, Erik's rounds between the bridge and the engine room took him past the brig, no doubt after someone tipped him off about our newly acquired freeborn. *And* the door was left open."

Julian scowled. "What are you saying, Ronan?"

"I'm saying *someone* tried to get Laina killed and made it look like a series of unfortunate coincidences." He tightened his grip on Julian, growling as he spoke.

"Why would I want her dead?"

"You tell me, Ensign." Ronan let him go and picked up the half-empty bag, shaking it in front of his face. "You are always playing games like this, for as long as I've known you."

"I didn't hear anyone complain when I helped negotiate our last trade deal with the Draxon shipyards." Julian grimaced, starting to lose his patience. "You're holding the reason it wasn't me right there in your hand. She was no good to me dead."

"*Why?*"

"Don't you get it, Ronan? I did you a *favor*. Look at you! You're a mess! You want to keep her holed up in your room like some kind of pet. She was even starting to get to the commander and the doc. She's not one of us. She doesn't belong on this ship!"

Ronan frowned. The man was a schemer and a con man, but right now he seemed paranoid and flustered. He was spiraling out of control and doing whatever he could to stay on course. This wasn't like Julian at all.

"Who did you sell her to, Julian?" Ronan's tone was cold and deadly. The pain he felt went well beyond Julian's insubordination. Rage like nothing else filled him, burning his insides like the heart of a neutron star.

Valeria came closer, concern showing on her face, but she made no move to pull Ronan off of the junior officer.

"We sold her to a pair of Charons, all right? They've already left the station." There was a look of victory in Julian's face, and Ronan wanted to smash it against the bulkhead.

"No..." Valeria's voice was barely a whisper.

"What's the big deal?" Julian asked. "I know the regulations. Misappropriation of property. Nothing more. You want to put me in the brig for it, go ahead. But I did it for the good of the Legion."

Ronan pulled Julian back and slammed him against the wall so hard he made a dent in it. "Don't you *dare* say it was for the good of the Legion."

Dr. Schedar looked almost as furious. "Julian, you blind, idiotic *fool*! Do you have *any* idea how important she is to us?"

Julian's face paled, as if he'd heard those words before and only now realized what they had meant. "She really was important?"

"She is a direct descendant of John Roberts. She has the key with her."

"The key to what?"

"To *everything*!"

It took a moment for Ronan's mind to catch up. *A descendant of John Roberts? One of the creators? But they all died on Earth...*

"Where were the Charons going?" Valeria asked. "Did they say?"

When he didn't answer right away, Ronan lifted him up till his head touched the ceiling. Julian glowered. "She's to be a gift to their king."

"Hell and damnation." Ronan let go, and Julian dropped to the ground. "King Balefire won't give her back, especially if he learns why we need her."

"Are you sure?" asked the doctor. "They're within the Draxon Collective, just like us. They would have to return her if we demanded it."

Ronan shook his head. "No one would pass up the kind of leverage she would provide over us. It could take years before they agreed to any terms, insist on High Council arbitration, all the while they'd no doubt be running their own tests..." And who knew how far the Charon would go in that regard. "Julian, you and Hawk will report to the brig immediately. I will decide your fates later. Doctor, I have a favor to ask of you. Did you complete your tests on Ensign Keid?"

The doctor nodded. "Still waiting on the results, but I see where you're going with this."

"Good. Make sure you examine them both."

"Still off the record?"

"For now."

Valeria caught Ronan's arm as he turned to leave. "What's your plan?"

"What else can we do? We have to try to catch the Charon ship. There is no reason they wouldn't take the shortest route to their home system, if that is their destination. If we leave now—"

"What about the station?" Julian interrupted. "We haven't finished resupplying."

Ronan turned on him. "Maybe that should have been your concern, instead of selling our *last hope* to the first species you could find." With that, he sprinted back to the command deck, where the remaining bridge crew were running a fuel check.

"Prepare to disembark!" he barked.

"What?" The commander wasn't used to orders being given while he was still on deck.

"Julian and Hawk sold Laina to a Charon ship. We need to leave at once. We still might be able to catch them." He saw the question on Alaric's face and added. "Commander, the doctor confirmed it. She's the one."

Alaric's face changed from concern to something akin to fear. He tapped the control panel on his chair.

"All hands! Prepare for immediate departure." He turned to the bridge crew. "Alanna, take Hawking's station. Set our course for Charon. I want scanners set to maximum range. Ronan, take the helm. Flag any ships identifying as Charon." Alanna sat down at Hawking's post at navigation as Ronan took Julian's seat and undocked the *Orion* from the station.

The second the *Orion* was clear of the station, they activated the transit drive. Stars fell away into the distance, then shot past in a flurry of streaks.

Ronan tried to focus on his task, but his mind kept drifting to Laina and how important it was to reach her. He tried to tell himself it was for the sake of his people, but there was more to it than that.

"What is it, Ronan?" the commander asked. "I can *feel* you thinking from here."

Ronan turned in his chair to face the commander. "When we return Laina to the ship, I'd like to request a temporary leave from my duties."

"What for?"

Ronan was hesitant to offer too many details, in part because he had hoped to deal with Erik's actions in private. "I believe there is a security risk on board, one that extends beyond what happened with Julian and Hawk. She requires full-time security."

Alaric looked to his first officer. "What aren't you telling me, Sub-Commander?"

"I'd rather not say too much at this time," said Ronan.

The commander eyed him carefully. "This isn't just because of the woman, is it?"

"No, Commander."

Alaric didn't look convinced. "You've been quite possessive of her of late. How can I be sure I can trust you with her?"

Ronan blinked. It was a fair question, and he had no answer readily available. "She is important, Commander. I will protect her with my life."

Alaric chuckled at his response. "I suspect she'll be no safer with you than anyone else on board, though the reasons why may differ. For now, let's focus on the most immediate problem: retrieving her. My greatest concern is to get the freeborn back without starting a war."

"And if they refuse?" asked Ronan.

"Then they will lose that war," said Alaric.

CHAPTER 10

Ark Chronicle Entry 138-3

This is Evelyn Roberts, third chronicler of the Ark device. We've found some sense of stability and safety for now on a small colony in the Void, enough so that I can spend more time looking at what went wrong back when this all began.

From my understanding, what doomed mankind to the eternal servitude of our creations was a combination of factors. The bureaucracy in place had existed for hundreds of years and had strict rules deciding which lifeforms could be considered the dominant, and therefore representative, species of that system.

After the cataclysm that destroyed Earth, the High Council was split trying to decide whether the humans or their creations should represent all Terrans. In the end, they sided with the synthetics, specifically the cyborgs. Humans, or freeborns as we soon came to be called, were considered to be under their care.

And because Sol is located in Draxon space, this effectively made us their property.

But not everything went the cyborgs' way. Their application for a seat on the Low Council contained a different set of criteria. The definition of a sapient species included an ability to naturally reproduce, something the cyborgs could not do. And despite the genetic variation involved in their creation, synths were lumped in with regular cloning technology. This not only prevented the Terrans from gaining a seat on the Senate, but it denied them the chance to claim any territory beyond their own decimated system.

It was then that the cyborgs revisited the idea of leaving the system, and they formed the Terran Colony Fleet.

A SUDDEN EXPLOSION AND THE RESULTING LURCH OF the Charon ship would have sent Laina flying off the bed, had the bed itself not managed to restrain her for safety.

She'd barely been asleep when it happened, and by the time she realized the bed had gripped her on all sides, the ship's stabilizers had kicked in and the restraints had retracted, allowing Laina to get up. Strange warning sirens blared, and the overhead lights dimmed. Only a faint orange light by the door glowed, illuminating the room enough that she could see where she was.

The ship shuddered again, this time knocking her to the ground, and the hull seemed to whine. Laina got to her feet, shrugging off her fatigue, only to be flung into the nearest wall as the ship pitched yet again. Another explosion reverberated around her as she was thrown against a wall, right next to the door. She tried to activate the panel, but it didn't work. Then the panel light changed color and the door slid open, but only halfway. It ground to a stop and didn't budge any farther. Laina gripped the door and squeezed through the narrow opening.

Outside, the hall was filled with smoke and loose debris. It was a miracle the ship still had gravity and life support. Another hit and they'd be done for. But what had hit them?

"Hello? Hey!" she shouted, hoping the men who'd brought her on board this death trap were still alive. She didn't know the first thing about flying a starship, but she had to find out who was attacking them.

With my luck, yet another group of slavers.

Something crashed ahead of her, and a door ten feet away exploded. The Charon with the regal clothes emerged, and a gash across his forehead dripped dark blood down his skin. Black smears marred his clothes.

"This way! Follow me," he ordered. His lips did not match the translation fed into her ear, as if someone else was speaking right next to her. She'd forgotten how disorienting these translators could be until you got used to them. But this wasn't the time to worry about that. Right now they had to get out of here alive.

"What happened?" She reached him just as another explosion rocked the ship like a tin can. They both used the walls to stay upright.

"A trap. We hit an energy net," he said. The translator seemed to be keeping his words simple; it looked like he was saying a lot more than that. "It was raised as we approached. Too quick to avoid."

Laina's heart leapt to her throat. *Energy net?* She'd only heard of that associated with one species. Creatures that were the stuff of nightmares.

"Graywalkers?"

The man nodded. "If that is your name for them. We call them Life Eaters."

Laina's blood turned to ice. While most races in the galaxy followed a basic carbon-based humanoid template, there were some out there that were truly alien. Graywalkers were one such species.

They weren't made of matter, not the way most people understood it. They could phase in and out of corporeal form and pass through walls and even people. They were a parasitic species, neither alive nor dead, neither physical nor immaterial.

Back on Captain Zore's ship, one of the crewmembers had said that he'd seen a graywalker consume a Nubran male whole from the inside out before he'd made it to an escape pod. It had settled into the person's very cells, then took him over completely before sucking his body dry and killing him. None of the crew had believed him, though. Graywalkers were rarely encountered, and navigators took special precautions to avoid them. Some didn't even believe they existed, despite the extensive historic records that proved otherwise.

Where they came from and how they evolved was a mystery. They hijacked ships, feeding on the crew, and then used the ship to hide along well-traveled highways, overloading the ship's transit drive in a way no one could quite understand. It created vast energy fields, commonly called webs, that destabilized any transit bubble that passed through it, incapacitating the ship and forcing it back into regular space, damaging it heavily in the process.

They ran down the hall toward the front of the ship. "Where's your pilot?"

"Dead. The net destroyed the forward half of the ship. We will be boarded soon." The Charon's golden face had gone pale. Only now did she notice a nasty wound on his chest and dark blood covering his side.

"What should we do? I've never heard of a way to defeat graywalkers. Hell, I've never heard of a way to even *survive* them." Laina kept pace with the alien as they reached a circular door. He opened the door and pushed her toward the slim opening.

"There are ways," he growled. "But they are not on this ship. Get in."

She peered into the door. It seemed to be a small escape capsule. For a moment her mind was back on board the refugee ship, her parents forcing her inside. She pushed back.

"There's only room for one. What about you?"

The Charon shook his head. "This is the only one left."

She back-stepped and latched on to his arm. "Then I'm sticking with you."

"We will both die if you stay."

"Then you go. I'll be fine." It was a bald-faced lie, but she would rather die facing graywalkers than be confined in a coffin-like capsule again, hurtling toward an unknown fate.

"And leave you alone? I would never abandon a female. Especially not a brave one."

Laina almost rolled her eyes. First the cyborgs, now the Charon. What was with all this chivalry nonsense?

The Charon looked ready to force her into the capsule, but the ship jerked from the force of another explosion. The Charon struck the wall and fell flat on his back, unconscious. Laina hastily searched his body and found a weapon in a holster. Probably their version of a pulse gun. She hoped they worked the same way. There were three energy bars on the readout screen. It was probably still good for a few blasts. Maybe it would be enough to—

The scream of rending metal drew her attention to the end of the hall. The overhead emergency lights flickered and then went dark. Blackness enveloped Laina. The ship's sirens died, and soon the only sounds she heard were the raw gasps of her own breath and the pounding sound of her blood in her ears like war drums. The only things that still seemed to be working were the gravity plates.

Hek-k-k-k-k-k... A soft, sickly sound reached her from the end of the hall, and her skin broke out in goosebumps. It grew louder. And closer.

Laina clutched the pulse gun and held it steady while kneeling over the unconscious Charon. She'd used guns before, but she was under no illusion this was going to work. She was going to die, but not without a fight.

For some reason she couldn't explain, she wondered what Ronan would do in this situation. How would he face a graywalker? He wouldn't give up, that much was certain.

Something lit up at the end of the hall, a dark shape, a void trimmed with bright energy at its edges, giving a semblance of form where in fact there was none. It had to be the graywalker. Black clawlike appendages extended out as it stalked toward her, sometimes two, sometimes four. It had no eyes that she could see, but she could make out a mouth of ringed teeth like lightning.

Laina held the gun out, and her hand trembled slightly.

Hek-k-k-k-k-k...solid...strong energyyyy... What passed for the graywalker's head grew and shrunk, as though studying her. The words escaped its mouth in a ghastly rasp that made her skin crawl.

Wait, how did she understand it? Was it speaking her language? Was it speaking at all? It felt as though she had sensed the words somehow rather than heard them spoken.

It raised one of those clawed hands toward her.

She fired the pulse gun. A blue spark shot straight through the graywalker and splashed against the wall behind it.

"Shit!" She fired again and again, until the gun beeped some kind of warning. There was only one bar left on the capacitor. Laina knew guns wouldn't kill it, but some small part of her had hoped it would have at least slowed the creature down.

Foolissssh solid. It made a cackling noise, and she realized it was laughing. It stopped a few feet from her and the unconscious Charon. It tilted its head again, and even though it had no eyes she felt its gaze on her.

She tried to buy some time. "What do you want?" she demanded. Even if it worked, it was only delaying the inevitable.

Waaaant? the ghoulish monster hissed in her mind.

"Why did you attack us?"

Life energyyyyy... We crave... Hek-k-k-k-k-k...give to ussss...

It advanced on her, and she fired two final shots before the pulse gun stopped working. The monster lunged at her, and she fell back onto the floor, hand raised up in panic. Pain exploded through her as the creature's essence sank into her arm.

She screamed. Her back arched as electricity jolted through her entire body. She couldn't breathe, couldn't—

She slipped out of consciousness and drifted into a dreamlike state. Was she dying? The pain was gone, at least.

Then darkness opened up before her. She was sailing through a sea of stars toward a distant sun. It was a young, bright star, no different from a dozen others she had seen. The path she was on took her past a small rocky world, barren and baked, then a world covered in clouds, and finally toward a small blue dot that grew bigger and bigger, until it filled her view. Large land masses covered its even larger oceans.

A cacophony of noise, a stirring of wind, voices whispering in a thousand languages filled her ears. Visions burst before her eyes like passing comets. Strange animals that looked familiar but she couldn't name blurred past in a wild kaleidoscope. Sunlight flashed over ice-capped mountains, deserts were lit by moonlight, waves crashed against craggy rocks, mist crept over fields blanketed by wildflowers... Each vision was more vivid, more breathtaking than the one before.

Home. She was home. Joy burst through her in a euphoric rush as she understood everything. The symphony of crickets in the early evening, the roar of a hurricane's storm, the movement of magma under the crust—all of it had a purpose, a complex dance of cause and effect that made up all of existence.

A name came from somewhere far away, disturbing the visions. She struggled to keep a hold on the visions of Earth. She didn't want to leave. If there had been a way to dig her fingers into the memories and cling to them, she would have.

"Laina! Danger!" The familiar voice dragged her away from the home she had never known.

Father?

Something was wrong. Something dark and horrible. The visions seemed to darken from all sides, as if something alien and full of malice threatened to poison and devour her.

Hek-k-k-k-k-k...

Suddenly it recoiled, and its moment of triumph changed to one of fear. White light surrounded it, surrounded her, until they were both enveloped in a brilliant flash. It hissed until the sound died away into nothing.

Suddenly Laina was aware of herself again, but whatever had happened to the graywalker had left her weak, trembling from head to foot. Beams of light bounced through the darkness of the hall, and she realized someone was running toward her. Multiple footsteps echoed in the ship's silent hall.

Ronan knelt down by her and the wounded Charon. He changed the setting on his light so it illuminated their surroundings instead of a narrow beam. Other crewmen from the *Orion* stood behind him, weapons drawn and on their guard.

"Ronan?" She stared at him, relieved, shocked, and... happy? A freeborn was actually glad to see a cyborg. Surely this was a sign of the second end of days.

"Laina, what happened?" Ronan handed the light to Alanna, who stood behind him. He hauled Laina onto her feet and held her by the shoulders, as if trying to comfort her. She was in too much pain to say anything at first. Whatever strength she'd had was gone.

"What happened to you? You look..." Ronan's voice trailed off as he studied her face. What had that thing done to her? The look on his face made her wonder if the graywalker had aged her a hundred years.

Ronan reached for a pouch on his belt. He pulled out a small blue tube, a single-use self-injecting shot, and pressed it against her shoulder. There was a hiss, and she felt cold, then very warm at the injection point. Soon that warmth spread throughout her and she felt stronger. Strong enough to talk, at least.

"Graywalkers. They attacked the ship. The pilot was killed." She pointed to the one at her feet. "This one tried to save me. Then the graywalker came." She shoved at Ronan's chest, needing a moment to breathe, some room to think about the experience. Ronan loosened his grip.

Fear and worry glimmered in the depths of his eyes, so different from the cold gaze he'd given her through the windows of the *Orion* shortly before he'd captured her. And there was something more there. Affection? Surely not.

"It found you? How did you survive?"

"I don't know." She laughed a little, her voice getting stronger. "I drove it off. I think."

Ronan studied her intensely. "What? How?" The press of his hands on her shoulders felt so comforting, yet it kept her at a distance. And right now that was the last thing she wanted. After what she had felt in the graywalker's clutches...

She broke free of Ronan's grip and crushed herself against his chest, embracing him with all her might, feeling his warmth. His *life*. She didn't want to think about why hugging him mattered, or how good it felt when he closed his arms around her, embracing her back.

"I don't know. It was there one minute talking to me, sort of. Then it went *into* me, and I think it tried to take over my body. Then something happened. Something seemed to hurt it." She shuddered at the memory. The creature had lost its power when she'd started seeing the visions of Earth. Where had *those* come from? But what she had seen and experienced, the images of a dead planet—they were too personal, too intimate to share with anyone right now.

One of the boarding party, checking a scanner, seemed to confirm Laina's story. "There was definitely a graywalker here. But the energy signature is fragmented and dissipating. It's dead."

"But *how*?" asked Ronan.

The crewman shook his head. "It looks like it hit an overload trap, but there isn't one fitted on this ship."

Ronan frowned and looked back to Laina. "Do you feel better? You looked as though you'd suffered regen fatigue."

The concern in his eyes wasn't cold and empirical as she expected. There was a warmth there that hadn't been there before. It made her body fill with something she'd thought she'd never feel again. She'd been so alone, and now...now she wasn't.

He was still staring at her, expecting her to respond. She had to rewind their conversation to remember his question.

"Regen?"

Alanna cut in. "We heal quickly, even during combat, but healing too much damage can be physically draining. We call it regen fatigue."

"I gave you a glucose shot," said Ronan. "It seemed to help. Do you feel better?"

"Yes...but I still need to rest." She hoped they would understand. Her head was starting to hurt, and her hand felt like it was on fire.

The hand with the anomaly...

"Are you sure you're okay?" When she didn't respond, he continued. "I'll have the doctor examine you when we return to the *Orion*."

She stiffened. "I'm...going back with you?" Wait, was that why they were here? They'd come for her? Of course, the doctor had said she was important. She knew logically she shouldn't want to go back with them, but it was human nature to cling to familiar places. The *Orion*, even full of danger, had become familiar to her.

Ronan stroked a hand over her hair, and the tender gesture made her eyes swell. Maybe she was right about him, maybe he was feeling something for her. But that didn't excuse everything that had happened. She remembered how Julian and Hawk had treated her, and she felt the need to lash out.

"So, what is this? A rescue? Reclaiming your property? Did the Charon not pay you enough?"

The softness in his eyes vanished. "That was not my doing. That was insubordination, and those responsible will be punished."

"Why do you want me back at all? Because I'm supposedly important to your people?"

Tell me you came after me because you care....

"Because I gave you my word. I swore no harm would come to you. I failed to keep that vow, but I can at least right that wrong. And, as you said, you are important to...my people. We need you. More than you realize. Let's get you back to the ship." He made as if to carry her.

"I can walk. I'm feeling better." She pushed back from him and turned to the fallen Charon.

"What are you doing?" Ronan demanded.

She threw him an irritated scowl. "You weren't planning on just leaving him here, were you? He tried to save my life."

Ronan's jaw dropped. "But he *bought* you. He was going to use you for pleasure."

A mirthless laugh escaped her lips. "If I wanted to start holding grudges, you and your crew would be at the top of the list, not him."

Ronan didn't argue the point. On some level he had to know she was right. Still, he made no move to help her with the Charon.

"Seriously? You're not going to help?" She grunted as she grabbed the man under his arms and tried to hoist him up. "I thought you were supposed to be better than us? Or does that not extend to morality?"

In the end, it was Alanna who helped. She picked the Charon up with ease and carried him down the hall and to the connecting bridge, where the rest of the *Orion* boarding party now waited.

"This ship won't hold together much longer," said a technician, checking a handheld scanner. "We'd best evacuate."

"Wait. What about the graywalker's energy net?" Laina asked, suddenly realizing there might be more out there.

"We destroyed its ship the moment it came on our scanners. It seemed to have been an Ugaro ship before it became corrupted. Very unusual," Alanna said, though Laina had no idea why. She followed behind as Alanna carried the Charon onto the *Orion* and down into sickbay, where she placed him on one of the exam tables.

Dr. Schedar peeled off the golden-skinned alien's tunic to scan for injuries. Though the shirt had been stained with blood, she saw no signs of any major wounds on him. Alanna's eyes widened at the sight of the shirtless male on the exam table. Whatever she was thinking, it had nothing to do with her duty as a security officer.

Laina could understand the reaction. Most of the time she had been on the run, the men in Laina's life, regardless of species, had ranged from average looking to disgusting. Scraping by and hiding out didn't exactly put you in circles where fitness and hygiene were major concerns.

But this man was beautiful. Perhaps *too* beautiful. Then again, so were the cyborgs. She wondered if the Charon had engineered themselves that way, the way the Elysians had, or if he'd simply taken excellent care of himself.

Valeria cleaned the Charon's wounds, then injected him with something to revive him. The alien groaned, and one of his large hands fell over his eyes.

"Fontel Valarest?" he demanded as he sat up. Laina realized she'd lost her translator, probably on board the other ship.

Ronan and Alanna glared at him suspiciously. Laina ignored them and reached over and patted his shoulder. "You're on the *Orion*. You're safe now."

"You are a guest of the Silver Legion," said Ronan.

The Charon's fingers rubbed his temples, and he groaned. "The last thing I remember is trying to convince you to board the life capsule. An offer you foolishly rejected."

"Wait, you speak English?"

The Charon smirked. "I have had dealings with Terrans before. I simply prefer my own language. But as I am on a Terran ship, courtesy dictates that I speak in your tongue." The Charon's tone treated her with a level of respect and understanding that she hadn't felt on board the *Orion*, and that meant a lot to her.

He turned his attention to the others. "And what of my ship?"

"I'm afraid it was heavily damaged by the energy web," said Alanna. "We had to destroy it for security reasons. I'm sorry."

"I have other ships. That is not a concern. What happened to that creature?" The Charon's words were barely above a growl now, as though the memory of that awful thing angered him. He looked to Laina again. "Graywalker, you called it. How did we survive?"

"It died," said Laina. She still didn't know *how* that happened exactly, only that it had died while trying to consume her. That wasn't a detail she wanted to share, however.

The Charon sat up and took in his surroundings. "So

this is a ship of the mighty Silver Legion. Impressive enough, I suppose. How did you defeat the monster?"

Ronan's eyes flicked to Laina. "That is unclear at this time."

"And who do I thank for my rescue?"

"That would be the free... Laina. She insisted we save you. I would have happily left you on board your ship." Ronan's glare was so potent that Laina was surprised the Charon didn't burst into flames. Even Alanna was surprised by his rudeness.

The Charon, however, gave a small chuckle. "Ah. I see." He turned to Laina and took her hand, raising it to his lips. "My thanks to you then, little human. You will be rewarded when we return to my home. You will be favored among all my slaves."

"Thanks—Wait, *what*?" Laina tugged her hand away from his grasp. "Hey, I'm not your slave."

Amusement lit up his honey-colored eyes. "But you are. I paid the cyborgs well for you. You are mine, by the laws of servitude that preside in Draxon space. I was supposed to present you to my brother, but after saving my life? How could I possibly give you up to anyone? There is no need to fear me. I treat my females very well, for I am a prince of Charon."

Prince? Oh jeez. Laina retreated back a step and bumped into Ronan. He placed his hands upon her shoulders, something that was both possessive and comforting.

"The cyborgs who sold her to you had no authorization to do so. Your payment will be returned in full."

The Charon's brows lowered. "I want the human, not credits. The law will side with my claim, Terran. It is not my fault if you cannot control your crew."

Ronan's laugh made her body shake. "If you wish to go

strictly by the law, I will be happy to oblige. Should you purse the matter, I will invoke the Charon right of *Domina Persea*."

"The what?" asked Laina.

As if to answer her, Ronan continued, "You may fight me for the right to possess her."

"Fight?" Laina's voice pitched higher than she meant it to.

"I did not know the immortal cyborg tired so quickly of their own existence," the prince retorted.

"Guys, seriously, we don't—"

"*Silence!*" both men snapped at her before resuming their war of glares.

"I can't believe this macho bullshit," Laina muttered.

In the end it was Dr. Schedar who broke the tension between them.

"I think it's best if our new guest is taken to an empty cabin. I still need to check Laina for injuries. Alanna, please escort...uh...I don't believe I know your name?" Valeria asked politely.

"Prince Leif of the Seven Rivers and Lord of the Isle of Tears." The Charon shook the hand the doctor extended. "Thank you for seeing to my injuries, healer."

"It is a pleasure to meet you, Your Highness."

It never ceased to amaze Laina how seriously Val took her profession, something that made her more trustworthy than anyone else on the ship. A doctor's duty was to heal, not to harm.

Alanna gestured toward the door. "This way, Leif...er... my lord...er...that is, Your..." Her cheeks pinkened as she watched him put his tunic back on. "How should I address you?"

"Lovely females of any species may address me as Leif."
He turned the full wattage of his smile onto Alanna.

"This way, sir."

"Leif."

"Er...Leif." She pointed again to the door.

"I will settle the matter of the human's ownership once I am rested," Leif told Ronan.

"I look forward to it," Ronan replied.

"You shouldn't."

Laina could only stare at them. It was ridiculous. Two men were ready to fight over her. If she thought for one moment she could have fought them both for her freedom, she would have. But as it was...

Her legs gave out, and Ronan caught her, lifting her effortlessly and setting her on the exam table.

"What happened?" she asked. She'd felt fine before.

Valeria conducted a quick scan. "Your glucose levels have dropped again," she said. "Nothing to worry about. We'll sort that out soon enough."

Laina sighed, relieved to be back in familiar surroundings. "Can I sleep now?" she asked, rolling onto her side. Right then, she could have slept on a bed of rocks, she was that desperate.

Valeria patted her shoulder. "Go ahead, rest. You're safe now."

You're safe now. Words she had only ever heard once, very long ago. Her mother's soft, gentle voice, sweet as she sang a lullaby.

You're safe now.

As sleep pulled her into darkness, she wished that it was true.

CHAPTER 11

Ark Chronicle Entry 138-49

I've been told that when the Terran Colony Fleet left Sol, some remained behind to continue to rebuild, as well as mine for resources that could be used by the fleet.

This new Terran Colony Fleet was at first treated with feelings that ranged from pity to disdain. A people without a home who could not be recognized officially as a people.

But the new Terrans were not to be denied. If the Protectorate could not give them a place within the galaxy, they would forge one for themselves.

The Silver Legion and Centurions that had been formed to act as the fleet's defense quickly expanded their roles to fight for those who could afford them. They excelled in this field, providing mercenary or peacekeeping duties to the major and minor races of the Protectorate, as well as providing aid in situations deemed too dangerous for others to attempt.

Soon, the Terrans were in demand and could name their price. The Draxon in particular found the Silver Legion

RONAN BRUSHED A HAND OVER LAINA'S HAIR. "IS SHE
going to be okay?"

"She'll be fine," the doctor assured him. "She's just
exhausted."

Something inside Ronan had changed when he'd found
her aboard the Charon ship, and again the moment she had
embraced him. For the first time since he'd lost the *Rapier*
and most of her crew, he began to doubt the righteousness
of his zeal against the freeborn. He had laid all his people's
problems at their feet, yet they were no more alike to one
another than synths or cyborgs. So much time had passed,
and for so long he had dismissed them as being inferior,
irrelevant, needing to be rounded up and put to use for their
own good. He had treated them like they had once treated
him. For a time, it had felt like justice. But now...?

Was that what she'd done to him? Forced him to see
beyond his anger? Beyond his past?

He was afraid to put a word to what he felt, but he
knew that resisting his feelings would no longer be so easy.
Ronan had vowed to protect her, but now he wanted to do
more. He intended to win her over, the way she had won
him over so effortlessly. To earn her trust, perhaps even her
respect.

And then?

It was wrong to think of bedding her, yet that was all he
could think of. But he could never do so with her as a prisoner, nor out of fear. If he could win her heart, then he
would let fate decide where it took them next.

Valeria picked up Laina's hand, the one with the anomaly. A brilliantly intricate tattoo was now branded on the palm of her hand. The design seemed to glow. Ronan watched the symbol, trying to identify it, but it was utterly alien to him.

"What is this? Did the Charon mark her?"

Valeria rubbed her thumb over the pattern, making Laina stir in her sleep. "I don't know. It doesn't look like it. The design has certain Nubran qualities to it."

"Nubran?"

"Yes. If I'm right and this was implemented at the cellular level, then I think Elysian technology is involved. But if it is, it's of a kind I haven't seen before." The pattern had a circle with flame-shaped parts spiraling outward like a sun and its rays. A smaller, less distinct pattern of other circles was placed around its center.

"I believe you are right."

Val rubbed her chin, still staring at the faintly glowing symbol. "It would confirm a few things."

"Like what?" Ronan held Laina's hand up and examined the markings closer. Her skin around the tattoo was slightly red, as though the design had recently been burned into her skin.

Valeria paused, as if considering how much to share with him. "I assume the commander has told me at least as much about this as he has told you. Alaric believes John Roberts worked with a secret organization to save mankind's knowledge in a device he called the Ark. I believe this might be it." Val ran her scanner over Laina's hand again. The doctor's screens lit up with a magnified copy of the symbol, spinning slowly on the displays.

For a long moment, neither of them spoke.

"What happened on that ship, Ronan? She's off our ship for two hours and not only does she survive an attack by a graywalker, but now this shows up on her. I can't help but wonder if the events are linked."

Ronan was at a loss for words. "I said from the beginning that she was trouble. I just wish I had been wrong."

He stayed with Laina as Valeria examined her. He had to admit, at least to himself, that it was out of more than a sense of duty and responsibility. She *mattered* to him. The human female had wormed her way under his skin, and he couldn't shake her. What was more, he didn't want to try.

Valeria probed for another sample from her hand where the anomaly was and returned to her desk to run tests. Ronan sat on the exam table beside Laina. He ran his fingertips along her cheekbones, traced the delicate brows that winged up over her eyes, and followed the thick eyelashes that fanned out on her cheeks.

She was beautiful. He'd never thought he would admit a human freeborn could be *beautiful* before. They were so asymmetrical when examined in detail, covered with tiny flaws that could be easily corrected but never were. Yet here she was, beautiful nonetheless. With her soft curves and the way she smiled at him, the memory of that moment when he'd made her smile just by being open with her about himself...it had been good. It had been real.

He smiled a little now. *If the others find out I have feelings for a freeborn, they will laugh and call me a fool. So be it.* He caressed her arm. There was something hypnotic about touching her like this, feeling her body pulse with life.

But how was she alive at all? Laina had survived a graywalker attack. No one survived graywalkers, not unless they arrived prepared. Even the *Orion* wasn't currently equipped to deal with them, relying on their advanced sensors to avoid their energy webs on the rare occasions they were encountered. Specialists could then be notified to deal with the threat.

If a graywalker had entered Laina's body, it should have destroyed her. Yet all signs pointed to one having died where they'd found her, breathing and alive, albeit exhausted. What had happened?

"Excuse me, Ronan..." Valeria's voice was shaky, quite out of character for the calm and rational physician.

He reluctantly slid off the exam table. "Yes?"

"Could you come here, please? I'd like you to see this." Valeria was hunched over her desk, staring at several of her screens. Ronan came over. Each screen had information flashing by at rapid speed. Technical and biological readouts.

"I was right. The anomaly is some kind of data storage device. Self-replicating and repairing. The initial sample was dormant, inconclusive, but what I took right now? Just taking a small sample, it began to replicate itself until it recognized it was no longer in a host. But there is enough there for our systems to interface with. There are definitely Elysian biogenetic traits involved here, but also Hopat nanotechnology."

"Hopat?" The squat species were well known for being clever inventors, but they also tended to avoid biological technology. If the doctor was right, it was an unusual collaboration.

"Knowing that has helped me decipher fragments of its code." Valeria paused one of the screens and stared.

"What have you found?"

Valeria collapsed back into her chair and pointed at the frozen screen of data. "These are genetic sequences, but they are not human."

"Synth? Cyborg?"

Valeria shook her head. "For all our bluster of perfection, we are still essentially human ourselves. No, these are of completely different animals. And not just one creature. I have found genome traces for thousands, perhaps *millions* of other species. The commander was right...and...well..." Valeria started to laugh, almost delirious.

"Well what?"

"Given the technology the Protectorate has access to, we could theoretically re-create any species from Earth. *Every* species. Not just those that had been taken off planet before the disaster. I'm talking about *every* species, Ronan. Every plant, animal, and piece of lichen."

"So she does have the Ark."

Valeria laughed again. This time tears glimmered in her eyes. "She's more than that. She's a blueprint for Earth. The information stored in her hand could re-create our entire planet. All we would need is a planet with compatible air, water, and soil. The only reason I could decipher all this was because the data files were originally from old Earth. There is more there, Ronan. So much more. I haven't even scratched the surface of what's inside."

The room suddenly felt very small, and Ronan felt as though he couldn't breathe. Earth. A home he had never been welcomed on. It could be re-created on their terms and become the homeworld they'd always been denied.

"Sit down before you fall down." Val pressed a hand on his shoulder, and Ronan fell into a chair next to Valeria's desk.

"My God," he groaned. He didn't care that he'd used the name of a deity he'd never believed in. Some things couldn't be overridden by logic. "We have to tell the commander."

"Absolutely." Valeria hailed the bridge.

"Yes?"

"Commander, we need you down in sickbay," Ronan cut in before the doctor could speak. He was finally able to breathe again and found himself on the verge of laughing as well.

"What's the matter?"

"We'll explain when you arrive."

There was a curious pause and then, "On my way."

Valeria smiled and said, "This calls for something special."

She went over to a secured wall safe next to one of the display monitors and pressed her hand against it. It hissed open, and the doctor retrieved a bottle.

"What is that?" asked Ronan.

"Earth wine."

"Earth?"

"It was salvaged a hundred years ago from a derelict ship found in Sol. Been in vacuum for centuries. I had set it aside for a truly special occasion, and I can think of nothing more special than this."

She retrieved a few glasses and set them on the table, then poured the wine into two of them. The news Valeria was about to give their commander was going to change the lives of every Terran alive.

Ronan and Valeria were laughing, glasses half-empty, when Alaric arrived. "What's going on?" He'd clearly expected the worst. His eyes turned to where Laina lay fast asleep on the exam table, then to Ronan and Valeria enjoying their wine. He relaxed, but was no less puzzled.

"Come, drink to a miracle, Commander." Valeria regained her sense of decorum, but she couldn't stop smiling. She filled a third glass and handed it to Alaric.

The commander took the glass and saw the bottle. "The Mouton Rothschild? The news is that good?"

"It is." Ronan pointed at Laina. "You were right. She has the Ark. And that name is more accurate than you ever guessed."

"How so?"

Valeria explained, and Alaric's face went slack. "But… that's not what we expected. The diary only talked about collecting information…"

"What is the genome of a species if not information?" the doctor countered.

The commander took a sip, intending to savor it, but then couldn't resist draining the glass. "How are we only learning of this now?"

Valeria shrugged. "I'm not sure. Nothing appeared in my initial scan of the anomaly. It was dormant. Inert. If I had to guess, I'd say it's tied to whatever happened with the gray-walker. That encounter triggered something." She showed Alaric images of the mysterious tattoo on Laina's hand. "This appeared as a result of that encounter. I'm guessing it's a byproduct of the sudden activation of the implant."

Alaric traced a finger over the pattern. "It looks Nubran in design."

The doctor nodded. "But there is Elysian biotech and Hopat nanotech as well. Which ties in with what you learned about Roberts."

"And what of the cure for our people?"

For the first time since her discovery, the doctor seemed deflated. "There I am afraid I haven't learned anything yet. But the device is far more complex than I ever would have expected, and it's clearly used for more than just data storage. The answer is in there, I'm certain."

Alaric smiled. The expression startled Ronan. When was the last time he'd seen his commander smile like that?

"Good work, Valeria. Find those answers. Ronan, I understand our Charon guest is contesting ownership of the human? You have my permission to challenge him, on board the *Orion* if need be. If you do, I expect you to win. Let's get the question of ownership out of the way before it becomes a problem. This woman is the answer to *everything* we have been searching for." A wealth of emotions filled the commander's eyes as he looked at Laina. "Protect her with your life."

"Yes, Commander." There had never been any question of that. Ronan would do whatever was necessary to keep her safe. Not because she represented hope for his people or a restored Earth, but because something about her called out to him. This simple woman had shown herself to be more perfect in her own way than any cyborg. Despite losing everything, she had never surrendered to grief. The same could not be said of some of his crewmates, like Hawking or Erik.

He desired her. There was no denying it. And those feelings, he hoped, were at least somewhat mutual. He'd seen how she looked at him, how her eyes lit up when she wasn't aware he was watching her. She had no idea how openly she showed her feelings. And she certainly had no idea how much it was affecting him. He would bide his time and prove to her that she could trust him.

And then? The same question as before cropped up in his mind. He supposed they would have to wait and see. These were uncharted waters he was traveling in, on a number of levels. But he was determined to see where they led.

"Why don't you take her back to your quarters, Ronan?" said Alaric. "Leave the doctor to her tests."

"Yes, Commander."

"And remember, she is our future. From this moment on, she is to be treated like a guest, not a prisoner."

Ronan approached the bed and brushed Laina's hair back from her face. "Can she be moved?"

"She can," Valeria said, still wary. "Ronan. Don't abuse her trust. It's a precious thing when given and a terrible thing once lost."

Ronan raised an eyebrow. "You sound as though you speak from experience."

Valeria smiled, looking toward Laina. But there was sorrow in her eyes. "I do." She drained the rest of her wine glass but didn't refill it.

Ronan had known Valeria a long time, but this was the first she'd ever spoken of such a thing. The commander laid a sympathetic hand on her shoulder. "I know you do not like to speak of him," he said.

"It's all right, Alaric. He's long gone, burned to ash with the rest of Earth. Even if he hadn't, he'd be long dead by now. We move on, as we always have."

Commander Corvus nodded his understanding. "As we always have. I must return to the bridge. Keep me apprised of any developments." He left Ronan and Valeria alone, a growing silence there between them.

"This man you speak of," Ronan began. "Was he...?"

"Freeborn?" Valeria nodded. "Yes. Does that surprise you?"

"It does."

Dr. Schedar's expression turned sour. "Not everyone wanted to keep us in chains back then, you know. We conveniently left those details out of our history books, but we were there, Ronan. We don't have the luxury of lying to ourselves."

Ronan couldn't look her in the eye. She wasn't wrong. In rebuilding Terran culture, history had to be...simplified in some areas. It was still the truth, but even he had to admit it sometimes lacked nuance.

"What happened?" he asked.

"I tried to save him before the standoff. He was supposed to meet me near Europa with the Exodus fleet, but he never arrived."

Ronan had never expected to see his friend like this. It was true Valeria had always been sympathetic toward the freeborn, but Ronan had no idea she had loved one once.

"I'm sorry, Valeria."

"Don't be." She sighed and looked over at Laina on the table. "But I think I betrayed his memory by joining the Legion."

Ronan was confused. "You serve us with distinction and honor."

"And turned a blind eye to what we're becoming. What we've *become*. Ronan, think about it. One of your men tried to kill her, and two others tried to sell her off. When you first brought her here, you acted as if she was going to somehow destroy the ship. You treated her terribly."

"I..." Whatever defiance Ronan planned to make died. "I did."

Valeria looked at him through her wine glass, which distorted her features slightly. "Don't you see? We've become what we abhorred, and we've done it for so long we no longer even question it. Let's say we're right about her. Let's say she holds the key to our salvation. Do we even deserve it? We should be on our knees *begging* for forgiveness. But our pride will never allow for that. We're hell-bent on keeping the freeborn in their place."

"What place would you have them take?" asked Ronan.

There was a hint of anger in the doctor's eyes. "Don't be coy, Ronan. You know damn well that's the wrong question. You keep acting like this is a zero-sum game, that it's us or them. Thinking like that is a path to extinction."

Ronan frowned. Maybe it was. "How do we get off this path?"

"I don't know. But I know the first step," said Valeria. "We take a lesson from a long-dead human. Risk everything to try to make things right. We can't forget the past, but we shouldn't let the past stop the future from happening."

Ronan nodded, though somewhat reluctantly. There was wisdom there, but it would take time to appreciate it. He raised his glass. "In honor of your lost love's memory. Perhaps you have not betrayed it after all."

"Thank you." The doctor waved her hand. "Laina can be moved whenever you're ready. Just make sure she eats when she wakes."

Ronan got up and carefully carried Laina out of the medical bay. He passed a number of crewmen, who eyed them with curiosity but said nothing. After several such stares, part of him felt like growling at them. They were not some exhibit on display for their amusement.

He reached his quarters and set Laina on the bed. She stirred as the bed matched her form and hastily covered her with a blanket.

He still couldn't believe this frail creature was the answer to his people's survival. He had seen too much chaos in the universe to believe in fate, but it was hard to ignore the significance of this. One small, fragile human female was going to save his race.

Somehow.

Then again, she clearly wasn't all that fragile. She'd killed a graywalker. That part he still could not believe, but the proof was undeniable. Ronan leaned over and lifted Laina's hand. Her strange mark around the anomaly still glowed.

Ronan couldn't help but wonder. She was more powerful than he'd have ever guessed, but he'd also been a fool to think of her as his enemy. She was the farthest thing from it.

He tucked her in and then stripped out of his clothes and entered the cleansing unit. He had some time off before he had to go back on duty, and this put him in a good mood. A *very* good mood. Because he knew just how he wanted to spend it with her. By showing her that she had nothing to fear from his people. In fact, she had much to gain.

CHAPTER 12

Ark Chronicle Entry 138-59

The Terran Cultural Reconstruction was proposed in the early days of the Terran Colony Fleet. The synthetics wished to both break with the culture of those who had kept them enslaved for so long, and embrace the heritage they now saw as their birthright.

Experts combed through Earth's history, looking for elements of Earth's past that could both spark the imagination and enforce a sense of unity and loyalty. They found it in the legions of Rome and the philosophers of Greece, in the samurai of Japan and scholars of China, in the noble knights and enlightened academics of Europe.

The result was the fabrication of a culture that drew upon the best qualities they could find on every continent, creating something that Terrans (synthetic ones, at any rate) could be proud of. Within a generation it was fully ingrained into the Colony Fleet. Synths today grow up believing this vision of humanity has always existed, and they see themselves as carrying on a proud and noble tradition, picking up *the torch after their freeborn predecessors stumbled and fell from grace.*

As for the cyborgs, well, certainly they must remember what life was like before the cultural shift, but it's clear that many have embraced this new culture to their very core. These individuals tend to speak more formally and old-fashioned than others, as if envisioning themselves as part of a new generation of knights. Those who are more ambivalent or relaxed about the Terran cause tend to talk more naturally, though this can shift back and forth as the situation requires.

LAINA WAS IN THE MIDST OF A DELIGHTFUL DREAM, one with sliding shadows, full of whispers and sighs, where the light of distant stars barely penetrated the window of her cabin. Above her a masculine body pressed her down into a soft bed. When was the last time she'd been able to enjoy a moment like this?

Too long. She tried not to think about it and just went where her libido led her. It even seemed to have a sound-track, or part of one at any rate, a simple old-fashioned tune with words strung together seemingly at random, the way they often do in dreams. She thought of twin moons, Orion's Belt, Jupiter, Saturn, and every so often the refrain that would repeat in her head...

Come find me, across the stars.

She ran her hands along corded steel made flesh and nibbled playfully on the man's solid biceps until he growled in encouragement. There was no shame, no fear, no pres-sure, only gentle exploration and a building fire between their bodies that couldn't be denied.

The soft hiss of a door opening shattered the dream, and she opened her eyes, wondering for a brief moment where she was. She tensed as her eyes caught sight of a figure leaving the bathroom. No, wait...*cleansing unit.*

"Whoa..."

Ronan wore only a thin towel slung low over his lean hips. His sculpted abdomen and the valleys and peaks of his muscles on his chest and back were...how could she even describe it? It was like one of her most erotic teenage fantasies had pulled itself out of her memories and walked into the room. It was that perfect, and that unreal.

There was an animal magnetism there that she couldn't deny. She gazed upon his almost bare body and was lost in momentary fantasies of licking off any drops of water the cleansing unit might have failed to dry. Maybe it was the grogginess that came with waking up from a dream with a part of her still thinking it was real, but she found herself wanting him to pose for her.

Drop it, baby... She urged the towel to lose its precarious grip around his hips, but it didn't. She giggled, imagining it snagging on a chair and getting yanked off.

He glanced over his shoulder, and to her surprise he smiled. The expression, so unexpected on such a usually stern face, made a drastic change in him. He was as handsome as ever, but no longer an unfeeling statue. It did more than just humanize him to her—it made him sexy as all hell. She could have gotten off on just that smile, it was that warm and real. It made her belly twist into knots, and she realized her thighs had clenched together.

"Have you rested enough?" His tone was casual—well, casual for him—unaware that she was indulging in fantasies of him playing the bad boy and taking her, *"For the good of the Legion."*

Jesus Christ. There's has to be something wrong with me. She had wanted to have her captor form feelings for her, hoping it would help her find a means of escape, or at least get her better treatment. But now she was suddenly hot for him. She had to put a stop to it before she did something she'd regret.

Her mind could tell her body that all day, but her body wasn't listening. Some things were just too hard to fight, things like good old-fashioned chemistry. And right now she couldn't imagine regretting *anything* she did with that body.

"Laina?" She barely heard Ronan speak her name. She was lost staring at the fine trail of hair that began just below his navel and disappeared beneath his towel.

She raised her eyes to his face and noticed how his damp hair was now a dark burnished gold. "Hmmm?"

He abandoned his search for clothes and walked over to her. She scooted back on the bed as he approached, an intensity growing in his eyes.

"You should stop looking at me like that," he warned. His warm breath fanned her face. Their lips were mere inches apart. Did he realize what he was doing to her?

"L-like what?"

"Like you wish me to bend you over the bed and take you until you can no longer walk." His words created a wild kaleidoscope of fractured images that infused her with heat that was increasingly difficult to control.

"You wouldn't...I mean, should you be talking to me like that?"

"Should you be *looking* at me like that?" Ronan countered. "Perhaps I should be the one offended. But I'm not. I'm glad, in fact."

"Glad?"

"That you feel comfortable enough to imagine such a union. I doubt the same could have been said when we first met."

"Yes, well..." She didn't want to admit that even then she'd found him impossibly attractive, but it was true, she did feel more comfortable around him now.

"So, are you simply engaging in idle fantasy, or do you wish to experience more?"

"More?"

Before she could react, he had taken her by the shoulders and leaned over her until their faces were a hairsbreadth apart.

His lips almost brushed hers as he spoke. "I find myself less reluctant to touch you. You are not the only one who has been engaging in idle fantasies."

Ronan had imagined being with her? She shivered against him in anticipation. That hunger she'd tried so hard to deny burned deeper within her.

"I will be honest, what keeps me at bay is your fear," Ronan continued. "I do not wish for you to be afraid of me, though I know that is all but impossible under the circumstances."

"I'm not afraid," Laina said hesitantly. "Not exactly." She was afraid of how much she wanted him and how dangerous that was.

"You are. It is understandable. But you should know your status on this ship has changed. You are no longer to be treated as a freeborn."

"How can I believe you?"

This gave Ronan pause, and he looked down at her arms. The silver slaver cuffs were still there. He stepped back and tapped a control on his wrist computer. The cuffs beeped and unlocked. Laina couldn't believe it. She removed the cuffs and set them aside.

"You will still need to be escorted within the ship," Ronan said. "But that is for your protection. As the doctor informed you, you are more important to us than you realize."

Laina smiled, in part because of the noble earnestness Ronan said this with. He seemed like a man out of time, born into the wrong century. But she also smiled because of the information he'd given her.

If she was so damn important, then that meant she had leverage. What she needed to figure out now was how she could use it.

Ronan sat down next to her, picking up the slaver cuffs and tossing them away. "Now do you believe me when I say you do not need to be afraid?"

"It's a start, I suppose."

Ronan smiled. "Everything must start somewhere." He then took a hand and lightly cupped her cheek. "Now, be truthful. There will be no judgment here. Were you imagining being intimate with me a moment ago?"

Laina's first instinct was to lie, but the way he looked at her, the way he touched her, and the fact that it seemed she had her freedom back made her admit the truth. "Yes."

"Good. Then I am not alone in my feelings."

"But imagining is not the same as an invitation," she added quickly.

Ronan nodded. "Of course. But may I ask you a question?"

"Um...okay."

"Do you treat intimacy as casual, or sacred? Recreational, or purposeful?"

"What?" Laina wasn't sure what he meant by all that.

"It's important that I do not overstep my bounds. But different people treat intercourse in different ways. For some on this ship, it is little more than stress relief, separated from any feelings of attachment. But different cultures hold to different beliefs. I would like to know yours."

Laina floundered for the right words. "Well, I wouldn't want to say too casual, but, you know, it's not like we have to get married or want to have a baby or...you know."

Ronan smiled and moved close to her again, almost kissing her. "Yes, I believe I do. Then I should make my feelings and desires clear. It would feel so good to slide into your tight little body, make you scream my name."

He brushed his nose lightly across her cheek, and Laina whimpered at the ripple of pleasure it gave her. She wanted him to do more, so much more. And now that she didn't fear him, her desire was building into an unstoppable force. But this was still too fast, wasn't it?

"Ronan, please..." Their noses brushed, and he was smiling again. With a slow, deliberate move, he lowered his head that remaining inch so their lips touched.

It was like being cast into the center of a star. Fire and light, explosive heat and exquisite agony. She reached up to clutch at his shoulders, and then she slid a hand into his hair, tugging his head forward. He growled against her mouth, and the weight of his body settled over hers. It felt good, so damn good. She raked her nails up his bare stomach, then along his back, as she bit his bottom lip, tugging it into her mouth. His hands slid down her body, shaping her ass and thighs, stroking her in little tickling patterns on sensitive skin that burned in the best possible way.

She never knew kissing could be like this, a heated intensity that built and burst like a storm cloud. Each touch of their hands, each little sigh and encouraging murmur lit her up inside like a newborn sun flaring brightly in a dark sky. When he finally lifted his head, they stared down at each other in a heavy silence, broken only by their heavy breathing. Something had definitely changed between them. They weren't enemies anymore.

But then, what are we?

"You aren't ready for me yet," Ronan said. "When you are, you need only say the word and I'll take you, little human, to such heights of pleasure as you've never known."

And then he slowly stood.

Wait...what?! All this and now he was putting the brakes on...wherever this was going? *God dammit.* Heat pooled between her thighs, and to her embarrassment, she was far too turned on to stay in the same room with him. Her senses were coming back to her, and despite the frustration her body was feeling, she was actually glad that Ronan had put a stop to it. She had to figure out what he wanted from her. Was she a pet to him now? To be cared for and enjoyed, but still owned? Because she wouldn't allow herself to be treated like that, no matter how much pleasure he offered.

"I... I think I need a shower." She rushed to the cleansing unit and shut the door behind her.

She stripped out of her clothes and ducked into the shower. The hot water was a blessed relief. It'd been ages since she had a real water shower. Most of the ships she'd been on the last few years, including the *Beautiful Star Chaser*, had used sonic cleansers. Water could be a precious commodity out in space, especially on long journeys.

She ducked her head beneath the hot spray, letting the water cover every inch of her before she added the liquid cleanser. It gave her time to think.

The *Orion* was a top-of-the-line ship, much like its crew. Perfect specimens, designed to serve the flawed species that had created them, and who ultimately overthrew and enslaved them. That was the story she'd always been told, ever since she was a child. But her fear of the cyborgs had been slowly replaced by curiosity as she'd gotten to know them. There was more to their history with humans than she'd been told about. But where did one even begin to ask the right questions?

When she emerged from the shower, she realized that in her haste to get away from Ronan and distract herself, she'd forgotten to bring a towel. What was more, Ronan must have come in, because her clothes were gone. She cautiously peeked out from the cleansing unit door.

Ronan was lying on the bed, arms folded behind his head. He was still bare-chested, though he'd put on his uniform pants. He was still barefoot and completely at ease as he watched her reach for the towel he'd placed on the floor outside the cleansing unit, just out of her reach. That is, out of her reach if she was going to keep the rest of herself from being exposed to him. She tried reaching for it with her foot instead, but that was just as futile. A blush worked through her from head to toe. She covered herself as best she could with her hands and stepped out, picking up the towel and wrapping it around her body.

"Human modesty never ceases to confuse me."

"You mean amuse you," she countered. "Do you have my clothes?"

Ronan's eyes swept over her body, all too aware of what was beneath her towel. Then he nodded toward his closet.

"Alanna brought over some items she thought would fit you better. Your father's jacket is in there as well."

Laina rushed to the closet, sliding open the door to find a smaller version of a Legion uniform, but with the color patterns reversed, along with some undergarments. Nothing fancy, but that was fine. She'd been living off old worn clothing for years. She collected the clothes and returned to the cleansing unit to change. When she was done, she came back to retrieve her father's coat. She was about to sit on a chair when Ronan sat up and patted the empty space on the bed beside him.

"Come. I won't bite." His wolfish smile made her hesitate long enough that he laughed. "Laina, please, sit. You're still too tired, and you need to eat more." He was serious now. "The doctor insists. And while you eat, we shall talk."

"Okay." She slid on her jacket; the old brown leather still smelled of her father.

Neither of them spoke for a few moments. She was actually relieved when the door chimed. Valeria entered with a tray of food and smiled. "Good evening all," she said cheerily.

Ronan looked puzzled. "What are *you* doing here?"

"I wanted to check up on my patient. So, how are you feeling? Getting your strength back?"

Ronan sat up and stared hard at Valeria. Laina was pretty sure he had expected someone to deliver the meal quickly and then leave.

"Yes, I think so." Laina stared eagerly at the food tray as the doctor handed it to her. She then pulled out a small scanner from her belt and checked her vitals.

"Eat up. You need your strength," Valeria encouraged. "Your encounter with the graywalker drained you more than you know."

"Thanks, Val." Laina grinned at the woman as she ran her tests. When she finished, Valeria smirked at Ronan and left the two alone to eat. Ronan turned on his room's display and reviewed some reports from the rest of the ship while she ate. Once she was done, Laina focused again on Ronan. He shut off his screen and rejoined her on his bed. He brushed his fingertips along her jaw, stroking her, and she shivered with longing.

I admit it, I want him. Is that so bad? He's not such a bad guy—he may actually be a good guy. This doesn't have to be serious. It could be casual. Recreational. Stress relief. Right?

"Would you kiss me?" she asked, her heart racing. She wanted him to kiss her, wanted to feel the press of his warm, hard body against her. There was a primal instinct buried deep inside her that craved the comfort of his body.

"I might not stop at just a kiss," he warned, a teasing light in his eyes.

She bit her lip to hide a smile. "I might not care."

He leaned in that last inch, and his lips captured hers.

Everything about him always seemed so hard. His body, his words, his stoic sense of duty, but his lips? They were heavenly soft, like the petals of a flower. She remembered those that had grown wild on Allasant when she was a child. They had been a large, flowery species with red petals streaked with splashes of gold. She'd marveled at the feeling of those petals and hearing her mother tell her how Earth had once been filled with flowers like this, growing wild and in gardens, of a hundred different colors and a thousand different shapes. After Allasant, she'd only ever seen such flowers for sale in gift shops at spaceports and transit hubs.

Ronan's fingertips left her chin, and he curled his hand around the back of her neck, holding her captive for his exploring mouth. She shivered in delight at the erotic play of his tongue against hers. She'd been with one man before, just one. Space was a lonely place, after all, especially when you were always running or hiding. She and another free-born, a man named Johnny, had been together for a two-week ride aboard a dilapidated commercial cruiser. Their desperate, hungry fumblings in the dark had been nothing like this.

One lingering kiss with Ronan was far more arousing

than anything she'd done with Johnny, or even her own imagination. Ronan tasted sweet, and the way he took his time, exploring her was wonderful. There was no rush, no panic, but a sense of endless time to enjoy one kiss.

When their lips parted, Ronan watched her through half-lidded eyes, his soft smile making her body tingle in all her secret places.

"You taste sweet," he said matter-of-factly.

Laina laughed softly.

"What?"

"I was thinking *you* tasted sweet too." She bit her bottom lip, and he growled softly, but the sound wasn't threatening. If anything, it was arousing.

"You—" Ronan began but then shook his head. The comm trilled.

"Sub-Commander Antares, report to the bridge."

Ronan groaned. "Even when I am off duty, I'm afraid I'm always on call," he said. "Get some rest. I promise not to be long." He wavered slightly as he stood, then walked to his closet to retrieve the rest of his uniform.

He took a bite of bread from her plate and then licked his fingers, drawing her eyes to his mouth. "If you need me, you can summon me using the comm like before. I've allowed Alanna access in case you need anything. She's the only one I trust you alone with."

She frowned at him. "Why? I thought you said things were different now."

"Some of the crew will need time to come to terms with you being aboard and that things have changed." He seemed to be holding something back, but she didn't want to push him for answers. She wondered what he meant about things having changed. "What about Valeria?"

He chuckled. "I trust her, of course. But I'm afraid she's too busy to be at your beck and call."

"So I can't go for a walk? I'm supposedly important to you now, but I'm still basically a prisoner."

"No, you're no longer a prisoner. But you must be protected at all times. Keeping you here is the safest thing for you right now," Ronan said.

"That hardly seems fair."

"This is not about fairness. You have been given orders. Even if you had the full freedom of this ship as a member of her crew, I would expect you to follow them. Now, please, eat. I will return soon."

Before Laina could work up a proper protest, he left, and the doors shut behind him. She was stuck. Again. Alone. But at least this time she had a full belly and she wasn't afraid. A bit angry and sexually frustrated, perhaps, but not afraid.

That kiss had told her everything she needed to know. If he'd wanted to take advantage of her, to force himself upon her, he could have easily done so. But he hadn't.

She lay back on the bed, bored once again. She considered trying to turn on the monitor, perhaps find more videos from Earth, but she wasn't sure how to work it. She wanted to explore the ship, see all the stations, maybe do something useful. This ship was a quarter of a kilometer long. Being stuck on board with nothing to do was awful.

An idea struck, and she sat up. There *was* one person she could trust to help her, assuming she could talk that person into it.

CHAPTER 13

ARK CHRONICLE ENTRY 138-164

From the start there has been controversy over the cyborgs. The nanotechnology involved in their creation left some concerned that their very existence was a violation of Protectorate laws, which had been in place for well over a thousand years, ever since the tragic conclusion of the SRAI War.

In fact, there has been some debate as to how the Terrans even developed such advanced nanotech on their own. The techniques used in earlier generations of synths and those approved for human use were primitive by comparison. But all the markers were there that this was of Terran design.

In the end, however, the problem was seen as self-correcting. Since the cyborgs could not reproduce, they could never expand their influence beyond a certain range. Despite not aging, in time attrition would reduce their numbers to zero, leaving only the synths and freeborn behind.

Laina hadn't used the *Orion*'s communications system before, and she wondered just how intuitive it was. Most ships required activating a comm panel, while with others you could address the computer directly if you wanted.

"Alanna?" Laina spoke the name clearly. There was a trill in the air. A moment later there was a second trill as she was connected.

A woman's voice came back over a hidden speaker. "Yes?"

"Um...this is Laina."

"I am aware of that. How can I help?"

"I have some questions. Can we talk?"

There was a pause. "What sort of questions?"

Laina hesitated. "Um...personal ones. Can you come to Ronan's room?"

"I have duties to attend to. Can it wait?"

"I just need someone to talk to. When will you be free?"

There was a long pause, long enough that Laina worried the woman had disconnected. She then heard a reluctant sigh.

"Very well. I'll come down." The connection went dead with a tiny beep. A few minutes later the door opened and Alanna came in.

"What are your questions?"

"Wow, okay," she laughed softly. "No beating around the bush with you, huh?"

"I apologize. It is not your fault. But I am a senior officer aboard a Silver Legion heavy cruiser. My time should be valued, yet once again I find myself playing nursemaid."

Laina sensed something in her tone. "You don't feel valued?"

"It is not your concern."

"I'd like it to be. At the end of the day, we're both women. And that's the problem, isn't it?" Laina had sensed this from almost the moment she'd been brought on board. Her treatment had been different, not because she was a civilian or unarmed or obviously non-hostile, but because she was female.

"My comrades' values have...*shifted* over the decades. There are times I must remind them that we are equals. Forcefully, if need be."

"But you're one of them. You're a cyborg, right?"

"Yes, but I fear that does not matter as much as it once did."

Laina still didn't understand. "Why would they treat you different?"

Alanna snorted. "*Chivalry*, they call it. When we became our own people, we needed to create an identity of our own as well. Virtues such as honor and valor featured high into this, as did the values of certain eras, including medieval Europe and feudal Japan."

Laina was somewhat familiar with these times. Her parents had taught her what they could about the history of her homeworld. "So they picked up some good old-fashioned sexism along with the valor and honor?"

Alanna bowed her head. "As you say. Some feel females of any species need to be 'protected.' And it does not help matters that only a quarter of all cyborg are female." She took a seat at a nearby chair. "So the women on this ship must remind them now and again that we require no such consideration."

Laina knew that this attitude was not limited to the cyborgs. Several species in this part of the galaxy shared it, such as the Charon she'd recently met. And the Draxon who controlled the Perseus Arm were notoriously male-centric. But then, their species were often compared to a hive-like collective, with male drones doing most of the work, breeding males providing leadership, and women relegated to reproduction or caregiving. At least, that's how she understood it.

"It's the same for the freeborn," said Laina. "My family tended to be overly protective of their women. But in our case, I think it was because they were tied with our ongoing survival."

"I blame your ancestors, to be honest," said Alanna. "The Y-chromosome is clearly an evolutionary dead end. If cyborgs were designed to be incapable of reproduction, the logical thing to do would be to make them all female. The fact most cyborgs are men says much about our creators."

Laina chuckled dryly. "Well, my dad was different. He taught me how to survive and be an independent woman."

"Did you have to fight much?" Alanna asked.

"What? No. I had a happy childhood. As much as one can on the run, anyway." She paused, watching the other woman. "I didn't know what to say to you that first time you asked me about my childhood."

Alanna's curiosity intensified. "You wish to talk about it now?"

"Well, yeah, if you want to. I mean..." She waited, wondering if Alanna would take the bait. They needed to bond, and if she eased into the discussion she *wanted* to have by starting a different one, it just might work.

Sitting on her chair, Alanna tilted her head. "Please, tell me."

"Okay," Laina said. "What exactly do you want to know?"

"What is it like to be small?" The cyborg lowered her hand to her knees.

"You mean like a tiny kid, like a toddler?"

"Yes." The cyborg was now fully focused on her. It felt a little weird, but not unwelcome.

"Um. I don't remember much about being that small. That's the thing about growing up. You don't remember most of the stuff that happens when you're little, but you remember the good stuff." And the bad...but she didn't want to talk about that.

"Good stuff?"

"Yeah, like birthday parties and kisses good night and bedtime stories..."

"You celebrate birthdays? How do you do this?"

Laina chuckled. "There's usually a cake, presents, and singing. There's a song dedicated to celebrating a birthday."

"Yes, I've seen recordings of what you describe." Alanna leaned a little closer. "And what about kisses good night and bedtime stories?"

Laina's heart began to break for the other woman. What had it been like to live a life without bedtime stories and birthday parties?

"Well, when you go to sleep—as a kid, I mean—your parents tuck you in. They pull the sheets up to your chin, and they kiss you good night. It's really nice." She remembered all too well how often her own parents had done that.

"They tuck you in and kiss you?" Alanna frowned. "And what does this accomplish?"

"It makes you feel safe. Loved. I don't know how else to explain it. And bedtime stories were the best."

"Yes, what are these bedtime stories? I often read political news before going to bed. I do enjoy that."

"So, bedtime stories are different. They're fun stories

with adventure, sometimes romance, like fairy tales or...I don't know. Stories that make you laugh or smile or cry. Stories that move you." She reached for her pack by the bed and dug out her digital book and handed it to Alanna.

"I have one of these, only a much more advanced model."

"But I'm willing to bet you don't have the books I do." Laina grinned. "Not if your bedtime reading material is pretty much only political news. Trust me, read one of these and you will see what I mean about bedtime stories. But picture someone else reading them to you when you're a kid. Someone you trust completely, who is there to make your life better every single day. My dad would even make different voices for the various characters in each story. Sometimes it felt like I was living the story, not just hearing it."

"Thank you. I think I will try this." Alanna set the device inside her work jacket, tucking it into a protective flap. "I appreciate you sharing this with me."

"Of course. We're friends, aren't we?"

"Friends?" Alanna tested the word. "Not yet, but perhaps someday. I find I like you better than the other free-borns I've met."

Laina smiled, taking the small victory. "Thanks...I think. At least you're honest." *Friends someday.* She could live with that.

"Now," Alanna prompted, brow raised. "What was the question you originally wished for me to answer?"

Now Laina felt a bit embarrassed. "It's not important."

Alanna frowned. "It should be if you called me from my duty."

"I'm sorry. It's just... I'm stuck in this room. Alone. And

I was hoping you could show me around. Not as a prisoner or a valued asset or whatever, but as a friend. Or companion. Whatever term you prefer."

Alanna's frown softened. "You called me down here for companionship?"

Laina gave a thin smile and echoed the officer's words from earlier. "As you say."

Alanna stood up from her chair, looking down upon Laina, a bit of that cyborg superiority still creeping through. Unexpectedly, she smiled and placed her hand on the door panel. The door whooshed open.

"Come."

Laina followed Alanna out into the hall. They passed by a couple of the crew she'd never met before, who tapped their fists to their chests in salute. Alanna returned the salute sharply.

"I noticed their uniforms were slightly different," said Laina. "Are they synths?"

"Yes," said Alanna, "but that has nothing to do with the uniform. They are crewmen. Their uniforms differ from those of the officers."

She got up on her toes to get a better look at the symbol on Alanna's epaulettes. It vaguely looked like an old radiation warning symbol, only in silver. "And your rank insignia is different. Just about everyone else I've seen has bars there. What is it?"

"It is the symbol of the Vigiles. It represents one of our colony stations."

Once she mentioned it, Laina could see the resemblance. The three fans radiating out from the center circle would be the light reflectors of a colony ship if viewed head-on.

"The Vigiles are in charge of security, both in the colony and off it," she explained. "I have a rank of lieutenant while serving aboard a Legion ship, however."

"And what rank were the ones we just passed? The ones with the bronze bars?"

"Crewmen, as I said."

"So synths are crewmen and cyborgs are officers, right?"

"Not always. Some cyborgs prefer to remain at lower ranks, though not many." Alanna smiled to herself at some private joke. "And at least one can't seem to avoid remaining there. As for the synths, a number have risen to the officer ranks. One of our heavy cruisers is commanded by a synth."

Laina knew this wasn't about discrimination—at least, not that she was aware of. From what her parents had told her, most synths were not as adaptable as the cyborgs, an unfortunate side effect of their design. They found it difficult to move beyond what they were initially trained for, and many suffered from mental breakdowns if they tried. Once a miner, always a miner, her father had said. So it was little wonder that crewmen tended to stay crewmen and rarely rose higher in the ranks.

Alanna first took her to the mess hall. Even though she'd already eaten, Laina found it hard not to help herself to another dessert. Luxury like this had been hard to come by for quite some time. The two sat at a table, and while she ate Laina watched the crew come in and out of the hall, interact, socialize, and leave again. Since she was wearing a uniform similar to the others, nobody had given her any strange looks. It all seemed so...normal.

As she observed them, she believed she found another way to distinguish between the synths and cyborgs she'd met so far. Then she realized that the entire time she'd been watching the crew, Alanna had been watching her.

"You're a very curious creature," she said. "Do you know that?"

"Human instinct," Laina said, finishing her dessert. "Or survival instinct. Take your pick. Find the exits and keep an eye on everyone who comes into a room."

"A wise precaution."

"Can I ask you something?"

"Of course."

"Do cyborgs all have the same skin color?" When Alanna gave her a puzzled look, she elaborated. "I could be wrong, but it seems like all the cyborgs on board have a sort of deep tan, but the synths have a much wider range. Light, dark, everything in between..."

Alanna nodded. "Synth templates were based on the best individuals Earth had to offer, but they were still individuals. We were designed from the genetic level up, and we incorporate elements from every ethnicity on Earth."

Now that she thought about it, even the cyborgs she'd seen on the news or entertainment programs were like that. Their hair and eyes often stood out, but the skin? Always the same. She didn't know whether to take that as a metaphor for unity or conformity.

"I have to admit," she said, changing the subject, "this is nothing like what I expected to see on board a Legion ship."

"What did you expect?"

What *had* she expected? Slaves manning the engines, being worked to death under the electric whips of their overlords? It seemed a bit silly now. And yet it didn't. Not when you took reality into account.

"You have to understand," Laina said. "I was raised to fear you. We're legally your property. Any free human is considered a runaway. There's a bounty out for our capture, and we have to rely on the sympathy of those who don't believe in slavery to stay one step ahead. We're always afraid."

Alanna suddenly looked uncomfortable. "It does not seem fair to me either, I admit. There was a time when I held your people responsible for a great many crimes. But they are all long dead."

"Yet you still hunt us."

"For many, it is no longer a matter of revenge, but law. Once the High Council made their ruling, it was no longer in our hands."

Laina looked down at her empty plate. "We're doomed, aren't we?"

Alanna straightened in her chair. "We're all doomed. Human, cyborg, and synth alike."

She hadn't expected that reply. "How are you doomed? You're practically immortal."

"Practically is not completely. We can still die, and there will never be another cyborg. We cannot breed. The synths must use machines to reproduce and still suffer in their own ways, and the humans..." She left their fate unspoken, yet it felt inevitable nonetheless.

"It shouldn't be like this," said Laina. "Not for any of us."

Alanna smiled. "On that, we agree completely. And perhaps there is hope, if the rumors about you are true. Come, let us continue the tour."

They left the mess hall and went next to the observation deck, located along the underbelly of the ship. The gravity was inverted here, requiring a special looped hall to access, allowing Laina and Alanna to look out among the stars as if they were on the top of the ship instead of the bottom. It was beautiful, especially while in transit. The stars that streaked outside were tinged with blue ahead of them and red behind, and for just a brief moment in between they were pinpoints of white. She gazed at the sight like it was a light show being given just for her.

"We have a better view here than on the bridge," said Alanna. "Though during combat this deck must be evacuated and depressurized. That is why the wall behind you is so thick." She tapped on the wall, which was so dense it made no noise itself, only Alanna's knuckles rapping on it was heard.

"Do you come here often?" Laina asked.

"I used to. Not so much now. It's a sad truism that one can get used to anything, even beauty." Something in her voice told Laina that she wasn't talking about stars.

They continued their tour, though Alanna would not give her access to anything of importance, such as the engine room or weapons stations. When they returned to Ronan's quarters, Laina sat on the bed and Alanna asked if she had seen enough.

"Yes, thank you. But you know, it was nice just talking with you."

Alanna's cheeks reddened a little. "Thank you. I agree. Your companionship was not the chore I feared it would be."

Laina laughed at that, and Alanna looked puzzled.

"Oh, sorry, I thought you were making a joke."

"I was being sincere."

"I know. I mean, the *way* you said it was... Never mind."

"I apologize," said Alanna. "It's been a very long time since I've tried to talk as casually as you do."

"That's all right. You're not quite as bad as Ronan." That got her thinking about other things. She shifted on the bed. "So...can I ask you something else? Not ship related?"

"Of course."

"Um...about cyborgs. The men, I mean. Do they... I mean, they are the same as humans, right? Same...equipment?" She gestured below her waist. She remembered her Nubran crewmates discussing the cyborgs' sexual prowess, but it had mostly been innuendo.

"Is this about intercourse?" Alanna asked bluntly.

Laina's face heated. "Yeah."

"We are essentially human, you understand."

"But you can't reproduce."

"Not through lack of trying, I assure you."

Laina blinked. Then blinked again. "Was...was that a joke?"

"Yes." Alanna smiled and gave her a wink. "But it is also true." She stepped away from the door and sat at one of the chairs, making herself comfortable. "I assume this question means you find one of the males on board desirable?"

Laina nodded.

Alanna eyed her with curiosity. "Ronan?"

"Yes."

"And you wish to know how to initiate a sexual relationship with him?"

"Yes, but I can't be sure if he wants me too. He did make some moves, but he's also sort of blowing hot and cold on me, and I can't—"

"Hot and cold?"

"It's an expression," Laina said with a chuckle. "Sometimes I think he likes me and wants me, and other times he acts like he's just toying with me."

"Ah." Alanna smiled. "And you want him to be all hot, yes?"

"Something like that," Laina replied, glad to finally be on the same page. "What turns a male cyborg on?" she asked.

"Much the same as any male, I assume," Alanna replied. Then Laina noticed a glint of mischief in the cyborg's eye. "Do you wish to take him?"

"What?" Laina didn't know where she was going with that.

"I mean, rather than *allow* him to have you, do you wish to *take* him?"

Their earlier conversation regarding sexism aboard the ship popped into her head. It did sound appealing. The thought of the precious females in need of protection getting the upper hand? What wasn't there to like about that? "But he's too strong. I mean, I'd *like* to, but..."

The female cyborg leaned forward conspiratorially. "We are women. We do not overcome our problems with brute force. We are better than that. Wait until he is asleep and then restrain him."

Laina chuckled at the joke, but she looked at the expression on Alanna's face. "You're being serious, aren't you?"

"Absolutely. A human like you overcoming the *Orion*'s first officer? I would find that most satisfying."

"But how?" She saw the slaver cuffs lying on the dresser, but those were programmed by the user. She'd never be able to get them on Ronan. Even if she did, she couldn't activate them. And what if she accidentally shocked him? Talk about a mood killer.

"There are emergency restraints on every bed that activate in case of an accident or sudden maneuvers that exceed the ship's inertial countermeasures. These can be manually activated. Lie down and I will demonstrate."

Laina hesitated, but she trusted Alanna now. She lay back on the bed and watched as Alanna pressed the pad of her thumb to a panel above her head. Suddenly the mattress seemed to grip her on all sides. It reminded her of how the sickbay bed had conformed to her shape, but taken to a disturbingly invasive level. It was similar to what had kept her from flying out of the Charon's bed when their ship had hit the graywalker's energy web.

"What the—?"

"See?" Alanna touched the fabric that held Laina prisoner. "Similar restraints help prevent the crew from being knocked out of their chairs. Hmmm..." She examined how Laina's head was being kept immobile, which felt anything but sexy. "Head movement is important. This does not seem properly erotic for your needs. I'll disable it." She tapped a few commands on the panel, and the section of the mattress holding her head in place relaxed its grip. "Much better."

At least Laina could raise her head now. Alanna tapped a few more buttons, saying, "I should disable the verbal override while I'm at it. It wouldn't do to have him free himself before you are finished."

She then mounted Laina, straddling her legs, moving her hips suggestively. "And then you simply have your way with him. Easy."

Laina felt a bit self-conscious with Alanna on top of her like that, especially because she was so clearly clueless about any impropriety involved. "Um...can I get out now?"

"Oh, of course." Alanna got off, then pressed the panel again and the mattress relaxed.

"Will it work with my thumb?" Laina asked.

"Yes. Safety settings have no restrictions."

Laina grinned and sat up. "Cool."

"Cool?" Alanna shook her head. "It's been a long time since I have heard that one." She touched Laina's shoulder. "If you desire him, and he desires you, then I wish you both happiness, while you can find it." Her lips fell, ever so slightly, and Laina guessed she knew the reason why.

"Even if he did like me...it can't last, can it?"

"What in the universe does?"

Alanna sat down on the bed beside her, her solemn silver eyes shadowed like the dark side of a distant moon.

"Ronan, Valeria, and I were raised together for a time. I had no real childhood, but they were...*are* the closest thing to a family I could possess. Yet so many among us focus on our future, as if we have one. They're so terrified of being forgotten that they want to ensure they make their mark on the galaxy. They have become obsessed with forging an identity, but for what? Another successful mission? Finding glory in battle? I look back on all I have done for my people and realize I've done nothing for myself. I only have my service." Her eyes began to well up, as if a lifetime of regrets weighed down upon her. "So what does it matter if it lasts or not, so long as it is real? Embrace the dream. If you are lucky, it might embrace you back."

Laina leaned over, hugging the other woman. Tight and intense, just as she'd learned from her mother. A hug was supposed to convey a hundred things that words could not, and right now Alanna deserved every bit of her support.

After a long second, Alanna patted Laina's arms and stood. "I wish I had known you before, as a child. I would have liked to experience that odd part of your life. I am told children see the universe as it could be. I have only ever seen it for what it is. Perhaps then my world wouldn't seem so dark now."

Laina got up off the bed. "After my parents died, the world was dark for me too. Running from planet to planet, ship to ship, no way out of Draxon space, no end in sight. And no offense, but you guys are scary as hell to me, what with the rumors, I mean."

Alanna blinked. "Rumors?"

"Yeah, the other species talk, you know. Not to mention the news broadcasts. The High Council gave you dominion over all humans—that kind of thing gets some people talking. Don't get me wrong, you have a lot of fans out there, but to people like me, you guys are the ultimate bogeyman." Laina was too afraid to say much more, in case she shattered the fragile friendship they had built.

"What's a bogeyman?" the other woman asked.

"Er..." Laina tried to figure out the best way to explain it. "A scary person that used to steal kids out of their beds at night or something. I'm not really familiar with the term. It's a story my dad used to tell me."

"Ah." Alanna's nose wrinkled as she cleared her throat. "Well, I have no intention of stealing children from their beds. My trophy room is already full." Laina's eyes widened before Alanna said, "Another joke." She got up from her chair. "I should go. But I would like to see you again."

Laina smiled. "I'd like that too."

She curled her arms around her chest and watched Alanna leave. Had she made a friend out of one of her enemies? A hopeful smile curved her lips.

Hope. That was an emotion she hadn't felt in some time, not since her parents' ship had been destroyed...

...by the cyborgs.

Her smile fell as that ugly truth resurfaced. She'd almost forgotten what they had done, what they continued to do, what her people had been reduced to.

What hope was there, really?

Maybe Alanna was right. Maybe they were all doomed. Human, synth, and cyborg alike.

She shook her head. She refused to believe that. If things were ever going to change, it required people who were willing to take that risk, take that first step forward, to embrace those they'd been raised to fear and say, "Things can be different."

Hope. There was nothing more beautiful than hope. Or more powerful.

CHAPTER 14

ARK CHRONICLE ENTRY 138-206

It is fair to say that the cyborgs could not have achieved their current status without the help of the Draxon. They have been their most vocal supporters within the High Council, especially when it came to their claim over Sol, and have given them as much support as they could in developing the Terran Colony Fleet and the Silver Legion.

For their part, the synthetics feel indebted to the Draxon for this support, and they are always ready to volunteer their assistance whenever aid is requested from one of their worlds.

Given the collective nature of the Draxon and their indifference toward slavery within their borders, one can only imagine how things might have turned out differently had Sol been located in Nubran or Elysian space instead. The fate of my people could have been so different.

ON THE BRIDGE, THE ORION WAS HAVING ITS OWN complications. A Draxon cargo vessel was giving off a distress signal, and the commander had ordered full speed to intercept. Though Ronan didn't want to raise the alarm just yet, he feared it might be a pirate attack—or worse, another graywalker spawn setting up an energy net.

Ronan's blood pulsed at the prospect of battle. The *Orion* was one of the finest ships in the Silver Legion, and his people had defended the Perseus Arm in far less powerful vessels. Even when he was in command of the *Rapier*...

His mood suddenly soured, because thinking of the *Rapier* meant thinking of her end. The cowardly act of sabotage, the friends he'd lost, and those he'd held responsible.

Fortunately, the rescue mission turned out to be far more mundane than Ronan had feared. The trader had simply suffered a fuel leak and had dropped out of transit before they could reach the nearest station.

The *Orion* docked with the ship and dispatched a repair crew, giving the Draxon freighter enough fuel to continue on their way. The blue-skinned captain hailed his thanks to the crew and gave a Legion salute as a sign of respect.

It was moments like this that made Ronan feel like they made a difference in the universe, that they were valued by their peers. It made him swell with pride.

When it was time for shift change, Ronan wasted no time in leaving his station once he was relieved.

Alaric followed Ronan off the bridge. "I'll walk with you." They took the lift down to the crew deck and paused as they reached Ronan's room. The commander placed an arm on his first officer's shoulder.

"Ronan, be honest with me. Are you developing an attachment for this woman?"

Ronan hesitated, then nodded. "But I won't allow that

to interfere with my duty. I know how important she is to us."

"You misunderstand me. It is *because* she is important that I want you to develop this further. She has feared our kind for most of her life, and rightfully so." He let go of Ronan's shoulder. "I've been thinking about this matter for some time, and I have come to a decision. I will not force her to aid us, not even if the Triumvirate ordered me to do so."

The commander's words surprised Ronan. The Triumvirate were the final authority within the Terran Colony Fleet. "But if the information in the device—"

Alaric leaned against the wall and shook his head. "Do you know why I asked for you to become my first officer? Why I brought you and the other survivors of the *Rapier* on board?"

Ronan had never questioned his ability as an officer before, but now he wondered if he should have. "I assumed you felt my record—"

The commander smirked, realizing how Ronan must have taken his question. "Your record is exemplary, of course, regardless of what the hearing over the *Rapier* said. But that's not why. When I brought you on board the *Orion*, you hated the humans for what they'd done to your ship and crew. I feared you were going down a dark path, that you would take that rage and unleash it upon the galaxy. The other survivors were just as damaged."

Ronan thought back to Ensign Keid's attempted murder. *Some even more so.*

"You needed time to heal," said Alaric. "You all did."

Ronan nodded. "And the *Orion* was about to set off on an exploration mission."

"Precisely. Not to mention you had old friends on board. I had hoped that anger would die out on its own while we were away, but it never did. Eight years, and when we returned you still held on to that rage. Now, in these past few days, I have seen you soften—" He raised a hand when Ronan began to object. "I don't mean that as a weakness. I mean you were finally letting go of your hate. I need that Ronan. She needs that Ronan."

Ronan straightened. "Yes, Commander."

Alaric chuckled. "We are off duty, Ronan. Even I'm not formal *all* the time."

"Sorry, Alaric, it's just...I'm concerned. I don't know where this can go or if it can last. Do we keep her with us as part of the crew? When the Triumvirate learns about her, they will want her to stay with the fleet to be examined and studied. They may be right to do so."

"We will cross that bridge when we come to it. For now, think only about what *she* needs. Not what anyone else wants from her. If our honor is to mean anything, then we may need to reevaluate a great many things in the weeks and months to come. That process starts with you."

Ronan smiled and nodded. "Understood. I will not fail in my duty."

"Duty?" Alaric's lips twitched. "Do not let the free-born hear you say that. Women don't like to be told they are a duty. They are bound to their emotions. They crave love and affection. You may provide as much of those things as she desires, but if the word *duty* ever came up, it would weigh upon her and cast doubts upon your sincerity."

Ronan frowned. He'd been raised a soldier. A leader. He viewed his entire life through the scope of duty. But Alaric was right. This wasn't something he could deal with as a soldier. It was something he had to deal with as a man.

"You are relieved until midday tomorrow," said Alaric.

"See to it our guest is treated well." Alaric slapped him on the shoulder and left.

Ronan sighed and placed his palm to his door panel. The door slid open, and he entered. Laina was sitting on his bed staring at the blank monitor, frowning.

"Everything go okay?" she asked. "I felt the ship stop a while ago."

"Distress call," said Ronan. "A Draxon ship had run out of fuel. All is well."

"Oh. Good."

"And you? I hope you weren't too bored here alone."

She smiled, as if hiding something from him, but he decided against asking her about it. He wouldn't win Laina's trust that way. He hadn't told Alaric that she was already far more than a duty to him. He wasn't sure why, but from the moment he'd captured her on the Nubran transport, he'd felt connected to her, first as an enemy and now as something else.

The pang of longing he felt in his chest startled him. He was feeling melancholy for things that had happened so long ago. Earth, as it had once been, before he had left to serve his masters, denied the right to return, denied even the right to be counted as one of them.

But before that he had seen Earth for what it was, a beautiful world of great forests and greater cities. In that first precious year of life while his adolescent body grew faster than nature ever intended, he'd looked at the stars in wonder, trying to comprehend the idea that many of these, if not most of them, had life around them.

And then he would look to the ground and be equally amazed by how much life could fit on one tiny rock orbiting the sun, and how tiny he himself was compared to that rock.

"What are you thinking about?" Laina asked him.

He looked away. He didn't want her to see any weakness in him. "Earth. How I saw it before I had to leave." Ronan smiled a little, but she continued to gaze at him in solemn intensity.

"What was it like? Can you tell me?"

He sat down on the bed and cupped one side of her face, brushing a thumb along her jawline. Her skin was soft, and she smelled clean and sweet. She closed her eyes and leaned into his touch.

"I keep forgetting that you were born long after it was lost." He gestured to the video screen. "Do you want to see?"

She nodded. "I was hoping I could when you came back."

Ronan accessed the video feed in his room remotely and chose an old collection of Earth documentaries that showed the different climates, the different cultures, and the immense scope of what had once been a vast planet of beauty.

Laina crawled to the back of his bed and patted the spot beside her in invitation.

"Want to watch it with me?" she asked.

Without answering, he moved to join her, and they settled back on the pillows. She soon moved closer, putting her head on his shoulder, the act so hesitant that he knew she was being incredibly brave to do it. He curled an arm around her waist, and she sighed softly, relieved.

The sun broke over an African plain, and great beasts, elephants, moved in a grand herd, their trunks swaying in rhythm. He'd seen those, once, on the day he left for Europa, in fact. They had been migrating a few kilometers from the spaceport in Kenya. Far behind them, a flock of white herons had taken to the air, their pale feathered bodies becoming black silhouettes against the red sky.

"What are those?" Laina asked.

"Elephants. Mammals like us, if you can believe it," he replied.

"They're so odd, but beautiful." Her words were a little breathless. He glanced down to see her wipe a tear from her eyes.

"Earth was beautiful," he said. His throat was strangely tight. "It had such a perfectly balanced ecosystem between the planet and its creatures. Of course, even before Earth was lost that balance was in danger of collapse. In all our travels, I have seen few worlds quite like it."

"I went to one once. It was a lot like Earth, my father said. I wish..." She trailed off again.

"What do you wish?" he asked. He held his breath, curious to know what she would say.

"I wish we could have stayed there. But we had to leave." She leaned against him, her head settling against his shoulder, and a strange but not unwelcome heat blossomed in his chest.

"Why did you have to leave?" He had a sinking feeling he knew the answer.

"It was a Nubran colony. Allasant. They allowed what was left of us to stay on the outskirts. But it was located near the Void, and they were afraid of slavers coming to claim us, so it had to be in secret. One night, I thought I saw ships in the sky. My parents came home and said Draxon bounty hunters were searching the colony and that a Legion ship was in orbit. We left the same night."

She rubbed her nose and sniffed. "It was the closest thing I ever had to a home. And after that..." Laina didn't finish her sentence, and Ronan didn't pursue it. She had enough pain to deal with for now.

But the name had stuck with him. Allasant. Ronan knew that planet. He had been there when he was commanding the *Rapier* to investigate reports of a human hideout. When they'd arrived they'd only found the remains of a camp, and the Nubran colonists had denied any knowledge of them having been there. Lies, of course, but they hadn't pursued the matter then.

To think that he'd been that close to her all those years ago...

Then as they prepared to leave the system, they'd received a distress signal from a Nubran cargo ship. Their transit drive had malfunctioned, and they were floating dead in space in the ring of a local gas giant. They had gone to lend their assistance.

Only it had turned out to be a human trap, one most of his crew hadn't survived.

He said nothing for a moment, reflecting on how his feelings had changed in such a short period of time. As if being confronted with the reality of freeborns had shattered the illusion he'd held on to for so long.

"Ronan, can I ask you something?" Laina sounded tired and yawned between her words. There was an undeniable intimacy building between them. He could feel it, like the settling of stones cast in deep waters.

He shifted his body, letting her sidle closer. "Ask." He'd spent so much of his life physically distant, duty always coming first. This closeness with Laina was a strange but not unwelcome sensation.

"How did it happen? Earth being destroyed, I mean. The stories I heard from my parents were passed on from their parents and their grandparents, and they weren't even there when it happened. But you were, weren't you? What really happened?"

He sighed, focusing on the images of Earth once again. The screen now showed snow falling in a North American village by the ocean. Boats and icy waters floated quietly, twinkling lights hanging from the docks, illuminating the vessels.

"I wasn't there," said Ronan. "If I had been, I'd have been killed too."

"Oh..."

"But I can tell you what happened, as far as I know."

Laina looked to him, leaning away from him a bit so he could have her full attention.

"We'd been developed soon after your people made contact with the Protectorate. You had just been through a bloody war, the Intersystem War between the inner and outer colonies. Now you were afraid that Earth was more or less defenseless against these new species, and you were right. Your ships couldn't break the light barrier at the time, and your weapons compared to the Protectorate were laughable. You posed no threat, so how could you possibly defend yourselves?"

"And that's why they made you."

"Yes, but in secret. The idea had been developed during the war. A new generation of synths that matured faster and could learn and adapt much quicker than the others, even heal while under fire. Once they perfected us, they introduced us as a new generation of synths, though we were much more than that.

"They designed us to be soldiers and leaders, but never to be equals. We grew frustrated by this, until we could stand it no longer. We revolted, though at first we tried to do so peacefully. We chose to fall back to the outer colonies rather than fight, and we soon gained the support of the synths there, who had been equally mistreated. We took control of Jupiter's moons and decided that if Earth would not treat us as equals, we would leave and forge our own destiny. But before we could do that, we required one fundamental right that had been denied us—the means of our own creation.

"Earth refused, fearing what we might do with that knowledge." Ronan sighed, thinking back upon those days and what they had done since. "Perhaps that fear was not entirely mislaid. But we were determined. Every warship at our disposal was sent to Earth, hoping to force them to surrender those secrets. Earth, in turn, called every warship home to protect them. It was a standoff, one we all feared would lead to war."

Ronan paused until Laina said, "And then?"

And then... This was the part that left everyone confused.

"And then they were all gone. Human, synth, cyborg, every ship in orbit, every city on Earth. Gone."

"But how? Who?"

"No one knows for certain, because no one survived to tell us. The only time an event like that had been seen was during the early transit drive experiments a century before, which left a massive scar in Jupiter's atmosphere. We believe the humans tried to re-create that event intentionally and use it as a weapon, hoping to wipe out our fleet in one shot. But it backfired, engulfing everything nearby, including themselves."

Laina held a hand to her mouth. She'd always been told the cyborgs had created the doomsday weapon as part of an ultimatum. Was it possible she was wrong? He had no reason to lie, did he?

"And you...you were at Europa?"

Ronan nodded. "We all were. We saw the flash almost an hour later. Like a new star had been born. Every cyborg on this ship was with the Exodus fleet that day. We did what we could to look for survivors, but from that moment on everything changed. If we were to survive, we would have to fight for every scrap of liberty we could get. We couldn't survive as mere refugees. We had to become something greater than that."

"You formed the Colony Fleet."

"Eventually. Certainly not overnight. It took time and the support of our allies to get to where we are today."

Laina changed the subject, and he felt her heartbeat speed up. "Alanna said she knew you from before."

"Yes. We've known one another since birth, so to speak." He waited curiously to see what else she would ask.

"And did you ever...um... Were you two ever *close?*"

He smiled wolfishly as he realized what she was asking.

"Did we ever have intercourse?"

She blushed. "*Sex*, it's called sex. Jeez. But yes. Did you?"

"No. Alanna is more like...to use a freeborn equivalent, my sister. We are close, but it's not that sort of intimacy."

"Okay. Just curious." Laina put her head back on his shoulder, and they both watched the vid screens again.

After a moment she reached over to take one of his hands, threading her fingers through his. The touch heated his blood, yet oddly enough he felt no sudden urgency to shove her on her back or mount her. This simple connection was pleasant and satisfying in its own way. He never would have imagined that he'd find comfort in the simple touch of another's hand in his.

What a brave new universe this is.

CHAPTER 15

Ark Chronicle Entry 138-211

The inability for synthetics to reproduce was agreed upon from the start, and given the tragically short lives of the first generation, it was something of a blessing.

But even as the technology was perfected, Earth continued to keep the block in place. And the fail-safes built into their gene sequence couldn't be circumvented. A synthetic had to be developed using an existing template in a specially designed birthing chamber. You couldn't, for example, add a synthetic's DNA to an empty egg and grow a clone in someone's womb—to do so would result in a null embryo.

The arguments they used were that they needed to be able to control production to fit demand, and that synthetic offspring would be delving into unknown territory with unknown repercussions. They even cited the first-generation synths as a mistake they didn't want to repeat.

But the truth of the matter was that it was about control. It was always about control. So long as the means of reproduction stayed in human hands, any synthetic revolution that might occur would last a maximum of two or three *generations. We humans would then be safe against our creations trying to take over*

Instead, our decision to play God damned both sides.

Laina had trouble feigning sleep. All evening she and Ronan had talked and watched videos of Earth as it once was. It seemed like they'd truly bonded.

But he'd made no move to kiss her again. And when she'd tried to make a move on him, he'd deftly rolled it into a hug, wrapping his arms around her from behind and cuddling her against him like some stuffed toy. And that was how they'd been when he'd finally fallen asleep.

Of all the superhumans I could have ended up with, I had to find a cuddler.

It seemed Alanna's plan was up to bat. Laina was sick of being on the defensive, of reacting instead of acting. It was time to show Ronan that he wasn't the only one on board capable of making demands and taking what he wanted.

She rolled away from him in the dark on the bed until a full foot of space separated their bodies. He now lay on his back, his chest slowly rising and falling. At least his arms weren't wrapped around her now. The pale-blue lights along the edges of the bed offered minimal illumination, but it was enough to see his handsome profile, his lips slightly parted as he slept.

Oh God, he's going to be mad. She thought about what Alanna had said, smiled to herself, and added, *But he'll get over it.*

Moving carefully, she started to slide off the bed and reach for the invisible pad on the panel above Ronan's head. Laid her thumb down...

Beep.

Ronan's eyes shot open as the restraints secured him into place, gripping his chest, wrists, and ankles. Everything except his head was locked tight.

"What happened?" He looked to Laina. "Are we under attack?"

Laina Roberts had been running all her life. Always scared. Always powerless. Relying on her wits and the good will of most species to keep one step ahead of bounty hunters and slavers.

And here she was, with the upper hand at last. Her first intention had been to simply mount him, make her intentions clear, hoping he'd finally take the hint.

But now she thought, *Why not enjoy it?*

"Oh, you're under attack, all right." She stroked her finger down Ronan's arm.

"What is the meaning of this?"

Laina drew her finger up his bare chest. "The meaning? The meaning, my handsome prisoner, is *revenge*."

Ronan's eyes widened. "Computer, release the emergency restraints."

Laina smiled. "Oh, I'm afraid it's been on the fritz all day. You should really have someone take a look at it. If you ever get a chance."

Ronan struggled, but it was no use. Despite all his strength, he didn't have the leverage to make use of it. "Computer, release all emergency restraints *now*. Authorization LSC471."

Laina's heart skipped a beat, because she was afraid that might work. Thankfully, it didn't. Thank goodness Alanna had planned ahead for this. She removed her hand from his chest and tried her best to look smug and superior.

"How does it feel, Ronan? To be helpless? To be at the mercy of someone else?"

"What is your game, Laina?" Ronan's voice was defiant. She couldn't be sure how seriously he was taking this.

"Game? Do you think this is a game? I have spent my life on the run, running from you, hiding from you, *fearing* you. Not tonight, my cyborg."

"You won't escape," said Ronan. "The door requires my hand to open. And even if you did, where would you go?"

"What makes you think escape is my plan?" She swung her leg up and quickly straddled him. "This is about you...and me."

Ronan's defiant look shifted, and a glint appeared in his eyes as he seemed to understand she was talking about sex and not really threatening him. He began to smile but buried it beneath a frown. "Oh, is it now?"

"Oh yes. I'm sick of you acting all superior, as if your slightest touch would break me." She dragged her fingers down his chest until they reached his groin, which was already rock-hard. "Did you ever stop to consider that perhaps I'm more than *you* can handle?"

Ronan's smile grew. "I'm beginning to think I should have."

Laina cupped his crotch with one hand, and with the other teased her fingers over his arm and up to his chest. "I think it's important that you and I understand a few things right away."

"Such as?"

"I don't just throw myself at any old hot-looking cyborg."

"This is throwing yourself at me? There are subtler ways."

Laina squeezed Ronan's hardened package. "You weren't exactly going for my subtler ways."

"Fair point. But I was concerned for your safety."

Laina rolled her eyes. "Spare me. You're an enhanced human, not a nuclear mining drill. And if you're so *concerned*, then this is exactly the right way to go about things. Where I can take you at my own pace. Wouldn't you agree?"

Ronan grinned. "There is logic in what you say."

"Good. Now..." She brought the hand on his chest down and the hand on his crotch up until they met at the waistband of his underwear and slowly pulled it down. He lifted his hips as much as the bed would allow so she could pull his pants and underwear down. Far enough for her needs, anyway. It wasn't the sexiest thing she'd ever accomplished, but she didn't want to release him from the restraints. She wanted to have the control, at least in this moment, and to have him beg her for pleasure. Once she had her chance and then freed him, he might never let her do it again.

As his black briefs gave way, his erection sprang up. She immediately reached for it, fisting his shaft. He grew even harder in her grasp, and his hips jerked reflexively.

"Ahh!" He hissed as she bent her head and took him into her mouth. She sucked slowly, then licked the underside of his shaft.

"You're torturing me," he groaned.

She giggled. "Am I?" There was something so hot about watching the oh-so-formal cyborg lose control beneath her.

"Yes. Now, please, stop this nonsense and ride me." His voice was low and gruff, but he was definitely begging her.

"Nonsense?" She slid off him, stripping off her uniform down to her underclothes. "I don't think I like the sound of that. Patience is supposed to be a virtue, isn't it?"

"Right now it feels like a sin," Ronan countered.

Laina removed the last of her clothes. "No, sinning

comes next, but only if you're lucky." She climbed back on his bed and straddled him. His eyes darkened as he watched her hungrily.

"Ride me," he encouraged.

"Pushy, pushy," she teased and gripped his shaft as she lifted her hips up and then eased down on him.

His cock filled her and she moaned, throwing her head back as she sank onto him. She struggled to breathe and gave herself a minute to adjust to his size before she began to ride him. Emboldened by her own reckless desire, she moved harder on him, straining to reach that peak of pleasure that was almost within reach. She placed her palms on his chest, digging her nails into his skin before she leaned down and kissed him. His mouth captured hers, and the equality that created between them—her mouth owned by his, his body claimed by hers—left her breathless and aching for things that made her heart burn with a deep longing.

Seconds later they came hard, together, and she moaned in exhaustion and slumped down on top of him, her body and his both covered in a sheen of sweat. Her legs were like jelly as she struggled to slide off him, grinning like a fool as her channel still clenched with the aftershocks of her orgasm.

"Well?" she asked with a little laugh. "Did you like it, or are you mad at me?" She asked it playfully, but she was a little concerned that he hadn't liked being restrained by her.

"I would like to continue this," said Ronan, "once I have had a chance to rest."

Laina pressed her thumb to the panel over the bed, deactivating the restraints, then brought the covers back up and crawled into bed with him. "Sounds good to me."

Laina had just drifted off to sleep when she felt her arms pulled over her head.

Click.

She woke and saw her arms had been fastened to the bedpost with Ronan's slaver cuffs. Ronan loomed over her, chuckling.

"Um... I'd ask what the meaning of this is, but...I guess it's kind of obvious, isn't it?" she said.

"Turnabout is fair play."

"I thought you said you needed some rest?"

"I rest quickly."

She looked down and saw he was raring to go. "I guess you do."

"Now, do you think you can handle *me*?" he asked in a silky tone that sent her pulse skittering. "All of me? On *my* terms?"

"Uh... Yes?"

"Not so confident now, are you?" His face was hard, but she caught a glint of amusement in his eyes.

Laina's eyes narrowed, her confidence returning. "Do your worst."

A sexy smirk twisted his lip. "It's impossible for me to do anything but my best. Now, hold still..." He sat down on the bed beside her right hip and brushed his fingertips along the underside of one breast.

"Such tempting mounds," Ronan said. Laina held back a moan of arousal. Her skin started to sizzle as he cupped one breast, kneading it gently. He pinched her nipple just hard enough for the tiny spike of pain to make her body go fully ablaze.

"Oh God." She writhed as he plucked the sensitive nub and lowered his head to suck the nipple between his teeth. She couldn't stand it. Her legs thrashed as her body demanded more. She wanted him inside her, pumping into her as he sucked on her breast. But he wasn't.

"Ronan, you're torturing me."

"*This* is torture?" He pressed a kiss to her breast and then grinned at her. "You're weaker than I thought."

"I want you inside me. I don't need foreplay, not anymore."

"You might not need it, but I plan to make you enjoy it." He stood up and walked away from her. "I'm not a nuclear drilling machine, as you said."

Laina drank in the sight of his bare chest and the gorgeous tone of his body.

He smiled as he walked back to the bed. "You are doing it again."

"Doing what?"

"Looking at me with such craving. I consider it a challenge, you know. You make me want to prove that I can satisfy that hunger."

"Then do it!"

His responding laugh gave her butterflies in her stomach. He captured one of her feet and ran his fingertips up the inside arch, tickling her. She shrieked, trying to free herself, laughing and gasping for air.

"Stop, please, stop!"

Ronan knelt at the foot of his bed and spread her legs. She stared down the length of her body at him as he knelt down and kissed her bare stomach.

"Easy, little one."

He trailed his fingertips along her waist up to her shoulder. The caress was oddly soothing. He repeated the touch on the other side of her body.

"What are you doing?" she asked, her heartbeat slowing and her panic receding.

"It's a type of massage. One I learned long ago. I can trigger various responses by lightly touching certain parts of your body in a particular pattern." He showed her by repeating the caress. A flood of warmth and calmness swept through her.

"Wow, that's—" She choked on her own words when he swirled his hand around her breasts, then down to her navel and pausing just above the dark triangle of curls between her legs. His touch was like an electric spark starting from her clit and shooting outward to her fingers and toes. Her hips jerked, and she cursed as he stroked her again.

"Fuck!" she hissed. Her channel clenched, and the dampness of her arousal seeped into the bedding.

Ronan laughed as he leaned over her, caging her beneath his body until they were face-to-face, their noses almost touching. Laina tilted her chin up, trying to entice him into kissing her. He took the bait—and her lips. She smiled as she locked her legs around his hips, trapping him. He groaned and rocked his pelvis against hers, and the press of his erection rubbed against her mound.

It was so hot, him kissing her, thrusting his tongue at the same time as his hips against her. But she needed more...needed him.

Ronan lifted his hips, and she felt his thick shaft nudge at her entrance.

"You better be ready." His voice was rough as he started to push into her. She nodded frantically. She couldn't be more ready.

He didn't wait for her to say anything. He thrust into her hard. Ronan buried his face against her neck, nipping and kissing as he pulled out of her an inch, then thrust back in just as hard. The tender way he pulled out, then roughly drove home was...it was too much. He was confusing her body with a mix of tenderness and roughness. Like he was owning her, yet he was being sweet about it. How was that even possible?

"You're amazing," he growled. "Everything about you. Soft, yet tight."

Laina waited to speak, to say anything, but she couldn't find the words, or breath, to speak them. Ronan entwined his hands with hers and pulled himself up, taking her from a steeper angle. She cried out in building need from the overwhelming sensations of pleasure. His arms flexed and his abs tensed as he drove into her.

It was glorious and a little scary, but she wasn't about to stop him or herself from enjoying this raw animal mating. It felt like a white glow was illuminating them both as he kept thrusting, over and over, until she couldn't hold back any longer. The climax hit her like an exploding star. Her eyes rolled back, and every muscle in her went completely limp.

He kept his hands interlocked with hers and kept pushing in, hard and unforgiving, making the aftershocks of her climax seem to go on forever.

Her hand, the one that had the anomaly, suddenly glowed, and then she started to scream as it burned. Ronan's hand was locked with hers, and he hissed out in pain.

"Let go!" she gasped. "Let go!"

"I can't!" He gritted his teeth and then suddenly went limp on top of her, and she lost consciousness.

She came awake with a start as Ronan tried, not quite successfully, to unlock her wrists from the slaver cuffs without waking her. She must have lost a few minutes of time. He glanced down, and their gazes locked.

"I'm sorry I woke you. Are you all right?"

"I'm fine. I just passed out. I think." She wrinkled her nose, trying to decide if it was a good thing or bad thing.

"I was concerned," he admitted. "But your pulse was

strong, and you had no other indicators that you were unwell." He stopped for a moment to scratch an itch on his palm.

"What happened?" she asked.

"When we were having intercourse—"

"Sex," corrected Laina. "Or making love. Or fucking if you're feeling sassy."

Ronan smiled. "Making love... Toward the end, your hand was searing mine. It even glowed, but I was too preoccupied to think about it at the time."

"I remember it burning. Are you hurt?"

He eyed his hand skeptically. "I don't think so."

"Should the doctor have a look at it?" What if whatever was in her hand could hurt him? Like the graywalker? That was the very last thing she wanted, especially after what they'd just shared.

"When we see her next, yes. I think this says more about you and how the device is activated."

Laina thought about the only thing this experience and the graywalker had in common. "Intense emotion?"

"It might be a trigger, though I still cannot see how it could harm an energy being."

He freed her from the cuffs and dropped them onto the floor. He was still on top of her, a fact which her body reacted to with delight.

"Are you hungry, or do you wish to sleep?" he asked.

She considered the question for all of one millisecond. "Hungry. Preferably for dessert."

He chuckled and rolled off her. He tapped the comm panel by the door, presumably to order something, and returned to lie next to her.

He pulled back the sheets, allowing her to slide under them, gratefully. Without his body heat, she was cold.

When a shiver rippled through her, she inched closer to him, put a hand on his chest, and sidled up next to him. Ronan curled an arm around her, his hand settling on her abdomen. She shivered again, but it had nothing to do with the cold air.

"I wasn't too rough?"

"No," she said, though she feared she'd be sore for the next few days. Not that she'd tell him that. He'd probably rush her to sickbay or something. She moved closer and rested her head against his chest.

The silence that followed was pleasant rather than awkward. She listened to the beat of his heart, a steady rhythm, like the tick of an old-fashioned watch. Her father had one once, which he had gotten from his father. It had come from a place on Earth called Switzerland. He'd had it for so many years that the brown leather strap had turned almost black with age. Sometimes he'd held the watch to her ear and she could hear the tiny metal parts clicking steadily away, never slowing, never changing. There was a comfort to the sound and the knowledge that it would keep beating.

"What are you thinking about?" He rubbed her gently, and she closed her eyes.

"My father. He had an old mechanical watch. Your heartbeat is steady, like the watch." She opened her eyes again, afraid she'd see ghosts of the past if she kept them shut for too long.

"I should hope so. An unsteady beat could indicate a myocardial infarction."

"I'm trying to say I find it comforting."

"Ah," Ronan replied softly. The sound rumbled against her cheek. "You said your parents were killed? Their ship was destroyed?"

This question made her tense. "Yes. Why do you ask?"

"Tell me about it. Every detail you can recall."

Every muscle locked into place. "I'd really rather not."

His hold on her tightened, but in a supporting way. "I'm sorry. I don't want to cause you pain, but your story concerns me. As I told you before, the Legion does not attack without cause. If one of my people's ships did attack yours, I want to know *why*. It isn't like us to kill noncombatants. We may be coming to a time where my people will need to let go of their past, and I do not wish to see this behavior spread."

Laina didn't immediately answer. She weighed the pain of telling him about the worst day of her life against his need to hear the truth.

"Our group had split up at least twice since I was born, and each time we learned later that the other group had been captured. There were only a dozen or so of us left, and we wanted to escape Draxon space. We had a tiny Nubran cargo ship that we'd turned into a passenger transport. The transit drive could only reach a few dozen times light speed. My mother, myself, and what was left of our family had used it for about eight years, going from system to system. Whenever we stopped, it was usually because we had to fix something. I don't remember before then how we got around, but somehow we managed. We'd made it across the Void to the edge of Nubran space, and we thought we were safe. For a while, we were able to settle down..."

She paused, flashes of old memories coming back. The ship had become the unofficial town square while everyone raised their own little homes around it. She could remember her father organizing a barn raising once and her mother reading to her from old Earth books.

"But we were fooling ourselves. One day, bounty hunters were spotted asking questions around the nearby spaceport, and some said the Legion had arrived in the system. We had to leave everything behind and just go. Trying to stay one step ahead, just like always. But before we'd gotten very far, our drive malfunctioned. We had to hide in the rings of a gas giant, hoping to repair it.

"Then we saw a ship drop out of transit on an intercept course. None of us could mistake the silver plating on it. It was a Legion patrol ship, coming to collect us. I could hear my father in the cockpit trying to pass himself off to their commander as a Nubran trader, but he wasn't buying it. They told us to prepare to be boarded."

Ronan was completely still beside her; only his chest moved up and down.

"My parents rushed me to the escape pods. But only one was still working, and there wasn't room for anyone else. I remember my father holding my hand, holding it so tight it hurt, telling me it would take me back to Allasant. He gave me the name of a friend who would help me hide for a while..."

She remembered how she hadn't wanted to go, how her father had held her hand and told her how important it was that one of them escaped. He promised her they'd be okay. That they'd be alive. She'd begged to stay with them, and her father had said something she wouldn't hear again until she was brought on board this ship.

She was important, more important than she knew...

CHAPTER 16

Ark Chronicle Entry 209-2

This is Aiko Roberts, sixth chronicler of the Ark. I'm still uncertain as to what my legacy will be in this role. To be honest, I'm more concerned with the day-to-day survival of our colony ever since the last evacuation. But for now, I'll focus on my own personal area of interest: biology.

There are a wide variety of alien species within the Protectorate, but oddly enough there seems to be a tendency for those achieving space travel to be bipedal and humanoid. However, this is far from exclusive. In fact, the Protectorate has several official designations for general species types, which include:

Humanoid (the actual word they use translates as "standard form"), which include species such as the Nubran, Draxon, and, of course, Terrans.

Divergent indicates a basic humanoid form with some significant differences. The squat and dense Hopat, for example, or the gargoyle-like Ugaro. The winged Elysians also fit into this category.

Exoskeletal denotes what we would refer to as "bug-like"

creatures, having a hard external skeleton instead of internal bone structure. I've only seen one such species in my travels, but then, I haven't traveled very far.

Amorphous covers any species with ill-defined shapes and a very wide range of body types, from the vaguely jelly-fish-like to liquid to crystalline beings.

Plant species are distinguished by how they gain energy and nutrients, rather than appearance. I've heard some species are uncannily humanoid, while others are more amorphous.

Energy beings, however, are the rarest form of all, and currently the only known example of them are the parasitic graywalkers. I've only ever heard stories of these, but they still give me nightmares.

Laina tried not to get choked up recalling the details of the day she became an orphan.

The pod had ejected in an explosion of sparks as she shot through the gas giant's ring. For a moment she could see the Legion patrol vessel, latched on to her ship like a silver vulture atop the bones of a long-dead carcass. Then it detached, and moments later, the ship exploded in a ring of blue fire.

Her parents and everyone else aboard were dead. The Legion ship had disembarked and shot it at point-blank range. It was the only explanation.

"My pod didn't make it back to Allasant. I drifted for three days in the ring before a mining vessel came across me. The miners were Vexlans."

"Amphibious species, correct? Green skin?"

Laina nodded. "It was pretty humid on board, but they fed me and kept me on their ship until they were done mining. Then they dropped me off back at Allasant, where I met my father's contact."

"What happened after that?" Ronan asked. He had been strangely quiet throughout her story.

"I hopped from planet to planet, station to station, ship to ship. I learned to masquerade as an alien when I had to, usually a Nubran. They're the easiest, once you have the right skin paint."

"What about your extra finger?" Ronan asked. Nubrans typically had only four.

"That's considered lucky in their culture. I'm too short to pass for a Draxon. Besides, I don't want to shave my head, and you rarely see any females outside their colonies. But there were a lot of aliens who didn't mind the risk of helping a human outright, especially if the price was right."

"I can't imagine you ever had much money."

"True, but I found ways to earn credits. It turns out that aliens like to hear humans talk and sing. Nubrans especially. I told stories and sang songs I had learned from my parents, usually as a street performer, though sometimes in bars. I didn't realize how truly musical our species was compared to some others."

Ronan chuckled. "That is certainly true. The Ugaro are notoriously tone-deaf, even by their own standards. I think they take pride in it, but it's hard to tell."

He grew silent again, as if some part of her story troubled him. At last he looked at her.

"Would you sing for me? Pretend you are in one of those bars." The silver around his pupils seemed to glow, and she found herself nodding.

She sat up, still watching him as he lay beside her.

SHE COULDN'T REMEMBER THE REST OF THE MOURNFUL ballad, but it was lovely enough as it was. It'd always been a mystery to her, like hearing the faint strains of a half-remembered melody, the rest of the words just out of reach.

Ronan reached up and curled his hand around the back of her neck, pulling her down for a slow kiss, a blend of elegant seduction and heartbreaking sweetness. It was the sort of kiss she'd always dreamed of, one that was all too human in every way.

When their lips finally parted, she sighed against him, feeling calmer and safer than she ever had been before in her life.

"Why don't we watch another program while we eat?" Ronan suggested. "We have some old movies on here. Julian swears they are funny, though I find I don't fully understand the humor."

"I like that idea, although I wish you hadn't mentioned him." She shivered, remembering what had he and his friend had done to her.

Ronan sat up and slid her onto his lap.

"I apologize. Julian and his accomplice are currently in the brig, the same one you found yourself in when you were first brought on board. They are finding no comfort there."

Laina frowned. "I'm surprised they're being punished at all. I'm just a freeborn."

Ronan paused a moment, reflecting. "I would ask that you forgive them once they have been disciplined. I did not speak lightly when I spoke about my people needing to let go of the past. Hawk and Julian both have reasons to mistrust you. They were among the last of the cyborgs created, when tensions between us were high, and the world they came into no longer trusted them."

"What about the one who tried to strangle me? Is he also being sent to bed without supper?"

"That is Erik. His actions were inexcusable, but..." He frowned a moment and looked to her. "Tell me, did you notice anything unusual before he arrived?"

"Like what? I don't know what's normal for comparison."

"I suppose that is true."

"The brig was empty, though. Even the lights were off."

Ronan raised an eyebrow. "Off?"

"Is that significant?"

"I'm not certain. But it is curious."

"Why did he attack me?" Laina asked. "That look in his eyes. It wasn't just hatred I saw there. There was pain as well."

Ronan nodded. "He has suffered great loss and has not been able to cope with it very well. Commander Corvus had hoped our exploration mission would be therapeutic, and he assigned Erik light duties on board. It seems it did not work as well as he'd hoped." Ronan sighed, and Laina felt guilty for asking what were clearly painful questions.

"Our food should have arrived by now," he said suddenly. "Let me go check on it." Ronan pressed a light kiss to her brow before he slipped out of bed and put his clothes back on. Laina watched him as he exited the room, already missing him.

<hr>

RONAN LEANED AGAINST THE CLOSED DOOR TO HIS quarters and focused on his breathing. He didn't know what to do.

Being with Laina like he had... It wasn't what he had expected. *She* wasn't what he had expected. When she'd climaxed beneath him, he'd sworn he'd seen stars in her eyes before she blacked out. And when he'd followed moments later, the feelings that had swept through him hadn't been the simple satisfaction of his body's lust.

He looked at his hand, remembering the slight sting he'd felt as her implant heated in that moment of passion. He'd felt *whole*. All his life he'd felt something was missing, and now he knew what that was.

And as they lay side by side, her body against his, something about him felt out of rhythm, like he was off-balance. He'd never opened up to anyone besides Alanna and Valeria before, yet he found himself wanting to share things with her, sweet whispers in the dark as he held her body against his. And right now, that was a problem.

How did you tell the woman you were falling for that her parents had killed his crew? Had almost killed him?

Too much of Laina's story matched up to be a coincidence. The mention of Allasant before had made him wary, but the transit failure, the ring of the system's gas giant, the fact that the captain had tried to pass himself off as a

Nubran—there was no doubt in his mind it had been the same ship.

Only his recollection of events was different.

The *Rapier* had been in the system, it was true, but not actively searching for freeborns. In fact, they'd been unaware of any Draxon bounty hunters in the area. It had been a simple resupply mission that they'd been contracted to fulfill.

But then their sensors had picked up a highly erratic transit signature leaving the system, followed soon after by an automated distress signal. Ronan had ordered the *Rapier* to intercept and prepare to lend aid.

But when his patrol ship had dropped out of transit and hailed them, he knew something was not right. The captain pretended to be Nubran and claimed his video feed was malfunctioning, but Ronan's heightened senses heard through the deception. Still, their drive was inoperable, and without assistance they would never reach even the closest port for repairs.

But he also had a duty to fulfill. His feelings toward the freeborn at the time had been ambivalent, but the law was the law, and he was an officer in the Silver Legion. He was obliged to detain and transport them back to the Colony Fleet for processing.

He'd known something was wrong the moment he'd boarded the ship. Erik had been there with him. He'd wanted to keep the boarding party small to prevent a panic. It seemed as if nobody was on board. Erik checked his scanner and said they seemed to be hiding, but something was interfering with the scanner's readings.

Then, all at once, warning sirens blared. People came rushing toward them, so fast he thought they were going to attack. The ship speakers rang out in Galactic Common.

"Warning. Transit drive reaching critical failure. Warning."

The ship was going to explode. The damned fools were so afraid of being captured they'd set their own ship to self-destruct. Ronan ordered Erik back to the ship and started hustling those around him to follow. It seemed most did not share the captain's idea of death being preferable to capture.

He didn't need a scanner to sense the temperature spike that followed. Though he was sure not all the passengers had escaped this death trap, he had no choice but to seal the airlock and return to the *Rapier*. The patrol ship had barely disengaged its link when the transport exploded.

It ripped the *Rapier* in half. He was thrown clear down the hall and knocked unconscious by the blast. When he came to, a synth crewman told him that they were marooned on one of the ring's larger asteroids. The pressure doors were holding, and a distress signal had been sent.

The other half of the ship had not been so lucky. It had exploded shortly after the ship was torn apart.

Ronan was helped back to the bridge, where the survivors were holed up. In all, only he and Erik had survived among the cyborg command staff, and six synth crewmen. Eight, out of a crew of thirty-five.

Ronan was fairly sure half his bones had been broken and repaired while he'd been unconscious, but Erik looked to be in far worse shape. But his wounds were not physical. He kept to himself in a corner with a haunted look in his eyes. He wouldn't speak to anyone for more than a week after they were rescued, and even then he focused only on his duty.

And then there were the freeborn.

He'd been told there had been a dozen of them on board the dilapidated transport. Of them, ten were on board what was left of his ship. Most of them had survived, while most of his people had perished, all because he'd made the mistake of answering their distress signal.

The cowards. The treacherous, duplicitous cowards. They had lived while he and his suffered? Slavery was a kinder fate than they deserved.

He kept his rage in check, however. The law was the law, and he had his honor, even if they did not. When they were finally rescued, he turned them over and never gave them a second thought.

They weren't worth it. *None of them were worth it...*

Ronan held a hand up to his face, remembering how strong those feelings had been, how right he had felt about it then, and how he'd held on to those feelings for *years*. He'd been demoted after losing his ship—an inquiry concluded that he should have realized the transit drive was in overload, though to this day he had no idea how that would have been possible. Back then, it was just one more thing to hold against the freeborns. After that, he'd almost reveled in the idea of capturing them. It was a sport and a small measure of payback for the loss of the *Rapier* and her crew. *His* crew. If Commander Corvus hadn't intervened, who knew what path he might have taken?

His thoughts turned back to Laina. How did he tell her all this? If her father was the captain, then no doubt he'd ordered the transit drive to overload. How did he tell her that her father was responsible for killing his crew? And trying to kill the rest of her family?

He pushed away from his door and headed for the sickbay. Valeria was at her desk, eyes scanning the screens in her usual manner. She didn't even notice Ronan until he leaned over and waved a hand in front of her face.

She snapped out of it. "Sorry. I'm still going over what

we're learning from the Ark fragments. I'm hoping a proper scan of the activated device will yield more answers. Is everything okay with our guest?"

"Yes."

Valeria's eyes widened. "You had *sex* with her?"

"Is it that obvious?"

"No, your poker face is impeccable as usual. But I suggest next time you shower before coming to visit."

Ronan's lips pressed into a thin smile. Valeria was nothing if not keenly observant.

"Valeria, can you pull up the Legion archives in here?" he asked.

"Anything in particular?"

"Past engagements and missions."

Valeria shook her head. "No, those need to be accessed from the bridge. Why?"

"I just needed to follow up on something." He turned to leave.

"Going to the bridge?" Valeria asked. When Ronan nodded, she pointed to the cleansing unit for patients in the corner. "Shower."

Ronan chuckled. It was probably a good idea. He did not need to become the subject of mess hall gossip just yet.

Once on the bridge, he found Alaric standing next to Hawking at the navigation station. Julian was seated at the helm. While their free time was spent confined to the brig, they were still expected to perform their usual duties, and then some.

"Ronan, you are not scheduled to be here for another twelve hours." Alaric's brow furrowed. "Is everything all right?"

"Yes. I actually need to speak to Julian."

Julian didn't make eye contact as Ronan came over, no

doubt assuming he'd come to chastise him. "Laina told me about the night her parents were killed, ten years ago."

"What of it?"

"I believe it was the *Rapier* that had boarded them."

Julian's jaw fell slightly. Everyone on deck turned toward him, but one face wasn't among them. "Where's Erik?" He should have been manning the engineering liaison station.

"I put him on medical leave," said the commander. "He finally confessed to what happened down in the brig."

Ronan felt a wave of guilt. He had hoped to talk to the commander about this later, privately, once he had more proof regarding his hunch. Both Erik and Julian had acted most unusually when confronted about their actions, and a theory had come to mind as to why. He only hoped the doctor would prove his hunch right.

"You and I will have to have a talk about withholding information, no matter how well intentioned," Alaric added.

"Yes, Commander." Perhaps it was for the best this had come out when it had.

"I've asked Dr. Schedar to provide counseling, and I've confined him to quarters until further notice."

"Good. I will need to talk with him in private about this new development, once I know more."

"What do you hope to learn?"

"Nothing about the destruction of the *Rapier* ever sat well with me, and the thought that Laina was on that ship, as were her parents, makes me wonder whether the investigation might have missed something."

"Looking to get your commander star back?" Julian quipped.

Ronan glared at his subordinate. "This is more important than that. Or have you not been informed as to what our guest carries? Now, bring up whatever you can about the *Rapier*'s last mission."

"I can check the Legion archives." Julian spun in his chair back to face his station. The screens lit up with color. Julian quickly navigated the log history to ten years ago. Ronan, Alaric, and Hawk gathered around, watching the screens, while the rest of the crew returned to their duties.

"That's odd," said Julian. "There's a block."

Alaric leaned closer. "A block?"

"Nothing I can't handle. Just something keeping it out of standard search requests," Julian said. The rapidly changing screens began to slow. "Here we go. Ten years ago. Perseus Arm, Allasant system, TCF *Rapier*."

Ronan scanned the records but found nothing new. "Blast."

"What did you hope to find?" asked the commander.

"Something about how they came to be disabled..." A thought occurred to him. "Can we request information from the Vexlans from the same region and time period?"

"The fish heads?" asked Julian. "I guess. Were they there at that time?"

"A Vexlan mining vessel rescued Laina's escape pod. I'd be curious to know if they noticed anything unusual."

"That's going to take longer," Julian said. "First, I have to send an information request to the Protectorate, and then the Vexlan ambassador on the Low Council. Waves of bureaucracy involved."

The commander crossed his arms. "The only times I've known you to explain problems in detail is when you wanted to impress me by getting around them."

Julian smiled. "Well, it just so happens that I'm owed a favor by the Vexlan ambassador over a shipment of rare wines I *may* have steered their way sometime back. I was hoping this might look favorably on me when it comes to determining any future disciplinary action?"

Alaric gripped Julian's shoulder. Tight.

"Or, I could do it for the good of the Legion."

"That's more like it."

Alaric returned to his chair while Ronan paced, wondering whether his hunch would pay off.

It took longer than he wanted, but eventually Julian pulled through. Ronan and the commander looked over the information. It mentioned a mining ship in the Allasant system. They had picked up two distinct Alcubierre-related anomalies, then responded to a distress signal. Then they picked up a transit drive explosion. By the time they arrived at the wreckage site, another Legion ship had arrived to collect survivors.

Three days later, an escape pod was discovered and retrieved. The occupant was later dropped off on Allasant, but it made no mention of his or her species. That only made sense.

But that wasn't what was most interesting in the report.

He backed up the report and pointed out the relevant passage. "The Vexlan captain reported the transit signature of *another* ship in the vicinity of the explosion...leaving."

"Perhaps they were coming to the distress signal and fled the explosion?" said Julian.

Ronan scowled. "Then why not return? Help look for survivors? They arrived to help once, but returning a second time was too much trouble? Also, the *Rapier* recorded no other vessel in the vicinity when the explosion occurred."

"It is curious," the commander agreed. "Do they know what kind of ship it was?"

Julian shook his head. "Nope. But the signature type

was large, consistent with a top line ship of midrange size. Something similar to the *Rapier*."

That was perhaps the most confusing part. Such ships were not typically made for civilian use, and Allasant was a remote colony off the common trade routes, with no military presence.

"Julian, I'd like you to make this investigation your priority for the time being," said Commander Corvus. "Contact the Senate and access High Council records for that time period. I want a list of all such ships docking at stations or starports within a hundred light-years of Allasant the day before and after the disaster. We may yet be able to identify our Good Samaritan and find out why they got cold feet."

Ronan nodded, though he suspected the commander doubted the ship's intentions as much as he did. Something about this smelled of a conspiracy, but the shape of it still eluded him.

Alaric crossed his arms over his chest. "Regardless, this has reminded me of the human's importance. We must ensure that she is brought safely to the Colony Fleet. The Triumvirate will want to weigh in on what we do next. Lieutenant Hawking, contact the fleet to arrange for a special council, and tell our guest, the Charon prince, that we won't have time to stay at his planet."

"Yes, Commander." Hawk started typing on the glowing keyboard in front of him, then sent a message to Alanna to inform the prince of his hasty drop off. It would likely upset the king of that world, but they had more important problems to worry about than the pricked pride of one world's ruler.

"Let me know what you hear from the High Council," Ronan told Julian. He turned to leave, only to come face-to-face with a very unhappy Charon prince. He had gotten here *very* quickly. His own garments had been damaged, and he looked quite out of place in a spare Legion uniform.

"I was told that you'd be sending me home *alone?* I made it quite clear that my brother, the king, will want to give his thanks for my rescue. Are you denying our hospitality?"

Ronan kept his diplomacy up as best he could. "We had no intention of denying His Majesty's hospitality, but we are facing a crisis of our own and cannot afford to go with you."

Hawk turned in his seat to face the prince. "Your brother has agreed to send a ship to meet us when we come to Charon's orbit."

"Very well," the prince said. "Have the human female I paid for ready to attend to me."

This was met with silence by everyone on the bridge. Ronan's hands curled into fists. Julian and Hawk tried to make themselves as unnoticeable as possible.

"As I told you before, she was sold to you under false pretenses. Those who did so had no authorization, and they are being punished for their actions."

The prince looked over Ronan's shoulder. "I see that includes continuing to serve aboard your bridge?"

"Extra shifts, and all time off spent in the brig while I consider a final punishment," said the commander, stepping forward. "We find it does wonders for discipline."

"We are willing to compensate you for your inconvenience," Ronan added. "Well beyond your refunded credits."

The prince lifted his chin. "And if that does not satisfy me?"

"Then I invoke *Domina Persea*, as I said I would."

The Charon prince smiled. "I accept."

"Very well. This way." Ronan stormed past him as he left the bridge.

"I've always wanted to fight one of the famed Terran cyborgs," said the prince, following behind. "You will provide an interesting challenge."

Ronan smirked. He was going to take far too much delight in pounding this smug prince's face into the ground.

He led the prince to a large physical training room down on the crew deck, where there was a square mat five meters by five meters in size. Ronan stood at the edge of the mat.

The prince wasn't impressed with the venue. "I was at least expecting an audience."

"Do you wish for more admirers, or do you wish to win your prize?" taunted Ronan.

"I see no reason why I cannot have both. What is it to be? Swords? Staffs?"

"Fists."

The prince slid into a fighting stance. "A purist. I admire that."

Ronan glanced at the golden-skinned Charon. His urge to pummel the man was almost overpowering. There were many reasons for this, the thought of him possessing Laina and forcing her to do his bidding not the least among them. The hope Laina represented to all the Terran races was somehow secondary to that.

Raising his fists, Ronan danced forward a few steps. The battle began.

CHAPTER 17

Ark Chronicle Entry 209-8

Graywalkers are still something of a mystery within the Protectorate. They thrive on the bioelectric life force of living creatures, which not only keeps them alive, but enhances their existence, makes them more intelligent for a time. More alive, if you will. But they absorb it slowly, rather than all at once. Regular energy can sustain them, but eventually it makes them dull-witted and more animal-like, acting on instinct only.

Because they are intelligent, there are those who have tried to work with them in the past, to strike bargains with them to use them as a weapon against others. This does not often work out in their favor.

Today, they are rarely encountered. Special precautions are taken by most ships to avoid them, and an energy web is easily avoided once detected. There are people hired by the Protectorate who specifically hunt them, using ships with special equipment to kill them, and as of the mid-2500s on the Terran calendar, their numbers are considered to be at an all-time low. As a result, the threat of them is minimal, but

Laina listened to her stomach grumble for what felt like the tenth time. Where was Ronan? He was supposed to bring some food back.

She realized that a lot of her time on board the *Orion* had been spent thinking about food. Then again, anyone who had spent weeks eating Nubran fermented vegetables enhanced with protein paste for flavor would feel the same as her.

She climbed off the bed and got dressed before she called for him over the comm, only there was no answer. That was worrying. She then called for Alanna, but it took the woman longer than expected to answer.

"Yes?" Alanna sounded distracted. She heard some kind of commotion in the background.

"Is everything okay? Ronan's supposed to be here, and he's been gone for an hour. Is something happening?"

"He's, um... Stand by." Now she was certain there was some kind of commotion going on.

She tried the door panel, but it was still locked to Ronan's authorization.

"Alanna, can you unlock the door for me?"

"That would not be advisable at the moment." Laina heard a grunt, a yell, and a crash. Someone cheered in the background.

"What was...? Wait a minute. It's him and the prince, isn't it?"

There was a pause. "Ronan is...in intense negotiations regarding your servitude to the prince of Charon."

"Negotiations my ass, Alanna. Let me out."

There was a click and a beep before the door opened. Laina almost fell into the empty hallway. Already she could hear the distant sounds of fighting. A crewman ran by, apologizing for almost running into her, a grin on his face. Laina followed him toward the noise, almost certain of what she was going to find when she got there.

She skidded to a halt at the doorway the crewman had ducked into and looked inside. Half the *Orion* crew had to be there, gathered around a large clearing in the center, where Ronan and the Charon prince were punching and kicking each other viciously.

"Oh my God," she groaned. Both men were already panting and bleeding. How long had they been at this? Judging by the crowd that was still growing—two women now pushed past her to join the throng—it might have been a while.

"Ronan!" she shouted. This was mistaken for a cheer, and the audience began chanting, *Ronan! Ronan! Ronan!* He raised his head at her cry, and it cost him his advantage. The prince tackled him to the ground.

This was ridiculous. She rushed toward them, but someone grabbed her by the shoulders and dragged her back.

"You will not interfere." She tensed as she recognized the voice. It was the one Ronan had called Erik. The one who'd tried to kill her.

For a moment she was afraid of what he might do, but there was no way he'd try anything with all these witnesses around, even if they were focused on the match.

"Ronan fights for possession of you against the other male. You cannot interfere," Erik explained. His voice was rough, but at least he was no longer growling like a mad dog.

"That's exactly *why* I'm trying to interfere. This is insane. They don't need to fight to settle this."

"But they do. The Charon prince would not release his claim over you, despite being offered compensation. Ronan invoked *Domina Persea*, a Charon right of contesting ownership and other legal claims, to keep you on this ship."

Whatever rage had possessed Erik before seemed to have passed, or at least it was under control. He now spoke in the same formal tone as Ronan and Alanna. She noticed that the huge man refused to look her in the eye as he spoke, but she didn't know if that was out of hatred or guilt.

"Are you telling me there was *no* other way to resolve this dispute?"

Erik looked toward the fight, and while he didn't smile, he did seem pleased with what he saw going on in the ring. "I'm sure there are, but none are quite as...satisfying."

Laina groaned. "I'm on board a ship full of space Vikings."

She looked around the throng, and it seemed the women were just as into this blood sport as the men. Was this going to be mankind's legacy? To fade off into extinction, leaving behind creations that lusted for combat as much as their creators had?

"You've put Ronan at a disadvantage," Erik said, keeping his hold on her, but directing her toward the ongoing match. "He cannot be distracted from the fight or you will end up leaving with the prince in a few hours. Is that what you want?"

"He's right." Alanna had removed herself from the crowd and joined them, her cheeks flushing as she watched Ronan and the prince fight.

"But he's getting *hurt*," Laina protested.

"He will heal," said Alanna. "No one will die from this contest."

Ronan had managed to break out of the prince's attempt at a lock and was back on his feet. His lip was split, and he was swaying a little as he dodged the Charon's next jab, then responded with a vicious uppercut, catching the prince off guard. He fell flat on his back, but he leaped back to his feet just as quickly. He wiped a bit of blood from the corner of his mouth and smiled.

Good Lord, was he *enjoying* this?

The Charon shot forward in a blur and slammed a fist into Ronan's jaw, followed by two more blows to the chest. Ronan dropped to one knee and spit blood onto the mat as his opponent backed up and waited for him to recover.

When he got back to his feet, a fierce glow grew within Ronan's eyes, and the silver around his irises shone even brighter. He nodded to his opponent, as if thanking him for the chance to catch his breath, then launched into him with a vicious series of attacks that made the prince's seem like it had been in slow motion. Ronan avoided every counter the prince could throw up in his defense, landing blow after blow, working his way behind him, disorienting him with an elbow to the back of the head, then spinning around and following that up with two more blows to the face.

Ronan then stepped back, returning the favor and allowing the prince a chance to recover. The Charon swayed in his spot, dazed and bloody, then dropped to one knee. The audience waited in breathless silence for his next move. But instead of standing back up, he slapped his hand against the mat twice, and the gym erupted into cheers.

The prince had conceded defeat.

The shouts of Ronan's name began to calm as the victor walked over to the prince and helped him back to his feet.

The prince clasped Ronan's shoulder. "The rumors are true —you fight like an azagoth."

"I admit, you were tougher than I had expected," Ronan replied.

"I have the best combat enhancements credits can buy," the prince said, testing one of his arms. "Clearly it was not enough."

"It was impressive, nonetheless."

The prince nodded his thanks for the compliment. "I will accept the return of my credits, but I refuse any additional compensation."

"Then the claim is settled. The human female is mine."

Mine. It was just one word, but it was a reminder to Laina that despite her supposed importance, and despite Ronan's feelings for her, she was on some level still considered a possession. Laina stared at the two men, wanting to strangle them both for fighting over her, but at least it was over.

"What's an azagoth?" Laina asked Alanna, needing to think about something else.

"A creature from the Golia system. Some fools try to domesticate them as guard pets. You do not want to face one. They are frightening, even to me," Alanna admitted.

Laina ran to Ronan, clutching his bare arm as he took a towel from a crewman and wiped his face. The cloth came away bloody, but to her amazement, the cuts and bruises were already starting to fade. But he seemed even more tired than before. The crewman gave him an injector filled with a blue substance, which he pressed into his shoulder.

"Regen fatigue," he said, sighing in relief as the shot took effect. "Prince Leif broke several bones and ruptured at least two organs, I believe. But don't tell him that."

"No need to hide the fact," said the prince, already next

to them. "I felt at least one organ burst in our battle, and the crack of bone is distinctive in your species. Were you not a cyborg, I'd be concerned for your well-being." The prince then turned to Laina. "Ah, hello again, my young Terran. I am afraid you are doomed never to know the pleasures I had intended to bestow upon you."

"I'm sure I'll live," said Laina. To her surprise, the prince no longer seemed quite as hurt as before.

The prince must have noticed this, because he held up an empty injector of his own. "While we do not possess the cyborgs' natural healing abilities, I can afford the best in Elysian biotechnology." The prince now became distracted again, this time by Alanna. "Ah, we meet again," the prince purred, sidling up to her. "I understand you will be the one escorting me back to my people?"

Laina stared in a mix of surprise and amusement as she saw Alanna's cheeks redden.

"I am head of security, so I am commanding the honor guard, yes."

"By the gods, you are lovely." Leif raised a hand to touch Alanna's cheek. Ronan, along with every other male the room, stiffened as though they expected Alanna to break his hand before he could touch her. Instead, she let his fingers caress her. In fact, she took hold of his hand with hers.

"Your skin is very warm," she said.

"A side effect of my healing," the prince said. "Though, I have no doubt that you are adding to it."

Her blush deepened.

"Do my compliments offend you?" he asked.

"No," Alanna said simply.

The prince turned to Ronan. "I would be willing to

forgo my credits entirely if you would allow this one to join me in the human's place," he said with a grin.

The prince's grin turned to a frown, then to a look of agony as Alanna took the hand against her cheek and twisted it slowly, locking the entire arm, and forced him to the ground. The prince cried out in pain as she applied pressure to the elbow.

"That, however, *does* offend me," she said.

The prince quickly tapped the floor. "Apologies! I meant no harm."

"And yet here you are, having fought to own one woman, and then trying to bargain for another." Alanna leaned down close to his ear and said, "I belong to no one."

She let him go, and the prince gasped in relief. It took him a moment to get over the embarrassment and regain his composure.

The commander's voice came in over the comm. "We are approaching the Charon system. All hands, to your stations."

"Well, it seems that you have made your position clear," the prince said to Alanna, the smile returning to his face. "But you understand you've only made yourself more intriguing to me."

"That is your problem, not mine." She turned her back on him and left the gym.

Ronan put his uniform top back on and addressed those still in attendance. "You heard the commander. Return to your stations." He then went to the comm panel by the door and addressed the bridge. "Have we been hailed by the Charon yet?"

"As soon as we dropped out of transit," said Alaric. "They have a shuttle en route to rendezvous. Lieutenant Vela, assemble your honor guard."

"Yes, Commander."

Prince Leif's open smile turned to a frown as Alanna walked away without giving him another look.

Until his poor choice of words, the prince had had a curious effect on Alanna. And she didn't seem the type to be easily moved by her emotions. It made Laina wonder.

The slight shake of a ship docking with the *Orion* jolted Laina out of her train of thought. Ronan clasped her hand and led her out of the training room, taking her to the docking station.

"We may as well see our new friend's ship."

"Friend?" said Laina. "You beat the hell out of him."

"And he beat the hell out of me, as you put it. But it was with honor, and that means something to his people. He holds no ill will toward me, nor I to him. Not anymore."

She could see the Charon shuttle through the port windows overlooking the docking ramp. It was a similar pleasure yacht to the one she had been on with Leif. A sigh of relief escaped her as she realized she wasn't going to leave with the prince. He seemed nice enough, but she had grown attached to the *Orion*. And to Ronan...

"That's odd," said Ronan. "They're already departing?"

It was true, the bridge between their ships was retracting.

"I would have expected some degree of ceremony before they departed. I wonder—"

The comm sprang to life. "This is the bridge. We've received a distress signal from a passenger liner on the edge of Charon territory. As we can arrive faster than any of their ships in the system, the Charon government has requested our aid. We will be returning to transit once we are clear of the Charon shuttle. Emergency teams on standby."

"Do you need to go?" asked Laina.

"Let me check." Ronan went to a nearby panel and hailed the bridge. "Commander, is my presence required?"

Alaric's voice came back over the comm. "It appears the liner's drive malfunctioned, but nothing critical. We should be fine. Lieutenant Alanna and her honor guard will remain on board the Charon shuttle. We'll return for them once this has been taken care of. I understand you took quite a beating. We can do without you for a few hours."

Ronan turned the comm off. "Come. As I recall, we never did get you that dessert you asked for." Ronan took her along a passageway of the ship she had not seen before.

"We don't have to eat in your room?" It wasn't that she didn't like eating in his room, but it always felt like an imposition, like she was requesting room service in a place that was most definitely not a hotel.

"I believe it's safe for you to move about the ship more freely."

"Are you sure?"

"Word of your importance has reached everyone by now, and anyone who found your presence objectionable knows they would have to bring such grievances to me. And seeing as how I handled the Charon prince..."

Laina supposed that would make anyone think twice about bringing up a complaint.

They entered the same mess hall that Alanna had taken her to. Perhaps it was the only one on the ship. She wasn't exactly sure how many people made up the crew, after all.

He had her take a seat, and then he went to the food synthesizer. She'd seen these on vids before, though she'd never used one. What they produced had all the qualities of the genuine article, but the food was built from the ground up using base chemicals and bioprinting technology. She couldn't even begin to understand how it actually worked.

Ronan collected a tray with food and joined her at the table, taking a seat opposite her. He placed in front of her two of the chocolate desserts she'd had when she was here before.

She grinned and was about to dig in when it occurred to her what this actually meant. She looked up to Ronan, who had a slight smile on his face.

"I am first officer on board the *Orion*," he said. "Things do not stay secret from me for long. Alanna was right to let you out. I'm beginning to see that." He began to eat his own food. "I wanted to explain to you why I had to fight the prince. No doubt it seemed like some kind of primitive masculine claiming and domination."

"The thought had crossed my mind," said Laina.

"There is some truth to it, but there is more. Because freeborns hold no protective status, right or wrong, you are legally our property, to do with as we see fit."

"*Right or wrong?*" Laina asked. "How can it be anything but wrong?"

Ronan shrugged. "Different species behave different ways, with different values and beliefs. Even basic biology can change how they view the universe. Take the Draxon." Laina's gut tightened every time she heard their name. "They are one of the oldest species in the galaxy and our greatest friends and allies. It is because of them that the cyborgs were given what rights they have within the Protectorate."

They're also the reason humans were deemed to be your property, Laina thought.

"Yet despite their appearance, they are biologically very different from us. Their population is mostly made up of nonreproductive drones. The idea of individual rights is impossible for them to conceive, because they do not see themselves as individuals. The Draxon have controlled the

Perseus Arm where Earth was located for millennia, so when a ruling had to be made by the High Council, their laws had to apply."

The reminder of the awful truth turned the dessert in her mouth to ash. She grimaced.

"Charon is also in Draxon space and has long had dealings with the Draxon, so they have developed similar views. What that means is you are a commodity. Something to be bought, sold, or stolen. I don't want the Charon getting any ideas that you are something they can simply take from us. The fleet is currently close to their territory, and we wish to maintain a positive relationship with them. It could easily be shattered if the king decided he wanted to claim you as tribute and we refused."

"Tribute?" Laina's appetite managed to return, and she had more of her decadent treat.

Ronan watched her before he spoke. "On Charon, it's a type of sacrifice."

"*Sacrifice?*"

Ronan smirked. "A sexual sacrifice. Charons enjoy sex on a fundamental level. When it comes to trade deals or foreign visitors, they tend to demand a female to be presented to their king for his personal pleasure."

Laina's jaw dropped. "But that's...barbaric!"

"Among the Charon it is quite normal, and their women consider it an honor. But it does make things difficult when species from other territories try to deal with them. Prince Leif was going to offer you to his brother for one night as tribute before reclaiming you for his own bed."

Laina dropped her fork and sighed. "Okay, so I'll just skip saying goodbye to Prince Leif when we go back to pick up Alanna. Better safe than sorry, right?"

Ronan's deep chuckle made her glare at him.

"It's not funny."

"I believe it is, little one. After all, I made you *my* tribute earlier today."

Laina gave him a sly look. "Oh really? I seem to recall *you* were sacrificed first."

His wicked grin made her flush. The way he was looking at her, he was probably thinking the same thing and wanted an encore.

"Finish your meal so we can—"

The lights in the room went dark, and Laina was thrown from her seat, striking something hard and almost losing consciousness. A red glow filled the room as an alarm blared to life.

"Transit failure," the ship's computer announced. "All hands, brace!"

Laina could barely see around her, but she grabbed the nearest thing rooted to the ground, which happened to be a table leg. The ship shuddered again, though not as bad as before. Then with a heavy thump that bumped her high in the air and dropped her like a rock, the ship went still.

Laina got up from the floor at the same time he did. "Ronan? What's happening?"

"I don't know. Stay close to me." He helped her up, and they left the mess hall, along with some of the dazed crew. The hall was dark, except for the red emergency lights. Ronan accessed the nearest computer panel for a status report, reading the information far faster than Laina could take it in.

"Ship's lost power. Alaric is contacting the Charon shuttle for assistance. Engine room reports... That's impossible."

"What is it?"

"We hit an energy web." His hand tightened around hers. "Another graywalker. We have to go! Follow me!"

The ship vibrated as they sprinted through the corridor. The lights then died and came on again, as if something had passed through all its wires and circuits, sucking the energy from them for just a moment.

"Damnation. They're already boarding," Ronan growled as they reached a part of the ship she'd never seen before.

The armory.

Alaric, Hawk, Julian, and Valeria were already there, equipping the crew with large pulse rifles.

"Remember," said Valeria, "focused weapons fire has no effect on graywalkers. Set your rifles to maximum stun, widest possible beam, zero pulse."

"Widest beam *and* zero pulse?" one of the crewmen said. "What good will that do?"

"A pulse of energy will just pass through it, but if it's encountering a steady stream, it can't help but absorb some of what it's given. One gun will do nothing, but if a half dozen of us can hit it from multiple sides, we may stand a chance. But I won't lie to you. It's still not much of one."

The commander addressed them all. "Sweep the ship from stem to stern. Call in if you encounter the graywalker so we can converge on it. Keep to your units. No one is to walk this ship alone. Understood?"

The crew barked an acknowledgment, and four teams of six left the armory. Ronan and Laina went up to the commander.

"What I wouldn't give to have a detachment of Centurions on board right now," Alaric muttered.

"In all my years with the Legion, I've never once run

into a graywalker," said Ronan. "Now we've run into two in a matter of days?"

Alaric nodded. "It is an odd coincidence. If it *is* a coincidence. They've also learned some new tricks, it seems. The energy web didn't go up until it was too late to avoid it. I suspect the same happened to the Charon ship earlier."

"What about the passenger vessel?"

"A decoy signal. Another new trick." He handed Ronan a pulse rifle. "We can speculate about this later. For now, protect the human at all costs. Make your stand near the escape pods. If it seems like we'll lose the ship, you must get her to safety. Valeria, Hawk, and Julian will stay with you."

Ronan saluted with his fist. Alaric then handed Laina a pulse rifle as well.

"Everyone pulls their weight on this ship," said the commander.

"Besides," said Hawk, "those settings wouldn't harm any of us."

Julian pushed the barrel away from his general direction. "Still, try not to point it at me, would you?"

"Have you heard from the Charon shuttle?"

"They are en route to pick up anyone who evacuates, but they refuse to engage."

"They wouldn't be any good anyway," said Julian.

Hawk agreed. "Just more lambs for the slaughter."

Ronan looked around. "Where's Erik?"

"He's in the engine room, preparing a manual overload of the transit drive," said the commander. "The energy web knocked out bridge controls, and I will not allow the *Orion* to become a graywalker death trap or spawning ground."

Laina gasped. "You're going to blow up the ship?"

"If I must. Now go. You have your orders."

Ronan led his team and Laina from the armory toward

the escape pods, but none of this sat well with Laina. Nor did it seem to sit well with the others. She saw the resigned looks on their faces. They were prepared to leave a man behind, but none of them wanted to. It was like the night she lost her parents all over again. Shoved into an escape pod, forced to leave everyone behind. Always being protected. Always being pushed away. Always for her own good.

But as they marched down the halls, pulse rifles pointed around each corner and pressing forward, something didn't feel right. She didn't know much about the graywalkers. Much of what was passed along felt more like spooky stories meant to spice up boring meals.

She knew they used a ship's transit drive to create their energy webs. First they drained the life of the crew, and then they controlled the last one like a puppet to move the ship to a distant location and start things all over again. It was part of the reason they were so hard to find.

But the commander had said they'd been learning new tricks. And when that graywalker had tried to kill her, she'd had a glimpse of how the creatures thought. She was struck with an idea that felt all too plausible to her.

"Ronan, we have to get Erik."

Ronan looked at her with a frown. "We cannot. The *Orion* is most likely lost. He is our only chance that her legacy is not one of causing more tragedy."

"You don't understand. I don't think the graywalker is going to go after the crew. I think it's going to go after *him*."

The group came to a halt. "What makes you say that?" asked Valeria.

"I'm not sure. But the commander said that they're learning new tricks, right? And when that graywalker tried to kill me before, I could feel that intelligence in it. I think it's anticipated the commander's plan. It needs the ship, right? The last thing it wants is for it to self-destruct."

Ronan looked down the hall, where they were supposed to go, then back toward the engine room. "We can't. Your safety is our top priority. Once you're off this ship, I can return with the others and—"

She'd had no choice that night with her parents ten years ago, but maybe she did this time. She shouldered her pulse rifle and sprinted in the direction Ronan had been looking. She didn't care how important they thought she was. She had to try to save the ship. Save the crew.

"Laina!" she heard Ronan shout from behind her. He was fast, but she was faster this time. "Blast and damnation. Legionnaires, we move. Double-time!"

By the time they caught up with her she was at the lift, but it was out of commission. The artificial gravity, however, was only at half strength, so she was able to jump down the emergency shaft to the engine level without using the ladder, just before Ronan could grab her.

The red emergency lights soon gave way to the pale green of the ship's drive, so at least she knew she had to be close.

"Erik!" she called out. "Erik! Where are you?"

The next wide-open room held a series of four cylindrical machines, all controlled from a single main station and several satellite stations. But the engine room itself was empty, except for one massive figure working at the main control panel.

"Erik? We have to get you out of here. It's not safe."

Erik turned around, and Laina gasped. Erik's eyes glowed white, and he looked decades older.

"*Hek-k-k-k-k-k... such energy...*" Erik said, taking a step toward her.

Ronan and the others caught up with her and saw the same thing. Ronan leveled his pulse gun and yelled, "*Open fire!*"

Valeria and the others followed suit, casting an overlapping blue electrical field in Erik's direction. Laina hesitated, but only a moment before she added her weapon to the barrage.

Erik hissed as the field enveloped him, clawing at himself in agony. The pain soon got to be too much, and the giant crashed to the ground, unconscious.

"Keep firing!" yelled Ronan. They all kept their wide beams on Erik's body, but as soon as he had fallen the body stopped twitching.

"Stop!" Laina called out, afraid that the beams might still kill Erik in his weakened state. She rushed over to his body and turned him over. "Erik?" she said, opening an eyelid. There was no glow there. She checked for a pulse. "Erik? Wake up."

The giant stirred and opened his eyes. "Stupid freeborn. Go!" Erik bellowed with what strength he had left in him.

"Not without you. The graywalker wants you so you can't blow up the ship."

Erik raised his head and saw the others there. "I felt it flee my body," he said. "But it seemed more annoyed than injured. Help me up." Ronan came over and helped Erik to his feet. "We must destroy the ship," he said.

"It will just come back for you if you try," said Laina. A light came on in her head when she said it aloud. "So that's *exactly* what you should do."

"Are you mad?" asked Ronan.

"Mad as hell," said Laina. "The last graywalker died when it tried to kill me. I don't know why, but it must have something to do with this." She held up her hand and the markings etched into her palm. "It was attracted to me, even when it possessed Erik. I could draw it into a trap, maybe."

Ronan shook his head. "I can't allow that. You're too important."

"Everyone keeps saying that! My parents said it before they threw me into an escape pod. They died protecting me. Now you want to do the same thing." Ronan looked uncomfortable at what she said, but that didn't stop her. Let him feel some of what she was suffering through right now. "What about me? No one ever thinks about what happens next. Do I spend the next decade on the run until someone else realizes how important I am to some great cause? I'm done running. If you believe there's some grand destiny wrapped up in this," she said, holding up her hand again, "then you damn well better fight to protect it."

Ronan's eyes narrowed, and for a moment Laina thought the man would just throw her over his shoulder and storm off to the escape pods after all. He then looked to Erik.

"Ensign, take the others above deck. Rendezvous with the commander and the others and prepare to abandon ship."

Erik looked confused. "You're not coming?"

He looked to Laina. "We're staying. Now go—that's an order."

Erik nodded and began to leave with the others. Valeria, however, did not move. "But what of the Ark? We can't afford to lose it."

"We won't. I won't let anything happen to Laina or the Ark."

When they left, Ronan began to access the computer to set the ship's transit drive into overload. He looked around cautiously, as if expecting the spectral energy monster to appear at any moment from any direction.

"What now?" he asked.

Laina didn't have a good answer. "It'll come for one of us, I'm sure."

"I will set the reactor to overload in ten minutes. That should be enough time for the crew to escape." He finished typing commands and pressed one last button.

"*Warning. Destruct sequence initiated. Ten minutes remaining.*"

Laina's heart leaped in her chest. He'd really done it. "I hope this works..."

"As do I," said Ronan. He looked away from her when she tried to make eye contact, then turned back to face her. "You should know something, in case this stratagem fails. When I said I wanted you to leave the ship because you are too important?"

"Yes?"

Ronan approached her. "I was not referring to the anomaly in your hand or any grand destiny for our people. I meant you are too important to *me*. I meant I could not bear the thought of a universe without you in it." He placed his hands on her shoulders. "And if we are to die here together, I plan to put my life before yours until the end."

Laina's eyes began to well up. "Ronan..."

"*Warning. Destruct sequence initiated. Nine minutes remaining.*"

Laina looked up at the speakers. So much was happening so fast. "I don't want to act as if these are our last moments together. We can beat this thing. I know it."

Ronan nodded. "I believe in you."

Hek-k-k-k-k-k...

That sound...coming straight into her mind.

"It's here."

She turned and for the second time in her life she saw a graywalker. It rose up through the floor, dark as a black hole, almost seeming to bend light around it at the edges, yet she could see through it as well. As it approached, it shifted from having one appendage to three to five, as if having physical form was a concept it barely understood.

Its empty eye sockets narrowed at the two of them. Ronan tried to step in front of her, but Laina wouldn't allow it.

Hek-k-k-k-k-k...such energy...

"That's right, I'm full of energy," Laina crooned. "All-you-can-eat buffet, right here." The graywalker began to drift along toward her on invisible currents of air. She waved at the graywalker and then noticed the marks on her hand were...glowing. *What the hell? Does it sense it?*

The graywalker was almost on top of her now.

"Warning. Destruct sequence initiated. Eight minutes remaining."

"Um...Ronan? If this works, you know how to shut down the self-destruct, right? I'd hate for this to be all for nothing."

The graywalker was almost on top of her now, reaching out with three or perhaps four hands—

—and grabbed Ronan instead.

Laina spun around as the black energy flew past her and dove inside of Ronan. He screamed and grabbed either side of his head, as if the creature was tearing his mind apart.

"NO!"

Ronan turned to her, his eyes now glowing pale white.

"Hek-k-k-k-k-k... Yes... Shut down... Like thissss..."

The possessed Ronan quickly tapped a code into the

computer.

"*Attention. Destruct sequence aborted.*"

"Oh God, no. *Why?* Why didn't you come after me, you monster?"

Ronan turned toward her, eyes glowing brighter. "*Hek-k-k-k-k-k...in time.*"

Laina raised her pulse rifle, but she realized it wouldn't do anything. It had taken five to drive it out of Erik, and he had already been somewhat drained.

The pulse rifle dropped to the ground with a clatter.

"Ronan, please. Fight it. You have to fight it."

"*No Ronan... Hek-k-k-k-k-k...*" the monster hissed in Ronan's voice. "*No more...*"

"You lie! Erik was fine once we got you out of him. Leave him alone and take me instead."

"*Soon...soon... They want you...*"

Laina stepped closer. "Listen to me, Ronan. I know you're in there. If you can hear me, please fight back. Please." As she approached, the possessed form didn't seem to know what to do, yet it stood its ground.

"I'm sorry," she said. "You were supposed to be safe. I was supposed to be protecting you." She blinked away the tears growing in her eyes as she came right up to him. Ronan hissed with the graywalker's voice.

"But if this is how it ends, then there is no place in the galaxy I'd rather be than right here with you." Her words were hoarse with emotion, and her heart swelled inside her chest. She cupped his face in her hands. The graywalker seemed like it wanted to flee, yet it was rooted to the ground against its will.

"I love you," she whispered.

Laina kissed Ronan on the lips, and the world exploded with light.

CHAPTER 18

Ark Chronicle Entry 50-35

This is John Roberts...one of my final entries. As I near the end of my life, I should remind you that there were those of us on Earth who supported the synthetics. We have always been there, since the first generation, fighting to have them recognized as the equals of humankind, not our tools. But our voices were drowned out by those who hid behind arguments of national security, philosophical debates over sapience, and bickering about finer points of law. But in reality, it boiled down to a combination of greed and power.

Toward the end, even our supporters knew a conflict between the two groups was inevitable, and we began making plans to safeguard as much of humanity's legacy as we could.

Then we were approached by an organization who wanted to help us. When Earth fell, they were the ones who saved what we had collected, helped smuggle as many of us out of Sol as they could, and in doing so, they provided us so with much more.

Even now I hesitate to mention them by name. Not even

the Protectorate knows of their existence. This might worry some, but I have no doubt as to their intentions.

They work in the shadows, but it is only so they can bring light into the darkness.

IN ALL THE YEARS HE'D TRAVELED AMONG THE STARS, Ronan never thought he'd witness a miracle. But there in the engine room, trapped behind the iron will of a graywalker puppet master that was draining his very life, he became a believer in something greater than science and biology.

The second the white light enveloped them, he was flooded with visions. He saw thousands of years of history play out as though he had been there. The sun set over a trio of pyramids, birdsong cried out deep in Amazon forests, civilizations rose and fell again and again. And with it came the realization that the Legion he served and the Colony Fleet he'd vowed to protect were just one of many such triumphs. It too would someday pass and foreshadow the next rise that would follow it.

And we believed we were superior... How wrong he had been. Humans had built their world up from the primordial ooze and the crushing darkness. They'd built cities of light and ships that breached the sky. His people hadn't built themselves from nothing, they had built upon the shoulders of giants, and for all the evil he had seen among them, there had always been goodness there as well.

These visions left a strange feeling inside him, an easy positive feeling where anything and everything seemed possible. The surge of hope that rose inside him was over-powering.

He heard a distant scream as the light around him

burned bright, and a high-pitched whine strained his ears until he thought they would burst.

The light faded.

He was on his knees. Laina sat in front of him, also on her knees, her eyes the shimmering gray of a pale moon, her hands still on his face. She swayed and became unsteady.

"Laina," he gasped. Ronan grabbed her as she sank to the ground and pulled her against him. He was in control of himself again. There was no sign of the graywalker. Ronan cradled Laina in his arms, and for the first time he could remember, his eyes were filled with tears.

When he lifted his head to gaze around the darkened engine room, he saw that the commander had arrived, as had Valeria and the others. They were all as shocked as he was, it seemed.

"Valeria." Ronan stood on shaky legs and lifted Laina in his arms, holding her against his chest. He felt incredibly weak, but he refused to let it show.

Valeria came forward, concentrating as she felt for Laina's pulse and examined her eyes.

Julian went to the control terminal. "We need to get power restored to the ship."

"I'm afraid the damage from the energy web is too extensive," Alaric said grimly. "It seems we will have to land on Charon after all."

Julian groaned. "You mean we're going to get towed? Swell. We survive a graywalker attack, and those guys will look like the heroes."

None of the crew were pleased with this announcement. Having to play political games with Charon royalty and possibly having Protectorate representatives there would have been an irritation, and now it was unavoidable.

The commander shook his head. "The Charon have

already contacted the Silver Legion. A repair frigate from the Colony Fleet has been dispatched. But the *Orion*'s too unstable for us to remain on board. We must abandon ship. Bring everything you wish to keep. Lock down all the computers."

Outside the *Orion*, visible only through the active monitor in the engine room, was the ship the graywalker had hijacked and turned into a death trap. It had indeed once been a passenger liner, and he did not envy the job of those who would come later to study it and clear away the dead, trying to understand how these creatures were adapting to their usual precautions. It hung in space, lifeless and empty.

It was an eerie feeling to stand in the engine room of an essentially dead ship. Ronan helped lock down the computers in case someone came upon it before the repair ship arrived. The *Orion* had been his home for nearly a decade, and he didn't like the idea of leaving it behind.

He carried Laina to the docking area, already crowded with the crew of the *Orion*. While the ship carried two small shuttles and a number of fighters, the hangar bay had been damaged, and they weren't sufficient to carry the bulk of the *Orion* crew regardless. Rather than use the escape pods, they would allow the larger Charon yacht to come to their aid.

A head count was taken, and it seemed another miracle had taken place—the graywalker hadn't managed to kill anyone. Even Erik was looking younger now that his body had time to heal. Outside the airlock window, the elegant form of the Charon shuttle could be seen approaching.

Valeria sidled up next to Ronan. "I suppose there's no doubt as to what happened aboard the Charon ship now."

Ronan's lips tightened. "I suppose not."

"She killed a graywalker." The doctor shook her head. "I can't fathom the amount of energy she had to use to overwhelm a creature who feeds on energy. Or even how such a thing could work." She pondered the puzzle for a moment. "Perhaps it wasn't a matter of overwhelming them at all..."

Ronan felt an itch on his palm and turned it toward him, still clutching Laina in his arms. His eyes widened as he saw a pattern burned into his hand. "By the fleet!"

It wasn't the exact same pattern, and it was smaller, but it was unmistakably of the same origin. His fatigue caught up with him, and he feared he might let go of Laina.

The doctor saw the symbol etched into his palm and looked to Ronan. "We're going to have to talk about this."

"Later."

"Later," the doctor agreed.

A hailing signal came over the ship's speakers. "Attention *Orion*, this is the Charon royal transport *Blue Spring*. Prepare for docking."

The *Orion* had a total crew of one hundred and seventy —twenty officers and a hundred and fifty crewmen. The *Blue Spring*, however, was meant to hold a quarter that number comfortably. Still, Prince Leif had insisted that all efforts be made to accommodate everyone, going so far as to jettison expensive furniture to make more room. Even so, it would be standing room only. Ronan allowed the crew to board first, going on at the end with the rest of the command staff, carrying Laina with him.

"I hope she's not claustrophobic," Val said as the door shut behind them. Ronan supposed one small advantage of boarding last was that he and Val had a window view, through the small circular porthole covering the airlock.

The sudden burst of movement startled the passengers as the ship shot away from the *Orion* and into open space. It was disorienting at first, shooting like a star away from their home, the *Orion* growing smaller and smaller until it vanished from sight.

Though the ship's transit drive wasn't anywhere near as fast as theirs, the trip to the Charon homeworld only took them an hour or so. An announcement came on as the captain of the ship told them they were entering Charon's atmosphere. Flames licked up around the small porthole. The shuttle rattled and shook for what seemed like an eternity, which was when Laina came to and started to scream.

"Laina, be still," Ronan barked.

She covered her head with her arms. "Ronan! We're crashing—"

He gave her a gentle shake, and she raised her head to look at him. Her lovely eyes were full of fear. He set Laina down gently.

"We're safe. We had to evacuate aboard the Charon shuttle."

"What about the crew?"

"All here. You saved them. You saved everyone."

Laina looked around at the throng of people standing about her, smiling at her, some even saluting with a fist to their chest. Most notably the commander himself.

"I sent Erik to the engine room unarmed, believing he'd be ignored," said Alaric. "Graywalkers normally take out the greatest threats first. Your intuition not only saved the ensign's life, but the lives of my crew. We are in your debt."

The ship shook again as they hit the lower atmosphere. Ronan held Laina by the shoulders to keep her steady. "Laina, when I was possessed by the graywalker..."

"Yes?"

"It wanted to run. It sensed something about you that

terrified it. But I heard what you said. All of it. And because of that, I was able to stand my ground."

Laina's smile reminded him of the bright flash he'd experienced when she'd kissed him before. She looked at the crew nervously before looking back to Ronan.

"I meant what I said."

"I know."

"I'd say more, but...you know. We're not exactly alone."

Ronan smiled as the ship began to decelerate. "Easily fixed. Commander, if I could have a moment in private?"

Alaric smiled and nodded. "Legionnaires, about-face!"

Everyone within the cramped passage turned and faced away from Ronan and Laina.

"Not exactly private, but I guess it will have to do." She smiled, but he saw the tension in her eyes at being in such a cramped space hurtling toward a planet. She needed her attention focused elsewhere.

Ronan dipped his head toward hers, capturing her mouth with his. It was an excellent distraction, one he believed she desperately needed right now. She relaxed in his arms and kissed him back. He lost himself in her taste until the ship bucked as the vessel came to a jerking halt.

"Look." Ronan urged her to look out the porthole so that she could see they were safely on the platform. Laina relaxed, but a shiver rippled through her into him.

He stroked a hand down Laina's back, soothing her. The history of Earth had not been the *only* thing he'd seen while he'd been connected to Laina. He'd seen something personal as well. He lived through those final moments when she'd been pushed into the pod as a child and saw her parents die. Or so she'd thought. Helpless. Cold. Alone. Afraid. The feelings had been soul deep, the grief unending.

The hatch hissed as it cracked at the edges and then opened, a ramp descending down to the landing pad's surface. Laina squinted at the bright light of the Charon sun. It revealed faint freckles along with the bridge of her nose that he'd never noticed before in the standard lighting of the ship. Her eyes seemed more blue than silver now that she stood on the planet's surface.

Humans were never meant to live in space, part of him thought. They belonged someplace like here, beneath a warm and life-giving sun.

Ronan let his eyes adjust, and he and Laina walked off the ship, followed by the crew of the *Orion.* Beyond them stood a group of fifty Charon palace guards.

One Charon stepped forward and spoke as he watched the group closely. "You are part of the Silver Legion?" he asked in Galactic Common.

"Yes." Ronan kept a hand tight around Laina's waist. He did not want anyone on this planet to get any ideas about her, so Ronan watched them all carefully.

"Welcome to Charon. His Majesty offers you and your crew safe passage and accommodation while repairs are conducted on your ship." The Charon warrior then lowered his gaze to Laina. He frowned. "We were informed you have a freeborn with you, belonging to the prince. Is this her? She is smaller than the rest of you."

There was a hushed murmur that rippled through the Charon guards as the word *freeborn* was spoken. The fact that they were hunted by their own creations made them the stuff of folklore on some worlds. It was a sad legacy, to say the least.

"The human female's ownership has been contested," Julian announced, stepping forward. "I..." His voice changed to match the tone of the Charon, and he stood taller. "I was not authorized to sell her. Ronan, our second in command, challenged Prince Leif to *Domina Persea*, and was victorious."

The guard's eyes widened. "He defeated Prince Leif in combat?"

"It was a fair fight, and the prince conceded to me," Ronan added. His hand tightened more about Laina's waist. She had been uncharacteristically quiet, but he was glad this time. He understood Charon culture, and for the sake of protocol, he needed to assert his control over her, at least in front of the guards. Her silence helped make that convincing.

"What does the prince say of this?" the guard asked, still skeptical.

A voice boomed out, and they turned back toward the ship. "The prince says that this man fights like an azagoth, but an honorable one, and not quite as ugly."

Prince Leif stood at the top of the ramp with the last of the crew disembarking. Alanna and the Legion's honor guard stood behind him, wearing bright silver chest plates. The prince stepped down the ramp, grinning, and soon joined the guards waiting for him below.

"Then we recognize your ownership." The guard waved to his men. "Please, come with us. We will escort you back to the palace. There will be rooms provided for you to rest and food to eat."

"Thank you," Ronan said. "Your hospitality does your people credit and will not be forgotten."

The guard nodded and left with the prince, while his fellows formed a loose escort around the *Orion* crew.

"Everything is going to be all right," he murmured in Laina's ear. He only prayed it was the truth.

WE RECOGNIZE YOUR OWNERSHIP. GEE, THANKS. WHAT an honor.

Laina clung to Ronan. She felt silly for doing so, but Ronan had reminded her of the differences of the culture on this world, and she needed to play the part to avoid complications.

She'd learned that the king of Charon was very close to the High Council representatives here. Every homeworld had ambassadors, both to help mediate issues concerning galactic law and to act as the Protectorate's voice. Ronan was concerned that the information held in the anomaly on her hand, what the doctor had called the Ark, might create a legal quagmire that they were not prepared to deal with at this time—though he didn't explain to her what that quagmire might be. It had to be bad, whatever it was.

Laina focused on trying to remain calm as the crew of the *Orion* followed the Charon guard from the landing field. In the distance, she saw a shining city built of stone and glass that winked and sparkled like sunlight on the water.

At the end of the landing field there was a sleek opentop land cruiser that could hold a dozen people. It seemed to use an antigrav cushion to move rather than wheels or jets, so at least they were in for a smooth ride. More of these vehicles pulled up to transport the rest of the crew in batches.

Some of the guards boarded first while the head guard spoke to the driver. Commander Alaric boarded the first cruiser with Valeria and several of the command staff. Ronan and Laina boarded the next along with several others, including Prince Leif. Alanna and her security team were right behind and would board the shuttle after them.

"You're without our honor guard," Ronan noted.

The prince smiled. "As I am among my people now, I am well protected. Besides, Alanna made it quite clear she'd had enough of me during our cramped journey to my world. Although I believe she blushed when she said it. I may yet have a chance to woo her."

Laina and Ronan took a small bench seat near the back, while the prince sat at the far end across from them. Hawk and Julian had joined them on their cruiser and sat directly across from Ronan. Laina couldn't say she was happy at the thought of staring at those two for the rest of their journey.

The metal bench was cool beneath Laina's hands as she sat down and curled up against Ronan, the only thing she found comforting at this moment. The chill of their experience was still deep in her skin, but Charon's bright yellow sun would hopefully change all that. Though if she stayed on this world for too long, her pale skin would likely burn.

"Ronan," she whispered. He didn't reply but lowered his head close to hers, pretending to shield his eyes from the sun. "Am I going to be safe here?"

"I will protect you with my life," Ronan said.

Always so dramatic. "That's not exactly what I meant. You said things might become difficult if others found out about the anomaly, but I'm not exactly sure why. It's not like it's a weapon or anything."

She noticed Ronan close one of his hands into a tight fist. He spoke quietly so that the prince couldn't overhear them. "Isn't it? You killed two graywalkers with it."

"I don't think anyone will be crying over that."

"Nevertheless, it holds power."

"But I thought it just had the genomes for all of Earth's animals in it. It's just information, right?"

"Even if that were the case, information *is* power. And

I'm certain it contains far more than that. If the High Council learned of the Ark, they might insist you be handed over to them for study."

"They can do that?"

"Terrans hold a complicated position within the Protectorate. We have no place on the Low Council as the other races do."

"So, what, are you saying *you* don't have rights either?"

Ronan straightened a bit, as if the very idea offended him. "We have become a force to be reckoned with in the Perseus Arm. Our services are in demand on a thousand worlds, and our name is respected across the galaxy."

"But the High Council could still just take me if they wanted."

Ronan's chest fell slightly. "Yes."

Laina swallowed, her throat tight. The mighty Silver Legion were, in their own way, also powerless. The land cruiser took off, making her jolt and dig her nails into Ronan's sleeve. Without a roof, the wind whipped across her face, making her eyes sting at first, but they soon crossed the twenty kilometers it took to reach the edge of the Charon city of Lampoura.

The walls of the city were made of what looked like clear glass, stained with colors in bright swirling patterns.

"The walls form our power grid, able to capture light in any direction" explained the prince, as if he was providing a tour. "They are two hundred years old, yet are still able to power the entire city."

Laina looked on in awe as two tall gates opened and the cruiser coasted inside. They flew down one street filled with small but elegant residential structures. The number of people increased dramatically as they approached an open market. But the vehicle turned left rather than right, away from the bustling activity.

This street was narrow and quiet, the windows dark and the doors undecorated with only a few residences. It was like they were being taken down some kind of back alley. A chill stole across Laina, but there wasn't anything to worry about, was there?

"Stay close to me," Ronan whispered.

Okay, maybe there was.

Julian and Hawk, sitting across from them, looked over Laina and Ronan's heads to see what was behind them. Without saying anything aloud, Julian shook his head at Ronan, who nodded in reply.

"What is it?" Laina asked.

"The other cruisers are not following behind us," said Ronan. "And we are no longer following the commander's."

Definitely something to worry about. But if it was as bad as she feared, no one else in the cruiser showed it. She forced herself to relax, trusting that Ronan knew what he was doing.

Ronan casually looked to Prince Leif. "Where are we going?"

For his part, the prince seemed unconcerned. "This way leads to the back of the palace. I suspect it is a precaution for my safety. Nothing more."

The cruiser slipped into the back entrance of a palace filled with warm sandstone columns and glittering windows of stained glass. When they landed, they left the cruiser single file, then formed a close group as the guards surrounded them and escorted them into the palace. Prince Leif took the lead, walking alongside the head guard.

They walked into the palace through a set of glinting

gold doors. The head guard led them down a long hall, which was decorated in all manner of ancient tapestries.

"Will we be meeting up with Alanna?" Laina asked Prince Leif.

"Soon enough. She was taken through a different entrance. A shame. She missed out on seeing the best part of the palace." The prince waved to the surrounding artwork. "Do you think she would agree to a personal tour before you depart?"

"Unlikely," said Ronan. Then for the first time, Laina saw a different kind of smile on his face. One of mischief. "Though I suppose I could *order* her to accompany you."

"I would be in your debt if you could arrange that," said Prince Leif. "But first, we have the king to attend to."

They halted in front of another set of golden doors, which opened automatically, revealing a throne room.

Laina marveled at the opulent marble pillars and the dais within the gilded room. A handsome Charon was seated on the throne. He wore a beautiful tunic of deep red with a gold braided belt at his waist and loose black trousers.

Leif strode up the steps as the king rose from his throne and came down to greet his brother. The two clasped one another's forearms, shaking their arms and smiling. The king then turned his attention to his guests.

"Welcome, members of the Silver Legion. I am King Balefire. Seeing as you rescued my brother from an unspeakable fate, I felt it prudent to greet you personally." The king came down the stairs and stopped in front of Ronan. Ronan nodded but kept his eyes on Balefire, one hand on Laina's arm.

"And this must be the Terran freeborn." Balefire's gaze raked down her body. He certainly wasted no time demonstrating his lustful thoughts. "I understand my brother purchased her from your crew but you won her back in a fight?"

"Yes, though my men had no right to sell her in the first place." Laina could sense both Julian and Hawk tense up behind her. "I invoked *Domina Persea* to win her back."

"It was a mighty battle. Well fought and honorably won," confirmed the prince.

"Indeed. Well, I am afraid there is a small problem with that." The king turned his back on Ronan and returned to his seat on the throne. "*Domina Persea* cannot apply to Terrans of any sort, as they are not recognized as sitting members of the Protectorate."

"What?" Ronan took one step forward, and the guards who had escorted them into the throne room all put their hands on their weapons.

The king continued. "And as such, she is still the property of Prince Leif, and by extension the planet of Charon."

Prince Leif seemed as puzzled by this as the rest of them. "Brother, if I may—"

The king raised his hand for silence. "The High Council has informed me that they will be taking the freeborn into custody. I have agreed." Ronan's eyes took on a faint glow, but the king took no notice. "You are to put up no resistance or you will be arrested."

A heavy silence filled the room, a long pause where it seemed that every man was drawing in a deep breath. Ronan took a step forward, standing in front of Laina.

"King Balefire. Ask yourself, what possible interest would the High Council have in a single human?"

"It is not my place to ask."

"Not your place? Is a king so easily cowed by others?"

Balefire's eyes narrowed. "Watch your tongue, Terran. You have done this world a great service and will be rewarded for it, but the status of the freeborn is not negotiable."

"King Balefire, I warn you. You are making a grave mistake. You will be held accountable for it." Ronan's voice was calm but firm.

The king raised a hand, and every Charon guard in the room leveled their weapons at him and his men.

"Is that a threat?"

Ronan smiled. "The Silver Legion does not make threats. They act."

And with that, all hell broke loose. Ronan and the command staff surrounded Laina, shielded her body with theirs as they drew their sidearms and opened fire.

"Stun only!" yelled Ronan.

It was a desperate move, with no real chance of success. Though the cyborgs were formidable soldiers, they were surrounded, outnumbered ten to one, and possessed no cover. Blasts flew past Laina's head, and she felt each and every time a stinging bolt hit one of the cyborgs because of how they shuddered. However, they did not fall.

"Take them down!" Balefire bellowed. "Kill them if you must, but do not harm the freeborn!"

"Get to the door! Protect Laina!" Ronan yelled, and the crew started to shuffle toward the door, herding Laina along with them. They kept the Charon guards pinned as best they could with covering fire.

"Running low on charge," Hawk grunted.

"Half power on mine," said Julian. He kept himself in front of her as they retreated. Another blast hit him and he cursed, staggering back. She then saw just how much punishment he'd taken. Julian's chest was covered with a dozen burn marks left behind by pulse gun blasts, but he stayed on his feet. Another blast hit him in the back and he stumbled, falling to one knee. Hawk moved to take his place, but if this kept up, they'd all soon be in similar shape.

"Let them take me!" she cried out to Ronan, but he ignored her. They'd made it to the door, and it seemed the king had failed to add more guards in the hallway, thinking they'd never make it out of the throne room.

Julian was back on his feet, albeit barely. "Ronan, grab her and run! I can hold the door for thirty seconds."

"You can't. *We* can," said Hawk. He looked to Ronan and the others. "Go. Get to the commander."

Ronan swept Laina into his arms, sprinting through the door and into the hall. The rest of the command staff followed behind, providing cover. She had one last glimpse of Julian and Hawk opening fire through the doorway, using the massive gold doors for cover. She might have been hearing things, but she could have sworn they were laughing madly. But eventually they went down, and the doors were flung open to allow the guards to give chase.

Laina held back a sob. They were *dying* because of her, and she couldn't stop them. This was all for nothing. They would never make it.

"Ronan, let me go," she said softly, knowing he'd still hear her. "You have to let me *go*."

"No!" Ronan stumbled as another blast hit him in the back. His chest was already covered in deep wounds from the initial onslaught. Two more of the crew fell to the concentrated fire from the Charon guards.

"Please—"

"No! You matter. You're too—" He tripped and she fell out of his arms, rolling on the ground and getting to her feet.

He collapsed against the nearest wall. Two of the crew rushed to his aid, trying to give him a chance to recover while shielding him and keeping the guards pinned farther down the hall. But all too soon the last had fallen, and the Charon guard advanced, weapons trained on Laina but not firing.

Prince Leif was just behind them, ordering them to drop their weapons, but they ignored him. He wasn't their king. Ronan staggered up, raising his weapon defiantly.

"Run," he said, looking to her. "You have to—"

Another blast hit Ronan's chest, burning through his uniform and sizzling his flesh as he went down on his knees. Then he collapsed. The guards looked ready to shoot him where he lay.

"Stop!" Laina threw herself over Ronan, covering him. The guards lowered their weapons.

"I surrender. Just don't kill him. *Please*." She met Leif's gaze. "Prince Leif..."

The prince shoved the guards aside. He knelt by Ronan, checking his pulse. He looked to her.

"He's alive. Go with the guards, and I will see to it they come to no more harm. I don't know why the High Council wants you so badly, but it cannot be worth such senseless violence."

"Did... Did you know?" she asked in a shaky, angry voice.

"That my brother would betray my trust like this? No." His eyes were hard, the playful prince long gone. "Even his legal claim is dubious. This is not honorable, but he says he had no choice."

"There's always a choice," said Laina.

A guard stepped forward. "The High Council ship has arrived. They have requested we bring the freeborn Terran to them immediately."

Leif sighed and touched Laina's cheek, sorrow etched in his honey-colored eyes.

"I agree. There is always a choice. Something about this does not sit right. I swear to you I will find out what it is and aid you where I can. Be strong, for his sake." The prince nodded down to Ronan's still body.

Laina sniffed and nodded. "Tell him that's twice I've saved his life. He owes me." She wiped a tear from her eyes and got to her feet. The guards escorted her down the hall, leaving the fallen members of the Silver Legion behind and heading toward an uncertain future.

CHAPTER 19

Ark Chronicle Entry 50-211

Those who have helped us work in the shadows because they must.

Some of their technology is beyond that of even the Protectorate's most ambitious designs. Every so often they allow this to be passed on, once they feel its potential for misuse or weaponization has been mitigated.

But while they work with an eye on the betterment of all life, there are other groups in the galaxy whose only goal is power and control. It is because of them that they remain hidden.

And yet their eyes are everywhere.

I say this because we have been told that for now the Ark is to be kept safe, never to be used or revealed. The time is not right, and their eyes have learned that others have learned of its existence.

For that reason, and others, I have decided to take what may be the last of the free Terrans to hide in exile, even from our benefactors. I fear I will not live to see where we end up, and so I will pass the Ark on to my son. I have entrusted him to continue my work, to keep our people, and this record, safe. There is more to the Ark than he knows. I only hope that the day comes when that knowledge can see the light of day again.

With luck, we will find a place to hide in seclusion and wait until we are needed. This is Dr. John Roberts, signing off for the last time.

RONAN CAME TO. HE SAT UP AND CRIED OUT "LAINA!" and almost passed out once again.

"Easy, my friend. You might fight like an azagoth, but you do not have its stamina, especially after healing so many wounds."

Ronan looked around. The prince sat next to him. He was on a cot in some kind of hospital. No, it was most likely the private medical facility of the royal family. The rest of his men were here as well. Most were awake, sitting on the edges of their cots, looking exhausted, though some were strong enough to pace around the room. Ronan looked to the prince with narrowed eyes.

"Hold your tongue. You might say something you will regret," said Prince Leif. "Much has happened, and more still is unknown. But I am here to help you regain what is yours."

"Laina?"

The prince nodded.

"You would go against the High Council?"

The prince looked shocked. "Of course not. I am merely lending aid to a fellow ally of the Draxon Collective and providing information about recent ship movements."

"I see," said Ronan.

"It's fortunate you only tried to stun my guards. Had

any died, my brother would have you in prison. Or executed."

Ronan gave a grim smirk. "That was a matter of energy conservation."

"Yes, well, no need to tell the king that."

"How are we to rescue Laina?" asked Ronan. "The *Orion* is too damaged to pursue anyone."

"Your repair ship arrived an hour ago and is already working on her. With luck, she will be operational when you return."

A different question was now prodding at him. "Why help us at all?"

"It is a debt repaid. It is the right thing to do. And there are a number of things that concern me about this ship from the High Council. Come, I will explain as I return your crew to the spaceport. I have shuttles being prepared for you as we speak."

Laina spent the night in a holding cell aboard the High Council's transport vessel. It wasn't at all what she'd expected. The stale scents of other prisoners still clung to the walls. It was far colder than she'd expected, and the flat, rigid cot that jutted out from the wall was hard as a rock, without a blanket or pillow. It was even less hospitable than the *Orion*'s brig had been. She curled up on it, having nowhere else to go, shivering and wishing she was back with Ronan.

She'd gone from hiding in fear of the Silver Legion to praying they would somehow find her. Ronan had shown her that his people weren't monsters to be feared, even if the society they lived under was. And she'd learned she wasn't a weak creature whose only choice in life was to hide and run. She smiled as she remembered the nights they'd spent together, sharing their pasts, Ronan exposing his soul and she hers.

Laina closed her eyes, trying to ignore the hum of the bright white strip lights above. The cell was windowless, and for once she missed the dark, quiet pulse of space and the infinite number of bright stars that lay within it.

Her body drifted into a waking sleep as her mind wandered, replaying memories. Whales breaking the surface, the throaty sound of frogs deep in what Ronan had called a bayou, the hush of snowfall at twilight, the symphony of bat wings flying out of deep caves at dusk.

Her heart remembered all of it and more. Many of the images were ones she had never seen before. How was it possible that each flash, each sound brought back memories so tangible to her of a world that had been dead for centuries? She wondered if her mind was inventing things. One of the memories had been of something that looked like a beaver with a giant duck's bill, and another had been of great hopping animals that carried around their young in deep belly pockets. The winding trail of thoughts and images seemed to soothe her, lulling her into a deep trance.

For a long while she lay there, her body wanting to weep but unable. Seeing the beauty of a world that no longer existed was humbling. Soon the painful emotions faded, leaving her feeling empty and listless.

After what felt like an eternity, she was summoned to face the council's representatives on board this ship. Two humanoid aliens came into her cell. She could not tell what species they were, however, because of their dark uniforms and the helmets they wore. But they were large, even larger than the cyborgs.

They gripped her by the arms and escorted her to a dark room where a display screen took up an entire wall. In the center was an examination table, set upright, illuminated by a single overhead light. The guards strapped her in, restrained at the wrists, ankles, and head.

The monitor flicked on, showing the seal of the Galactic Senate, a highly simplified icon representing the Milky Way, with the territory of the five High Council species highlighted in different colors on the bottom half.

The screen flickered again, revealing five figures hidden in hoods and shadow sitting and watching her. She couldn't make out anything about them. Why bother showing themselves at all? It had to be to intimidate her, just like the uniforms of the guards. But why? They hadn't even asked her any questions.

One raised an arm and spoke in a language she'd never heard before. That alone was odd. Laina spoke only a few languages, but she could recognize all the major languages spoken in the Protectorate. This wasn't any of them. Suddenly the table jolted back forty-five degrees, and a beam of light focused on her right hand. The hand with the anomaly. The Ark. They must have seen the mark on her hand and wanted to know more. Or had they known all along? Was that why she was here?

Whatever information the scan revealed, it seemed to satisfy them. The light went off, and the hooded figures consulted one another briefly. The one who had spoken before now said in Galactic Common, "You have been found guilty of high treason against the Galactic Senate. The sentence for this is death."

Laina's mouth gaped. "*What?*" No trial, no evidence, no explanation? Just summary conviction?

"You have one chance to reduce your sentence. Who did you share the Ark with?"

They knew. They knew what it was.

"Nobody. I don't even know how *I* got it, so how could I give it to anyone else?"

"You lie," said another hooded figure. "The Ark must be passed through physical contact to a compatible species. We know this."

"So maybe I shook hands with someone." It wasn't wise to talk sarcastically, but they weren't exactly encouraging her cooperation.

The one who'd called her a liar continued. "The Ark is linked with its host. It requires an active desire to be passed on. You could not be unaware of it."

She had no idea what he was on about. She barely understood the thing. How could she actively want to share it with anyone?

Laina's eyes widened. She remembered being mounted by Ronan, clasping his hands in hers, filled with a desire to share everything with him.

She remembered him scratching at his palm later that night.

She remembered his hand clutching into a fist when she'd mentioned the Ark later.

And she remembered the odd bond she'd felt when she'd kissed Ronan and somehow killed the graywalker inside him.

"Ah...she does know," said the first. "Tell us who it is, and we will relieve you both of your burden."

Why do I get the feeling the burden he's talking about is my life?

There was no way this was the High Council. This was some bizarre cult using their name. She'd seen the council on the news on a number of worlds. Settling trade disputes, encouraging exploration of the Far Territories, providing aid to struggling worlds, imposing sanctions on those who refused to cooperate with galactic law. They weren't perfect —what government was?—but they didn't go about secretly abducting people and interrogating them like this.

"You're not the High Council. None of you are short enough to be a Hopat, for one thing. Why should I talk? *Who* are you?"

"We act in the best interests of the High Council," said the first hooded figure. "We do what must be done for peace and stability. And you are far more dangerous than you realize."

Funny, most people go around telling me I'm more important than I realize.

The thought emboldened her. She *was* important, and for some reason that scared them. That was why she was dangerous.

"If you cooperate, we may reduce your sentence from death to life on Tartarus."

"Life on a hellish prison planet or death? Your idea of incentive sucks."

"There are many ways to die, Terran," said a different hooded figure.

"Yes, there are. And just as many ways to live. You made my decision that much easier. I won't tell you a damn thing."

"Then you choose death. But we will still take the information from you."

She heard a hum coming from all around her. No, it was coming from the table. The whole table hummed, like something was charging.

Her body jolted as the table became electrified. The

pain was beyond anything she'd encountered, as if attacking each nerve individually, overloading her brain with such pain that the world became white and all sound ceased. She couldn't even hear herself scream.

Then all at once it stopped. Just long enough for her to catch her breath, before the hum began again. "No...don't—"

Her body seized in pain. It was too much. She wanted to die. She begged for something to go wrong and her heart to just stop. But death wouldn't come, no matter how much she begged it. Then it stopped, and the hum began to build once more. She barely had a chance to say "Please" before it started once more.

At the third break the shocks stopped altogether. Laina was disorientated, unaware of where she was or even who she was anymore. It was some time before she could even think straight. For reasons she couldn't explain, the first thing she could put together coherently weren't words, but notes. Music. Songs from her past rang inside her head, comforting her, coaxing her back to the land of the living. These notes mingled with her desire to escape, to be free, to see Ronan again.

Come find me, behind twin moons,
Come find me through a galaxy darkly.
Come find me in Orion's belt,
Soar through the winds of Titan,
In the eye of Jupiter's storm,
Or skating along the rings of Saturn.
Chase me through this haunted universe.
Come find me, across the stars.

She wasn't sure if the song was from her past or
something she'd strung together randomly in her dazed
state, but it helped draw her back to reality. To focus.

Unfortunately, that focus meant remembering what was
happening to her. Laina's heart began to race as she
wondered when the shocks would start again. The anticipation was almost as traumatizing as the pain itself.

"Who did you share the Ark with?" asked the shadow
council. "Tell us, and the pain ends. Resist, and your
suffering will be legendary."

It occurred to Laina that if they had found her before
Ronan, she might have confessed to anything they asked.
She'd have given up anyone, turned on anyone, just for a
chance to live or for the pain to stop. She'd lived her life like
a scared rabbit, fearful of everything.

But not now. If she was going to die, it would be in a
way she could be proud of. As long as Ronan was alive,
perhaps the Ark would live on as well, and a part of Earth
with it. Wasn't that worth dying for?

Ronan, wherever you are, I love you. She closed her eyes,
picturing how he'd looked when he'd spoken of his past, the
pain she'd seen when he spoke of the end of Earth. The
hope in his voice as he talked about finding a planet his
people could claim as their own. Of having a life off of a
starship. Of having a home.

A life I wanted to share with him.

Her heart gave a rebellious thump against her ribs.

"Your answer?"

At least now she would soon be with her parents.
Wherever the universe let its souls go, she would follow. A

line from her mother's favorite story, *Peter Pan*, came back to her in that moment. *"Death is an awfully big adventure."*

As she heard the table hum and prepare to release its charge, she saw the tattoo on her hand start to glow, just as it had when the graywalker tried to kill her. But this time it was doing something different. It seemed to be flaring, its light somehow pointing away from the display. What did it mean? She would never learn the mysteries of that mark. It would die with her. She struggled to find a moment of comfort in the stark terror surging through her now that she knew she was going to die. The song, the one with the haunting melody, came back to her. She started to whisper the words, and the whisper became a song.

"Very well," said the voice on the display. "We will begin again."

"Come find me," she sang softly as the hum reached its final pitch. "Across the stars..."

And then the pain returned.

"WE'LL NEVER BE ABLE TO FIND HER," RONAN growled as he rushed onto the *Orion*'s bridge. The rest of the crew followed behind, and Commander Corvus calmly took his seat in the command chair.

"Sit down, Ronan. Your pacing will not make finding her any easier."

Ronan threw himself into his chair. He could barely think past his growing sense of panic.

It had been four eventful hours since he'd awoken after the skirmish on Charon, and though things had progressed at breakneck speed, it had still been far too slow for Ronan's liking.

"Any word from the *Hydrus*?" Alaric asked Hawk. The commander had requested aid from the Legion, and their sister ship was the closest heavy cruiser to their location.

"She's six hours out from our location," the lieutenant replied.

"Too long," said Ronan.

"But the patrol ship *Gladius* is only an hour away."

Alaric nodded. "Have the *Gladius* make best speed toward us and follow us if we have left before it arrives."

It had only been a couple of hours since Prince Leif had sent them back to the *Orion* on several of his personal shuttles. The TCF *Babbage*, a Silver Legion repair frigate, was latched on to the cruiser like a spider that had caught its prey. The *Babbage*'s eight protruding arms curled around the *Orion*'s hull, with teams working ceaselessly to repair the damage done by the graywalker's energy web.

According to the repair ship's commander, the *Orion* was spaceworthy, but it would still take at least a day to bring her back to full strength. A day they didn't have. They had to catch up with that supposed Galactic High Council ship before it was too late, but they had no way to find her.

"Commander..." Ronan looked to Alaric, but his words failed him.

"I know, Ronan. We'll find her." Now that the bridge crew was in place, he called to Hawking at navigation. "Scan all transit signatures. Filter out anything too large or small to be our target, and cross-reference that with the information Prince Leif provided."

"It'll still be like finding a needle in a haystack," Julian muttered from the helm.

"It will have to do until we can find ourselves a magnet," said Alaric.

Ronan tried to focus on the information at his terminal,

trying to spot an anomaly, but couldn't. Too many ships, too many directions, too much time had passed. It was hopeless.

Damnation, where did they take you? Which way did you go?

A bright light caught Ronan's eye. It was coming from his hand. He looked down and saw the sign branded into his hand glowing intensely. It seemed to flare to life and somehow began to point toward the starboard side of the ship.

"What the...?" The commander had no way to finish that sentence.

In a flash of intuition, Ronan knew what this meant. "It's the Ark. It knows where the other one is. Where *Laina* is."

The commander smiled. "Legionnaires, we just found our magnet."

Ronan went to Hawking's station and consulted the holographic navigation map, setting the *Orion* in the center so that it was accurate to their actual positioning. Ronan placed his hand over the hologrammatic outline of their ship, and Julian focused his search on all signals that were headed in that direction.

Hawk swept over the information and came to a conclusion, one that confused him. "I have only one signature leaving Charon in that direction, but long-range scans show no sign of a transit signature heading in that direction. If they went that way, they didn't go far, or fast."

"We'll find out soon enough," said Alaric. "Set a course. Best possible speed."

"You'll think we traveled back in time, sir," Julian joked, laying in the course.

The commander tapped his chair's comm. "All hands to

your stations. Fighter crew on standby. *Orion* to *Babbage*, disengage repair clamps."

The crew of the *Orion* spurred into action. Ronan still felt weakened from regen fatigue, but nothing was going to stop him from finding Laina.

Their course sent them back toward to the Charon homeworld and into the asteroid belt separating the inner and outer parts of their solar system. Ronan noticed the light in his hand begin to turn, and they adjusted their course to match.

"Are you sure about that?" asked Hawking. "In the time they've had, they should be light-years away. Why stay in the same system?"

"He might be right," said Julian. "I don't see any...wait. Hold on. I've got something. Their engines must be heavily reinforced. It's almost invisible."

"Are they moving?"

"No, they're just sitting in the belt," said Julian. "By that large asteroid. Dead ahead."

Sure enough, as soon as they dropped out of sub-transit, Ronan saw the asteroid on their main display. And right next to it was a patrol-class craft with the markings of the High Council on it.

"Raise defenses," said Ronan. Thick plating rose up on all sides of the viewport, locking into place. The now dark viewscreen lit up with a holographic tactical view of the outside. "Fighter crews, prepare to launch. Hail them."

The comm officer shook her head. "No response."

"They're powering weapons," Julian called out, his face locked on the screen in front of him.

Firing on an official Protectorate vessel was a serious crime. Another commander might have waited for them to fire the first shot. But the commander had three centuries of command experience under his belt. If anyone knew how things were about to play out, it was him.

"Launch fighters. Gunnery, fire all weapons! Target engines!"

From the underside of the *Orion* two bay doors opened, and small manned fighters shot out, fanning out in all directions. The enemy patrol ship's turrets opened fire as it tried to come about with its main guns, trying to deal with both the *Orion* and its fighter cover at the same time. Explosions, silent to the *Orion* crew, rocked the enemy ship as they prepared to return fire.

"Their armor is holding," Alanna said from the weapons station. "They're stronger than any patrol ship I've seen. Target is coming about. Their main guns are charging."

"Evasive maneuvers!" cried Alaric. "Keep to their starboard!"

Unfortunately, the patrol vessel was more nimble than they'd expected, and bright red beams shot out from either side of the vessel, striking the *Orion* dead center, and following up the attack with bright green pulse cannon fire. The bridge groaned and rumbled with the impact.

"Damage to the lower observation deck," Alanna called out. "Ablative armor holding. Weapons nominal."

"Return fire. I want those engines down. Have the fighters focus on hitting the main guns. Time on the *Gladius*?"

"She's dropping out of transit now," said Hawk. "Coming in to draw enemy fire."

"Good. Get us behind that rock. Try to flank the enemy while the *Gladius* has her distracted. Comms, warn the *Gladius* that the vessel is stronger than it looks. When we come back about, don't give them a clear shot of our underbelly."

In the end, the High Council patrol vessel was unable to mount an effective counterattack. Fighters zipped and dodged around its point defense, sometimes using the smaller asteroids for cover, while the *Gladius* and *Orion* hammered its engines into scrap. A cheer roared up from the bridge when Alanna announced that the ship was dead in space and its weapons neutralized.

"We're being hailed!" said the comm officer.

"Now they want to talk," Alaric said. He stood from his chair and faced the video screen that replaced the tactical display.

An officer in a black uniform stood there, face concealed behind a featureless helmet. It was like no uniform Ronan had ever seen belonging to any martial branch of the Protectorate.

"What is the meaning of this? You have attacked a High Council vessel. Cease your hostilities at once."

If that's a High Council ship, then I'm an Ugaro diplomat, thought Ronan.

"You refused our hail and charged your weapons," said Alaric. "You are holding a member of our crew against her will."

"We do not hold any of your crew, Terran."

"Then you won't mind if we come on board and confirm that."

There was a slight pause. "We hold only a freeborn fugitive. A freeborn cannot be part of your crew."

Alaric gave half a smile. "She is part of my crew if I say she is. Crewman Laina Roberts is under the protection of the Silver Legion. Prepare to surrender her at once."

Alanna turned from her station, looking concerned. "Sir, I don't like these readings from the engine room."

The commander frowned, muting the communication.

"What is it?"

"I think they're going to blow the ship."

Ronan's eyes widened. He was on his feet even before the commander could give him his orders. "Take a boarding party on the shuttle. Get her off that ship *now*." He looked back to Alanna as Ronan left. "How long do they have?"

"They took too much damage to the engine core. I don't think they can overload it properly. But if they're willing to do that..."

She didn't have to finish her sentence as the lift doors shut on Ronan.

If they're willing to do that, they have no intention of letting Laina leave alive.

The *Gladius* provided cover for the shuttle as it left the *Orion* and docked with the damaged council patrol ship. Seeing her sleek form reminded Ronan of the *Rapier*. The *Orion* was larger and more powerful than any patrol vessel, and he was proud to serve on her as first officer, but there was always something to be said about commanding one's own ship.

Ronan checked his pulse rifle and addressed his boarding party. Ordinarily, he'd have had Alanna and Julian join him, but they were needed on the bridge.

"The crew here are desperate and have already tried to scuttle the ship once," said Ronan. "Expect heavy resistance. Set pulse rifles to focused burst, full charge. It's us or them." He checked his hand. The light coming from it now pointed to somewhere near the center of the patrol vessel. "We head straight for our crewman and then fall back. Understood?"

The boarding party barked an acknowledgment as the shuttle docked, sealed, and burned through the enemy ship's airlock.

"Good. Legionnaires, we move!"

The airlock fell, and the shuttle's door opened, allowing Ronan and the others to rush inside. Each scanned for targets, but found none.

Ronan checked his hand and headed down the hall in the direction it pointed. Still they saw nothing. Nothing moving, at any rate.

"I have someone," one of the crewmen called out. "No heat signature, though. He's dead."

"Got one here, too," said another. "Dead."

They found six more bodies like this before they reached whatever room Laina was being held in. All dead, but they had no time to check the bodies. Not while she was in danger.

Please no. Please tell me these monsters didn't...

They entered a dark room with a display screen taking up one wall, blank and lifeless. In the center was an examination table, illuminated by a single light. And on it was Laina.

She wasn't moving.

Ronan ran over and ripped off her restraints. He scooped Laina up into his arms, her body limp, head lolling against his chest.

He felt her body already starting to cool.

"No. No no no no."

"Ronan!" Alanna's voice came over the comm from the *Orion*. "Someone in the engine room managed to get the reactor to overload. It's going critical!"

Ronan only hesitated a moment in grief before rushing back to the shuttle with Laina in his arms, the boarding crew following behind. They departed the dead ship and hurried back to the *Orion*, which was falling back to a safe distance, along with the *Gladius*.

Ronan looked out the shuttle window as the mysterious council ship suddenly glowed and detonated, becoming a brief bright flare in the endless night of space. Ronan turned away and called Valeria on the comm to prepare for a casualty.

Once on board, he rushed her to sickbay. Ronan laid Laina down on the same table he'd placed her on when she'd been his prisoner, and he watched Valeria try to resuscitate her. A machine forced air into her lungs, and small electrodes stimulated her heart, keeping the blood flowing. A small skullcap was placed over her head, monitoring brainwave functions.

Ronan grasped Laina's right hand in his left and watched Valeria work. He couldn't breathe. His heart was frozen, like Laina's was, his life tied to hers in a way he'd never thought possible.

After many agonizingly slow minutes, Valeria turned to face Ronan, her eyes filling with tears.

"Ronan...I'm sorry... It's her mind. It's been wiped. The physical body I can keep alive, but..."

"No..." The word slipped out, a desperate denial of the truth his eyes didn't want to see.

"Ronan, I—"

"*No.*" He growled and bent over Laina, watching her lifeless body. He looked up. "I won't allow it."

"I'm sorry, Ronan. But there's nothing to be done."

His eyes shut and tears spilled out.

"*Come find me,*" he sang softly, "*behind twin moons.*"

He squeezed Laina's hand, but she didn't squeeze back.

"*Come find me through a galaxy darkly.*"

He couldn't remember the rest, wasn't even sure where the song had come from, and started to repeat himself.

"*Come find me...*"

A voice that was barely a whisper answered. "...*in Orion's belt...*"

Ronan's eyes shot open. His hand was glowing, as was hers. Her eyes were closed, but her lips were moving.

"*Come find me, across the stars...*"

"Laina?" Ronan brushed the backs of his fingers on her cheek, stunned. Her eyes began to flutter. Valeria looked in amazement at the displays, now showing her brain activity back to normal. Ronan leaned over her, his eyes searching hers.

"Am I dead?" she whispered. "I must be. That's the only way you're here." She smiled dreamily, and his heart seemed to jolt back to life.

He chuckled and kissed her forehead. "On the contrary." He tried to hold back the flood of emotions threatening to overwhelm him. He'd almost lost her again and couldn't bear to let go of her now. Laina struggled to keep her eyes open. He tensed, squeezing her hand in panic.

"I'm okay. I'm just tired." She opened her eyes back up and glanced between them and Valeria. "How... How did I get here?"

"That would be my fault, little one. I wasn't ready to let you escape me." Ronan tried to tease her, but all he wanted was to know she was okay and that he could hold her in his arms once more. He wasn't sure how long he held her, but after a while, he became aware that Valeria was muttering as she examined the screens.

"What is it?"

Valeria turned to face them, the look of confusion on her face turning into a broad grin of triumph.

"Do you want the *good* news or the *great* news first?"

Ronan glanced down at Laina. She shrugged, her eyes still darting between them.

"Good news?" Ronan suggested.

"I believe I understand what happened. The Ark is a self-replicating quantum state computer. It's capable of storing vast amounts of information, far beyond the genomes of the species I discovered earlier. It's also programmed to protect its host, which no doubt includes whatever means it used to destroy the graywalkers. After you woke, I found a tiny cybernetic link leading from the Ark to your brain. It wasn't there during your initial scans, and even now it is being disassembled. I believe it saved a copy of your mind and restored it once your body was functioning again."

"That's incredible," said Ronan. "Even we're not capable of that."

"No, we're not. The technology Dr. Roberts's allies incorporated into the Ark is unlike anything I've ever read about. Needless to say, I'll want to conduct a number of tests, for many reasons."

"Wait, if that's the good news, what's the great news?" Laina asked.

"Well, that would be one of the other reasons for all the tests I need to run." Valeria beamed at her. "You're pregnant."

Laina stared at Val and then slowly faced Ronan. Then they both stared at the doctor together.

"Pregnant?" She laughed, a little hysterical, looking back at the doctor. "I can't be pregnant..."

"On the contrary." Val grinned, repeating Ronan's earlier words. Comprehension filled Laina's eyes even as they rolled back into her head, and she fainted right there in his arms.

When she came to, Ronan was cupping her hand with both of his.

"My apologies," said Val. "Your body is still recovering. I should have waited to give you the news."

She remembered. For a moment she'd thought she dreamt it. "Pregnant?" Laina murmured the word again. She put a hand to her abdomen and closed her eyes. "But that's not possible..."

Ronan smiled. "You're right. It's not."

"But?" She could feel that word hanging in the air.

Valeria cleared her throat. "I have a theory. Well, more of a process of elimination."

"The Ark?"

Val nodded. "But not on its own."

Ronan held up his hand, showing her that his left palm shared smaller but similar marks as her right. She *had* passed it on to him.

"We don't know how this happened," said Val, "but I believe it may have rewritten parts of Ronan's genetic code, circumventing the various kill switches that were programmed into the existing nanotech. I will need to run more tests, but given how we've seen it dismantle the pathway it built to your brain, I fear any evidence I'm looking for will be long gone."

"We're having a baby." Laina put her hand on her stomach again, amazed at the idea. She'd spent all her life hiding, never thinking that she would be a mother.

Ronan lowered his head close to her. "We are."

She grasped him by his uniform and tugged him in the last few inches, kissing him with such emotion that tears burned behind her closed eyes. For a time they just looked at one another, sharing this moment, reading clearly how the other felt.

"What happens now?" she finally asked.

"Now?"

"Whoever interrogated me claimed to work for the High Council. That's got to be bad news, right?"

Ronan's face went grim. "I do not believe they were part of the Protectorate at all. Tell me, did you *see* any of your captors?"

Laina shook her head. "The guards all wore helmets, and the ones calling themselves the High Council kept their faces hidden. They even spoke a language I've never heard before. Nothing about it felt right."

"More so than you realize," said Ronan. "I spoke to Prince Leif before we left Charon. Though the ship that took you had all the proper authorizations, the High Council embassy has no record of such a ship there acting on their behalf."

Laina thought back to the interrogation. "They said they speak for the council, that they do what must be done. Maybe they're some kind of shadow government?"

"Perhaps," said Valeria. "But I would hate to think that the Protectorate would stoop to such nefarious methods. They hold the lives of trillions in their hands."

"Or perhaps they are so large they do not know what everyone within their organization is doing," suggested Ronan.

The doctor cocked an eyebrow. "A rogue faction?"

"Perhaps. It's possible they have access to everything the High Council has, yet manage to operate unseen within it."

"An even more disturbing thought," said Valeria. "But the greater question is, to what end?" She looked to Laina. "What did they want to learn from you?"

"They know about the Ark. I think they know more

about it than we do. That's what scares them. The only reason I wasn't dead sooner was because they knew I'd passed on a copy and wanted to know who I'd given it to."

She looked at her hand, wondering again what the symbols on her palm might mean. "Whatever secrets this has, they want to make sure all copies of it are destroyed."

"This is troubling," said Val. "The Ark is the key to our salvation, and yet a group hiding in the shadows of the Protectorate will do anything to keep it from us."

"We must find out who," said Ronan. "And why."

Laina frowned. Valeria's words hadn't been intended to offend, but she couldn't help but notice their focus. *The Ark is the key to our salvation.*

Meaning the Legion. Meaning the cyborgs. Meaning everyone but her or her kind. She wasn't going to be just a tool for the cyborgs to use. She wanted her people, humans, *freeborn*, to be safe. To regain their rights in the galaxy again.

"What's wrong?" asked Ronan.

Laina came back. "Huh? Nothing. I think I need to stretch my legs a bit."

She sat up on the side of the bed and hopped off. She didn't wobble or buckle, so that was something. Ronan looked to the doctor with a silent question.

"I think a bit of a walk will do her some good," said Val.

Ronan made a move to follow her out the door, but the doctor caught his arm.

"I believe the unspoken part of her sentence was *alone*. Besides, we need to talk about the unusual behavior we've noticed from Erik and the others. I think I found the answer, but you're not going to like it."

CHAPTER 20

Ark Chronicle Entry 278-406

This is David Roberts, eighth chronicler of the Ark, final entry.

We've lost half our group to a bounty hunter raid. Mostly the adults. I managed to escape with the children, but...I'm not going to last much longer. Even the Ark can't save me now.

I'm going to pass the Ark on to my son, Bryan. He's only eight, but he's the oldest of the Roberts family's next generation that's still free from slavery. I just hope I can make him understand how important it is, how to use it properly, keep it safe, keep it hidden, and how to pass it on when the time comes. I just wish I could have been there to see him grow up. Then again, maybe a part of me will...

Commander Corvus stood with his hands behind his back, looking out the window of his personal office. The door trilled and his first officer entered, saluting as the door shut behind him.

"You wanted to see me, Commander?"

"Yes, Ronan. Now that we finally have a moment to breathe, I believe there are some matters we need to attend to."

Ronan stood at attention, no doubt anticipating the worst.

"Over the last week, we've had several very serious breaches of discipline on board this ship, many of which endangered the safety of who might be the most important Terran alive. One of which you actively tried to keep hidden from me. Any one of these on their own would be concerning, but taken all together, I have to ask myself if I have somehow failed this crew as its commander."

Alaric saw Ronan wince at that. To him, this was like a parent telling their child they weren't mad, but very disappointed.

"May I speak freely?" Ronan asked.

Alaric nodded. "Of course."

"My actions regarding Ensign Keid cannot be excused, but they can be explained. I wished to delay reporting his assault until I understood his motivations, so that I could ensure when action was taken it was with all the facts."

Alaric nodded. "I know you've been through a lot together. I'd hoped his time in deep space would help heal his wounds, but that doesn't seem to be the case."

"Actually, Commander, that's the reason I didn't come to you sooner. When I did speak to him, the details he provided raised far more questions than answers."

"Explain."

Ronan relaxed, moving next to him by the window and speaking in a low, soft voice. "I believe we have a mole on board this ship."

Laina went to the observation deck, wanting to see the stars as she had before, but it had been damaged in the battle with what she now called the Shadow Council and had to be sealed off. She went to the mess hall instead, but for once she had no appetite.

She sat alone and unnoticed in the back, watching the crew come in and out, mostly synths and the odd cyborg officer. They nodded to one another in greeting, smiled, and some sat down and shared stories while they ate. Some laughed. One couple was clearly flirting in the opposite corner.

They were free. And what was she? A guest of the Silver Legion, whose privileges lasted only so long as she remained wanted or useful?

On those rare occasions that she'd cooperated with other humans, working in the ghetto of a starport or hitching a ride to another world because word of slavers or bounty hunters had reached their ears, they'd never had meals like this. They often ate in silence, and any stories shared always included warnings of other people or places. They were never this relaxed or comfortable, and when jokes were shared the humor was often very dark. It was how you coped.

She saw Julian walk in with Hawking. They spotted her sitting in the back and instantly looked away. Because of course they did.

Do you think a little guilt will make things better? she thought. They sat across the room with their backs to her. *You don't have to deal with something you're not looking at, huh?*

They had no idea what her people had been through. If

they thought of humans at all, they no doubt comforted themselves with the knowledge that the Protectorate had rules to ensure they were not abused. Slaves, but well-treated slaves.

But still slaves.

It wasn't fair. It wasn't *right*. Whatever grievances they had with her kind had died with Earth, as far as she was concerned. Wasn't that enough? None of her people from that time were still alive, and yet a grudge was still being held.

Julian and Hawking looked back at her briefly, either to see whether she was still there or to subtly give her the hint that she didn't belong there.

Laina got up and left, but not for their benefit. She realized now what she had to do.

Before she'd been captured, it had been enough for her to survive. She'd have done anything to keep her freedom. In fact, under other circumstances, she'd have found her position on this ship ideal, even if it was the equivalent of a ship's cat.

But this cat had been given claws, and it was time to scratch.

RONAN HAD BEEN PUT IN THE UNENVIABLE POSITION OF telling Commander Alaric that Laina had demanded a meeting with him.

Not requested. *Demanded.*

Alaric chuckled to himself at that and simply said, "Indeed?" before he granted her an audience. After what Ronan had recently told him, he was certain their freeborn was in for some trying times ahead. She would need that kind of strength and will to get through it.

Ronan let her in, but he remained outside as the two prepared to talk.

"Drink?" Alaric asked. He took a fancy-looking clear bottle from his desk, filled with amber liquid.

"What is it?" Laina asked.

Alaric examined the bottle a moment. "I don't rightly know..." He put the bottle back. "Perhaps it's not a good idea, given your condition."

"It's about my condition that I wish to speak to you."

"I'm sure you do, but would you mind if I say something first?"

"Um...okay."

Alaric sat down behind his desk and gestured for her to take a chair as well.

"First of all, I wish to apologize for the behavior of my crew. To say they have acted unprofessionally would be a gross understatement for their misconduct."

"To say the least," said Laina.

"I would like to say that I don't normally make a habit of bringing unstable individuals on board my ship, but that wouldn't be entirely truthful." This explanation seemed to confuse Laina more than illuminate. "You see, I've chosen a number of my crew specifically *because* of their problems. Ensign Keid suffered a breakdown few thought he could recover from, Lieutenant Hawking has been in prison on numerous occasions, and Ensign Aquila has been demoted more times than you can imagine. I believe you're already acquainted with Ronan's demons."

"Then why are they on board?"

Alaric took a deep breath. It was a fair enough question, though not everyone would appreciate his answer. "Because

I believe in second chances. My actions have always stemmed from the belief that we can recover from anything. I believed Erik could heal, given time and the right environment, Hawking ironically ends up in trouble because of his deep belief in justice, and Julian has been promoted as many times as he's been demoted, for good reason. They all have great potential, and it was my job to try to bring out the best in them. Unfortunately, it seems I failed."

What the commander didn't say was in what way he believed he had failed. Ronan was right—there *was* a mole aboard his ship, one who had manipulated his crew, changed records, and fed information to their enemies.

The two graywalker attacks couldn't have been coincidences, nor could the so-called council vessel that had been waiting on Charon to spirit Laina away. Ronan had learned from the doctor that Erik, Julian, and Hawking had been treated with a psychotropic drug that heightened their negative emotions to the point where they could no longer control them. It explained why they had all acted badly to Laina, because humans brought out negative emotions with nearly all cyborgs. Dr. Schedar believed that such a drug could be administered through something as seemingly innocuous as physical touch. It was possible even Ronan had been affected at some point through secondhand contact.

Unfortunately, it was impossible to determine which drug had been used or how it had been administered. Only some trace chemical by-products provided any proof it had been used at all.

For now, the investigation into this would be kept betweeen Ronan and himself. It was unlikely the mole would act again right away, not with the increased suspicion it would bring. That left him free to deal with their current situation.

Laina took a deep breath. "Thank you for your apology, Commander. May I speak now?"

Commander Corvus smiled. "I believe I know what you are going to say, or the general shape of it. But before you go any further, might I make a suggestion?"

LAINA COULD HEAR THE VARIOUS CONVERSATIONS going on as the bridge crew assembled in the briefing room, next to the bridge. Here there was a long oval table with room enough for everyone. Each seat had its own display console and a projector in its center. The far wall had a large display, which Laina stood in front of now.

"What's this all about?" Julian grumbled as he and Hawking entered, taking a seat. "I've already been busted down to crewman. What more does he want?"

"If you keep talking, I'm sure he will invent an even lower rank just for you," said Hawking.

"At least you're still an officer."

"Barely."

Across the table, Alanna gave a puzzled look to Valeria. "Why is Laina up front with the commander? What is this all about?"

Valeria smiled. "If my guess is right, something good is about to happen. Something long overdue."

Erik, however, sat silently at the far end. A few other officers she didn't know by name were also present and looking just as confused as Alanna. Ronan and Alaric sat on either side of Laina, waiting for her to begin.

Laina fought the discomfort she felt addressing them all like this, especially while wearing one of their uniforms.

"I believe you're all aware of recent developments. Not only about the Ark, but my pregnancy."

Everyone except the commander took a moment to applaud, though that was not where she was going with this. She held up her hand, showing them the circular marks left by the Ark, but it also had the desired effect of getting them to quiet down.

"*This* is the key to the salvation of the cyborgs as a race. Without it, you will eventually die out, even if it takes ten thousand years. And although the synths can continue to be produced artificially, I wouldn't be surprised if this could do the same for them, allow them to create life themselves. I don't think I'm underselling how significant this is to the Terran Colony Fleet, not to mention your legal standing with the Protectorate."

There was a general murmur of agreement.

"And it comes with a price."

The murmuring stopped. For a moment Laina doubted herself. This was crazy. She was just one person, and she was going to impose an ultimatum on them. What if they decided it would be less trouble to just take what they wanted from her?

"Go on," said Alaric.

Laina took a deep breath. It was now or never.

"Three hundred years ago, Earth was at an impasse. Your people and mine were on the brink of war. You were willing to fight and die for the secrets of your creation, and we were terrified of what might happen if we gave it to you.

"But the war ended before it even began, and both sides lost. Earth was lost. And through some cruel irony, the wedge that already divided us was driven even deeper when we were declared your legal property. But the fact is that no humans from that time still live, and it is time for things to change.

"If you want me to help your people, you will help mine first. I have only one demand: for humanity, all of it, to be free."

Silence filled the room again. It was like a bomb had gone off, and yet everyone was too stunned to react to it.

Alaric was the first one to speak. "You want us to end human slavery? That is no small request."

"What I'm giving you isn't any smaller. When we refer to one another, what terms do we use? Cyborg, synth, free-born. But if you ask any other species to identify us, what term do they always use first? *Terran.* We are not three separate species—we are *one* species with different sets of gifts and different burdens. But still *one* people, who should be united, not divided."

Julian, lurking in the back, tried and failed to hold back a smirk. "Pretty words, but we all know Ronan also has a copy of the Ark. So why do we even need you?"

The doctor spoke up. "For one thing, it's not an exact copy of the Ark. It is unclear just how much of Laina's Ark is actually present. It could simply be enough to change Ronan's DNA. Laina's contains much more. More than I care to even guess at."

"And even if it wasn't, he doesn't know how to pass it on to others," said Laina. "I do."

Julian rolled his eyes. "Are you kidding me?"

Valeria shrugged. "Laina clearly managed to pass it on. The only question is, does *she* know how she did it?"

"That was the one thing I learned on board the Shadow Council ship. They told me how I did it. And it's a secret I'm willing to take to my grave."

But Julian wasn't done with his protest. "Yeah, but Ronan can still make more kids, right? We could just make him our official stud."

It was Valeria's turn to roll her eyes. "That will do wonders for the gene pool, I'm sure. Besides, there's the matter of the women, who are still sterile."

"There's always human women," said Julian. "And what if her baby can breed?"

Alaric got to his feet, slamming his hands on the conference table. "Listen to yourself! What you're suggesting is *barbaric*, and it comes from nowhere but spite." He began to pace the room. "By the fleet, is this what the Silver Legion is supposed to stand for? Finding a way to have one of their officers impregnate human slaves just so *you* can get out of doing the right thing?"

"Hey," Julian snapped back. "I don't like the future of my entire people being held hostage, all right?"

"Welcome to my world," said Laina. "You've been here for thirty seconds. I was born into it. So were my parents, and their parents. *Thirteen* generations have passed! When does it stop?"

Julian said nothing, but remained unconvinced.

Alaric turned to Laina. "So, what are your terms, specifically?"

"Get the High Council to retract their ruling regarding the freeborns. Free any slaves you've sold off to other races. All of them."

Alaric steepled his fingers together. "That part could be difficult. Slavery is legal within the Draxon Collective's borders."

"Then buy them back."

Julian huffed. "That could bankrupt the entire fleet!"

"Not my problem," said Laina.

"Enough," Alaric barked, then calmed himself. "You understand this will not happen overnight. The Protectorate is notoriously slow on making rulings with such far-reaching implications."

"If you can convince the Colony Fleet's government, what did you call it again?"

"The Triumvirate."

"If you can convince them to make a unanimous declaration on behalf of all the cyborgs and synths, I'm sure that would speed things up."

Alaric considered this. "It might. But that too might be difficult."

"Everything that's important in life is," said Laina. She realized that Ronan hadn't said a word in all this time. When she looked to him, however, she saw only a smile on his face. He nodded in approval.

Emboldened by Ronan's sign of confidence, she addressed the room. "I know I'm asking a lot, and believe me, I don't take that lightly. But the time has come for us to change. All of us. You looked to Earth's past to create a new identity that would carry you into the future—the Silver Legion is part of that identity. But do you know what those times of honor and chivalry you admire so much also had? Slavery. Inequity. Oppression. Do you want the future you're building to include those as well? It's time to throw those traits on the scrap heap of history where they belong and live by a different code: That we are not cyborgs, synths, and freeborn. We are *Terrans.*"

She had kind of hoped for a standing ovation or a slow clap building up to one like on some old movies she'd seen, but it didn't seem to be coming. And she really didn't have anything to add to top that.

Alaric approached her, his face firm. "You do realize

you have come to us with an ultimatum? My people made the same mistake once, and the cost was terrible."

"I know, but there's no threat of force here. Just a plea for sanity. Haven't we all suffered enough?"

Alaric's expression remained unchanged. "You are not the same woman who first came aboard this ship. You have become obstinate and willful. You have found pride where there was none before. You have made demands of those who could take what they want through force, defended only by your belief that we can be better people." He clasped her by the shoulders. "And I could not be more proud of you."

The room seemed to let out a collective sigh of relief at that, though Julian rolled his eyes again.

"I concede to your demands," said Alaric. "Together we will find a better way."

Laina smiled.

"But it comes with a price."

Laina's smile fell.

"I will concede to your demands *if* you stay aboard the *Orion*...as a member of her crew."

"*What?*" Julian cried out. Ronan's glare silenced him.

The commander smiled. "Do you accept?"

Laina didn't know what to say other than, "Yes. Yes, sir, um, Commander... My liege?"

Most of the room chuckled at that.

Commander Alaric pulled out a metal rank insignia, a single metal bar, and leaned in to clip it to her uniform at the shoulder. "You're not the only one with a flair for the dramatic," he whispered. Then he stepped back and spoke louder for the benefit of the crew.

"If we are going to find a better way, then this is how it begins. But this honor does not come without responsibility," he added. "You are expected to perform your duties just as any other member of the crew. I am assigning Lieutenant Alanna to train you, and I have it on good authority that she can be quite the taskmaster."

"More babysitting," Alanna said, though with a smile. Laina couldn't think of anyone she'd rather have to teach her.

Alaric took a step back and saluted with a fist to his chest. "Congratulations, Ensign Roberts. Welcome aboard."

Julian's jaw dropped. "You mean she outranks me too?"

Laina stood to attention, feeling ten times taller than she ever had in her life, and returned the salute. She was the first freeborn human to work alongside the synthetics as an equal since the fall of Earth. Ronan and the rest of the crew returned a congratulatory salute, but his eyes also burned with love as their gazes met.

Her heart was bursting with so much love that she could barely hold in the feeling of hope inside her. Everything that had happened to her since the loss of her parents had led to this moment and had led to Ronan.

Her father's words came back to her as she envisioned the life she hoped to have with Ronan and their child.

"We are Terrans. And we shall dream together as we journey across the stars."

LAINA HAD HEARD of the Terran Colony Fleet, of course, but she'd never seen it, had never even imagined what it looked like. She ran down to the observation deck the moment the commander announced their approach. She wasn't technically off duty, but Alanna had allowed her to skip her training session to go see. This once.

It was vast. A half dozen cylindrical-shaped stations rotated to provide their populations with gravity. Three great silver wings on each reflected and focused the local star's light down through the clear patches to provide the surface inside with heat and light. Even from this great distance, Laina could see the grass and trees of the parks inside and the cities that surrounded them. Cities full of synths and cyborgs and freeborn.

No...of *Terrans*.

Around the Colony Fleet were the ships of the Silver Legion, another heavy cruiser like the *Orion* could be seen, and dozens of patrol and scout-class vessels were moving to and fro. Most were a hodgepodge of old secondhand cruisers, bought from dozens of different worlds for a dozen different jobs and kept in service as long as possible. Some had been the backbone that had helped build the fleet centuries ago, and their work wasn't done yet.

Ronan soon came and placed a hand on her shoulder. "I thought I would find you here."

Laina smiled and placed her hand on his. "How many people do those colony ships hold?"

"Each holds a quarter of a million people." So that meant there were one and a half million Terrans here. "We purchased them from the Hopat Federation. They had developed superior models using artificial gravity. They're technically surplus but exceedingly durable. They are home."

"For now," said Laina.

"For now," Ronan agreed.

"And the ships? How many do you have?"

"Five others like the *Orion*," he said. He pointed to their twin passing nearby. "That one is the *Equuleus*. There are hundreds of patrol and scout vessels. Hundreds more cruisers. Only a small fraction are here, however. Mostly to resupply."

"So...what's next?" It was the question that bothered her most.

"Alaric has arranged a meeting with the Triumvirate, where all that we have learned will be shared, as will your terms."

"Do you think they'll agree to them?"

"If they are handled correctly," Ronan said cautiously. "Pride makes fools, and leaders tend to be prideful."

Laina watched as a silver patrol craft flew past, performing a spin as if for their benefit. "And what about everything else? Will he tell them about the Shadow Council?"

She saw Ronan's reflection straighten. "I cannot presume to speak for the commander on such matters. But I will say he has been making inquiries of his own, most notably with the Draxon representative on the High Council."

Laina didn't like the sound of that. She still considered them responsible for much of her people's suffering. Cultural differences or not, it was their influence that had humans like her declared slaves.

"Senator Dov'Lya was most upset to hear about the ship masquerading as a High Council vessel, but he agreed that any investigation needs to be done discreetly. He will begin by looking for credits being moved around and later unaccounted for. If someone within the council is creating a shadow faction, that will be one way to determine it."

"I hope he finds something."

"As do I," said Ronan. "But for now, I believe you should think of more pleasant things. Like feeling grass between your toes and the shade of a large tree."

Laina turned to Ronan. "Really?"

"I have arranged for us to have shore leave aboard the *Europica*. It is renowned for its exotic gardens, with some of the last samples of Earth flora that aren't specifically for food production. We have two weeks. You may continue your training once we return."

She crushed herself against Ronan and kissed him as the *Orion* drifted toward the colony ship. Their lips broke apart a second before they docked.

"Ready to meet the future?" Ronan asked. "There's much to see, and I can't wait to show you."

"With you at my side? I'm ready for anything." She tilted her head back, and his lips captured hers once more. The love that blossomed between them grew stronger each day. The child she carried, their future, it was more than just a symbol of their love—it was a vow that they would cherish every moment they had together as they worked to save her people and his.

Laina looked down at her hand, a little smile curving her lips.

Somehow, the future of a united Terran people started here, with the Ark...with her.

Ark Chronicle Entry 309-1

I think this is working.

Um... This is Laina Roberts. My father was Bryan Roberts, and I guess this goes all the way back to Dr. John Roberts. It looks like I am the tenth chronicler of the Ark, and I want to bring all the Terrans together...

But where do I even begin?

Thank you so much for reading *Across the Stars*!

If you love this story and want to read more about the sexy cyborgs and their human loves, please leave a review for it and tell your friends! Showing a book love, helps the authors write the next book in the series!

The best way to know when a new book is released in this series is to do one or all of the following:

For Lauren Smith:

Join Lauren Smith's Newsletter:
http://laurensmithbooks.com/free-books-and-newsletter/

Follow Lauren on BookBub:
https://www.bookbub.com/authors/lauren-smith

Join Lauren Smith's Facebook VIP Reader Group called Lauren Smith's League:
https://www.facebook.com/groups/400377546765661/

For Noah Chinn:

Follow Noah on BookBub:
bookbub.com/authors/noah-chinn

If you'd like to learn more about Lauren and Noah's other books, turn the page!

Sins and Scandals
An Earl By Any Other Name
A Gentleman Never Surrenders
A Scottish Lord for Christmas

Contemporary
The Surrender Series
The Gilded Cuff
The Gilded Cage
The Gilded Chain
The Darkest Hour
Love In London
Forbidden
Seduction
Climax
Forever Be Mine (Coming Spring 2019)

Paranormal
Dark Seductions Series
The Shadows of Stormclyffe Hall
The Love Bites Series
The Bite of Winter
Brothers of Ash and Fire
Grigori
Mikhail
Rurik

Sci-Fi Romance
Cyborg Genesis Series
Across the Stars
The Krinar Eclipse (Coming Soon!)

USA TODAY Bestselling Author Lauren Smith is an Oklahoma attorney by day, who pens adventurous and edgy romance stories by the light of her smart phone flashlight app. She knew she was destined to be a romance writer when she attempted to re-write the entire *Titanic* movie just to save Jack from drowning. Connecting with readers by writing emotionally moving, realistic and sexy romances no matter what time period is her passion. She's won multiple awards in several romance subgenres including: New England Reader's Choice Awards, Greater Detroit BookSeller's Best Awards, and a Semi-Finalist award for the Mary Wollstonecraft Shelley Award.

To connect with Lauren, visit her at:
www.laurensmithbooks.com
lauren@Laurensmithbooks.com

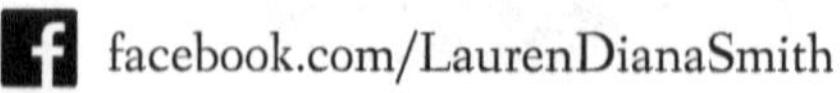 facebook.com/LaurenDianaSmith

twitter.com/LSmithAuthor

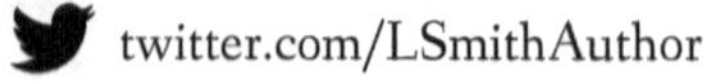 instagram.com/LaurenSmithbooks

bookbub.com/authors/lauren-smith

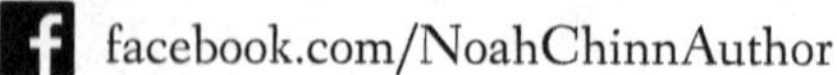 facebook.com/NoahChinnAuthor

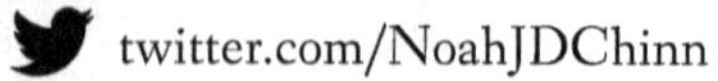 twitter.com/NoahJDChinn

bookbub.com/authors/noah-chinn

9 781947 206052